THE JUNE BOYS

D0029529

Also by Court Stevens

Four Three Two One
Dress Codes for Small Towns
The Lies About Truth
The Blue-Haired Boy
Faking Normal

PRAISE FOR *THE JUNE BOYS*

"The final reveal is surprising and chilling."
—*KIRKUS*

"Stevens takes a good swing at resolving lost faith and trust while trying to rebuild the strengths and bonds of family and friends."
—*PUBLISHERS WEEKLY*

"Tense and haunting, *The June Boys* is not only a terrifying story of the missing, but a heartbreaking, hopeful journey through the darkness. Beautifully written and sharply plotted, this is a story that lingers long after you turn the final page."
—MEGAN MIRANDA, *NEW YORK TIMES* BESTSELLING AUTHOR OF *ALL THE MISSING GIRLS* AND *THE LAST HOUSE GUEST*

"Masterfully plotted with stunning twists and turns. Hang on tight, *The June Boys* is a fantastically crafted suspense that keeps you guessing until the last page!"
—RUTA SEPETYS, INTERNATIONAL BESTSELLING AUTHOR

"*The June Boys* by Court Stevens is a gripping suspense that hooked me from the first sentence. Fabulous characterization and a layered plot with tension that escalated with every page. Highly recommended!"
—COLLEEN COBLE, *USA TODAY* BESTSELLING AUTHOR OF *ONE LITTLE LIE* AND THE LAVENDER TIDES SERIES

"I just finished *The June Boys*, and I loved it. The feeling of the intensity of friendship at that age, the tension of the chase to find Welder, all the twists to get to who it was—I was hooked and couldn't stop reading. I wanted to cry with Aulus every time I read his letters and felt that Thea was that friend everyone needs. Though flawed, she is devoted to her friends with a ferocity that I loved."
—CATHERINE BOCK, BOOK BUYER FOR PARNASSUS BOOKS

THE JUNE BOYS

A Novel

COURT STEVENS

THOMAS NELSON
Since 1798

The June Boys

© 2020 by Courtney Stevens

Published in Nashville, Tennessee, by Thomas Nelson. Thomas Nelson is a registered trademark of HarperCollins Christian Publishing, Inc.

Interior design by Emily Ghattas
Maps by Matthew Covington

Thomas Nelson titles may be purchased in bulk for educational, business, fund-raising, or sales promotional use. For information, please email SpecialMarkets@ThomasNelson.com.

Library of Congress Cataloging-in-Publication Data

Names: Stevens, Courtney C., author.
Title: The June boys : a novel / Court Stevens.
Description: Nashville, Tennessee : Thomas Nelson, [2020] | Summary: High school senior Thea Delacroix, aided by her friends, seeks to catch the Gemini Thief, who abducts and releases boys unharmed--including her cousin--but begins to fear the criminal is someone very near.
Identifiers: LCCN 2019036744 (print) | LCCN 2019036745 (ebook) | ISBN 9780785221906 (hardcover) | ISBN 9780785221944 (trade paperback) | ISBN 9780785221913 (epub) | ISBN 9780785221920
Subjects: CYAC: Kidnapping--Fiction. | Community life--Fiction. | Single-parent families--Fiction. | Mystery and detective stories.
Classification: LCC PZ7.S84384 Jun 2020 (print) | LCC PZ7.S84384 (ebook) | DDC [Fic]--dc23
LC record available at https://lccn.loc.gov/2019036744
LC ebook record available at https://lccn.loc.gov/2019036745

Printed in the United States of America

20 21 22 23 24 LSC 5 4 3 2 1

For Ruta Sepetys, my friend and mentor.
You are a bell ringer for so many, especially me.
Genesis 6:22

"The truth is like a lion.
You don't have to defend it.
Let it loose.
It will defend itself."

—St. Augustine

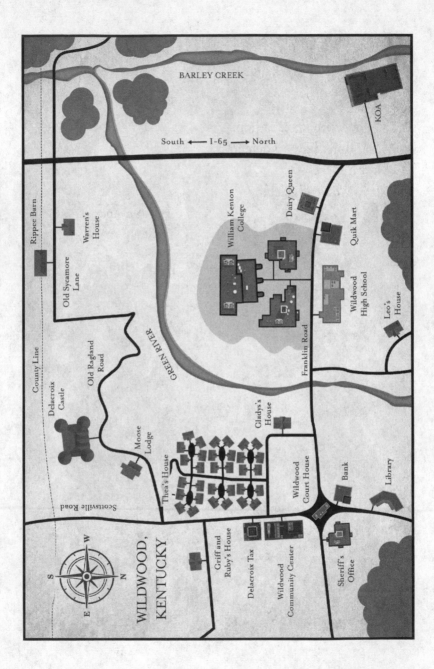

SAGE ADVICE

You don't owe your truths to everyone.

Those were my father's exact words.

There were upside-down spoons in our mouths, ice cream thawing on our tongues. The hard rock maple table held our elbows. It was midnight and I smelled like Johnson and Johnson. Dad tapped his watch and gave me the inevitable *you should have been asleep hours ago I'm probably a terrible father* grimace.

Trouble was, my new classmates at Wildwood Elementary were going to wonder about my mother. Dad spoke around a mouthful of mint chocolate chip. "Don't tell them anything," he said. When I argued that they'd ask, they'd definitely ask, we swapped bowls and he shrugged. Not like my question didn't matter. More like the people asking didn't.

I remember his lip curling into my favorite smirk and pink dribbles of Neapolitan clinging to his mustache. I remember *Riverdance* sounds as he clacked the spoon between his bottom

1

and top teeth. Then the precise shape of his lips saying my name. "Thea." And I remember what came after.

He shoved the bowl toward the lazy Susan and placed his hand over my eyes. "I want you to picture a basement," he said. He gave my imagination time to populate the darkness. To spot the blackish-green mold clinging to the plaster, hear the boiler gurgling in the corner, hang a single raw bulb from the ceiling. His fingers smelled like sugar. "Now," he said, "take all your favorite truths and secrets, the things you're not sure about, the things you love most in the world and put them down there." Almost as an afterthought he added, "Where they'll be safe."

"Like you letting me stay up past bedtime?" I peeked between his fingers.

"Definitely." He winked. "And tough stuff too. Like Mom leaving." I spotted a momentary wave of regret before he said, "Whatever, whoever you want. When that's done, lock the door." His face grew animated and he explained that his basement had an ancient door with a cool skeleton key.

"Like at Nana's old house in Nashville?" I wanted to know.

"Yes, like at Nana's old house." Then he said something that's wedged in my memory. "Imagine there are only three keys to the basement and the people with keys, they get to know about Mom. Everyone else gets a shrug."

"Do I lie?"

He parted the hair on my forehead and planted a kiss along my worry wrinkle. "Only if you're desperate."

That was 2001.

The Gemini Thief kidnapped the first crop of boys that year.

MAY

We'll pass the billboards in another mile.

They'll smear by.

The five of them.

Last September they sprouted in the field along I-65. Their font coal black and Apple Store white; huge block letters that demanded attention from motorists. The quintet is weatherworn now, and as far as advertisements go, can't compete with Bojangles's new spicy chicken sandwich or TriStar's four-minute ER wait.

I'm staring out the passenger window of Nick's Civic, watching the landscape pass, wide-eyed and afraid to blink. "They're just ahead. After the water tower." I tap the glass, leaving my fingerprint smudges for him to wipe away later. To appease me, he slows to a honk-worthy speed and we squint against the rising sun.

The Gemini Thief could be anyone.
Your father, your mother, your best friend's crazy uncle.

Some country music star's deranged sister. Anyone.
Someone is stealing Tennessee's boys.
Report suspicious behavior.

A tip line number follows. The byline explains the Check Your Neighbor Campaign is funded by Families of Gemini Victims. These days the billboards are ants in the rush-hour parade. Another bit of empathy fatigue for the daily commute.

Unless your whole life is on those signs.

Aulus McClaghen's my cousin.

Maybe you know the name. Maybe you don't. In the media, he's nobody yet. To Nick, he's the Kentucky boy among the current three missing from Tennessee. To me, he's the million-piece puzzle I've been working since childhood. It's not just me fascinated either. Nearly everyone in Wildwood could reel off four or five Aulus facts without blinking. That's the kind of person he is. Was? Is.

Like:

He worked the cash register at Quik Mart.

He once raised seven hundred dollars for St. Jude's reselling Hershey's Kisses.

Dude loved his car—an Audi Quattro that he tipped the Wildwood High shop class to handsomely accessorize.

He wrote letters to famous people and for some reason they always wrote back. His favorite, and mine: J. K. Rowling. (The letters are framed in the Wildwood Library, near the family bathroom.)

A person isn't a grouping of stats or a list of strange accomplishments; that's reductive and insulting. But take a snapshot of Aul's life on any day, and you'd love him instantly.

Nick returns the Civic to an above-normal speed. "I hate what those signs do to you."

4

"I like them," I whisper. It's nice to count on something in this case that doesn't change.

He runs his index finger inside the looping Western Kentucky University lanyard attached to his keys. We reach for the radio at the same time and scan through the stations twice before giving up. He says, "We can always wait. Find out on the evening news." Nick makes another loop on the lanyard.

The FBI found a body in Baxter, Tennessee, this morning.

Juvenile. Male.

Dumped on the side of the highway and phoned in by a motorist who had to pee and couldn't wait.

Dana, Nick's sister and one of the lead agents on the Gemini case, wouldn't confirm the body was a Gemini victim—she's not allowed—but the implication . . . clear. She called Nick. Nick called me. Thirty minutes later he arrived with breakfast and a full tank of gas.

I toss the pastry bag in the back seat and sigh.

"Didn't think I'd get any calories into you," Nick says.

"I can't eat if he's dead."

In nine years the Thief has never killed. Never been violent with the boys, as far as the reports indicate.

I clear my throat. "Dana tell you where in Baxter?"

Nick shrugs but doesn't look worried. I piggyback on his confidence even though we're on a fishing expedition for flashing blue lights and federal vehicles in some remote county east of Nashville. "You want to talk? You don't have to if you're tired."

I am tired. I went to bed at eleven, fell asleep around two, and answered Nick's call at five a.m. "I don't know what I want. For that body not to be Aulus's." *Except, is that wishing for Zared or Rufus or Chris to be dead?* Tension squeezes every muscle in my neck and shoulders. "Sorry," I say.

Nick pumps my leg twice like my knee needs CPR. "Don't be sorry." He sips his coffee to the dregs and rattles ice against the plastic cup.

It could be Aul, his eyes say when he looks sideways.

I know, mine answer.

The Civic eats miles like candy.

We reach Nashville. We pass Nashville. I can't bear forty more miles of silence so I say, "Uncle Warren" (who is not really my uncle, but might as well be) "says calls dribble in occasionally."

"Huh?" Nick asks. Then, "Oh, on the tip line?"

"People ask if there's a cash reward. They find out there isn't and hang up. Did I tell you that already?"

"Thee." My name empties the air. "Has this gone unsolved for so long because people never consider that someone they know might be guilty?" He nibbles skin on the side of his thumb. "Like . . . you and I have discussed every bizarre fact of this case and not one time did I—" He stops midsentence.

I intend to wait him out but can't. "Not one time, what?"

His sigh, both deep and long, feels shaped by shame instead of fear. "I never asked myself if my mom or dad or a neighbor or Dana or anyone I know . . . could be responsible for taking Aul." Nick's eyes aren't so much a specific color, but you'd call them blue if you had to call them something. They don't pierce; they lean at your calf like a dog. "I mean . . . Have you?"

I can't think of anything worse. "Everyone I know is pretty great. They don't seem the kidnapping type."

"But you'd report him?"

"Why wouldn't I?"

Twelve kidnappings are attributed to the Thief. They're all boys. Most were abducted from homes: bedrooms, backyards, driveways. One was riding a neon green bike with black racing stripes. Another was last seen begging his mother for strawberry ice cream. That kid was in a grocery store alley near Jackson.

The crimes started as early as 2001; the FBI acknowledged the pattern to the public in 2007. The pattern is this: On June 1st three boys disappear; no ransom is requested. The kidnappees are harbored in an underground bunker through June 30th of the following year. Thirteen months. Thirteen. Then they're released, dropped somewhere along I-40.

A fallow season follows.

A dormant year. Sometimes two.

But he always steals again.

Three boys. Tennessee. June 1st.

And he's gotten away with kidnapping twelve times. Thirteen, if you count Aulus. In 2009, Aulus's year, he took Chris Jenkins (five years old) from Oak Ridge, Rufus Cohen (fourteen years old) from Portland, and Zared Parker (fifteen years old) from White House.

One is dead on the side of the road in Baxter, Tennessee. Russian roulette. So, back to Nick's question, would I tell? Yeah, if I had the faintest suspicion of the Thief's identity, I'd scream his name from a mountaintop.

Nick taps the steering wheel. "I'm only asking what happens if we consider the possibility that the Thief is a dude from Wildwood who gets up in the morning, pushes tomato soup through a crack in his cellar wall, and goes off to . . . drive his school bus or, I don't know . . . provide legal aid or plumb toilets? He could have kids or a wife or a chinchilla named Biscuit."

"That's not exactly the profile, and I doubt the Thief's from Wildwood."

"You're probably right . . ." Nick's hand's in mine and I'm not even sure who made that happen. I let him lift our fingers to his lips and kiss our laced knuckles.

"Love ya," I say.

"You too," he says from a long way away.

Locating Dana's slew of federal agents happens without much fuss. They're blocking the shoulder of I-40, clogging the Baxter exit. Vehicles dog-paddle along, their drivers rubbernecking the scene. Nick angles the Civic over the rumble strip. An uncomfortable assumption roils my stomach that if we crack the windows, we'll smell who died. Nick swallows hard, rests his forehead against the wheel. "It's not him," he says, fingers paused on the door handle.

I crane toward the winking reds and blues. There's a cop bent over in the bushes, hurling.

"It's not him," I repeat, but it probably is.

"That's Dana's." Nick points at one of the dozen SUVs. "Remember, she won't look happy to see us."

We leave the car and pick our way toward Nick's sister, me still attached to his hand. Cigarette butts and gravel litter the ground. Grass quickly creeps over the edge of my flip-flops and swats my toes. The May heat bats against our faces as semis whoosh by. I hold my breath until it hurts. This shoulder's a ravine, dropping swiftly into a fenced-off wooded area that doesn't garner much love from the highway department. It's amazing anyone noticed a body; you could hide a circus in a grove this thick. An officer spots us and yells that the area is closed and if we're media we can move along. We keep walking and he makes a fuss that stops the scene.

"Tommy," Dana snaps at her coworker. "That's my brother and his girlfriend. Let 'em through."

After thinking long and hard about whether he should, Tommy steps aside. His partners follow suit and an aisle opens.

The crime scene raises its ugly head.

On the ground there's a box. No, a suitcase. A multicolored tweed holdover from the Kennedy administration. It has burgundy handles, water marks, and grass stains. The zipper . . . the silver teeth have eaten hair and skin.

Bloated blue-gray skin.

Blondish-red hair.

Nick stops like someone suddenly nailed him to the earth. "I . . ." He starts to say *can't*. The word cowers behind his clenched teeth.

I don't know which of us is more ashamed. Him for the inability to move closer. Me for charging robotically forward.

Four to five yards away from the scene, Dana squats. Her eyes rove the disturbed space around the boy and suitcase. She's brave to stare. I try to be brave.

The body's small.

I look away.

Dana keeps staring.

I check again.

Too small to be Aulus. Far too small.

Another agent drops to Dana's level and swaps her clipboard for an evidence bag as they discuss body identification and keeping the press out of the loop until the family is notified. Good luck with that. The press skulks toward the woods with cameras and microphones. If I had to guess, the connection to the Gemini Thief is already playing on every major network.

Dana adeptly wipes her cheek with her shoulder before jockeying the plastic bag from one hand to the other. Then she stands, walks to me, and angles our backs to the body. "Nick?" A crevice appears between her brows.

I point to the Civic.

"I shouldn't have called." She lowers her voice. "It's not Aul . . ."

"Chris Jenkins," I say.

She nods, then I find myself swallowed by Dana's arms. She has been up most of the night. She's wrung around the edges and red in the eyes. Still, the Jones warmth devours me. I hope I give her half what she gives me. She's going to need it.

We break apart. The plastic evidence bag that was banging my ribs dangles there for viewing.

Inside, a silver key chain.

I bend closer.

Dana tightens the plastic around the object so the features are visible.

A castle.

Two turrets. Three arches. One dangling camo key.

I'm telling myself it can't be and asking, "Where did this come from?" at the same time.

Dana leans toward me, whispers, "From the body. In his mouth," and then makes a show of saying, "Tell my brother to drive the speed limit home. You know you can't hang around a crime scene."

Dana gives away nothing to her team, but she's seen that key chain before.

2

Chris Jenkins is dead.

The media circulated a photo after his initial disappearance that showed mischievous green eyes, a matching checkered button-up, and adorable aqua sandals. His jeans didn't meet his ankles. I can imagine his mother cooing, "Chrisy-Chris, stop growing up so fast."

He's done growing now. Maxed out in less than three thousand days. He probably still believed in Santa Claus. Probably wanted the training wheels off his bicycle. Probably liked grape jelly on both sides of his peanut butter sandwich. Maybe he complained about whole wheat bread.

He died with Aulus's key chain in his mouth.

I haven't managed anything except a seated position. I'm curled around the glove box, cheek and nose buried in the dashboard dust. One of Nick's arms drapes the wheel, the other massages my shaking shoulders. "I'm not driving until you tell me who's dead."

"Chris." The name tastes like horseradish. "Sorry," I say because I am crying and I'm not sure whether the motivation is grief or relief.

Nick frames out like a jockey who has stopped starving himself—small, not tiny. He crosses the console, scoops me against his chest, and hugs me like an octopus. It's stunning, really, the amount of arms on this boy.

I'm not sure I can make myself say everything once, much less twice, and Gladys and Tank still need to be told. "Can you drive and let me tell you everything at the WCC?" I ask.

"Thee?" He has no intention of waiting.

I wriggle away and lift my pack from the floorboard into my lap. "Evidence on the body. This." I hold a twin key chain of the one in the evidence bag. A key chain I've been led to believe is two of a kind. *"Nick."*

He speaks my thought. "Now we're sure."

Aulus was with him.

And if I'm right, trying to get a message to us.

The sun bakes the car. More than one officer has tapped the window and asked us to move. We're not being defiant. It's hard to drive knowing what we know. No matter what I do, that tiny body and suitcase returns, and I can't stop thinking: all the images I've conjured of Aulus over the last year—the basement, Welder, endless cans of soup—they're true.

It's quite a thing to be right. Quite a terrible thing.

Nick lifts my key chain and stares at it, through it. He fists the silver ring, knuckles reddening as he squeezes. "There's a good chance we might be those people who know the Thief," he says, nearly emotionless.

This seems like a leap. Still, there's a new fear, half dressed and

12

exposed, in his eyes. "You're tied to this," he says. "You. Not just Aulus." And though he speaks with uncertainty, his tone betrays him. His brain is now a Rubik's Cube spinning in perfect algorithm. The colors are lining up.

After that, we drive.

A NOTE FOR THE READER

To the best of our knowledge the following letters, hereafter referred to as the Elizabeth Letters, were penned in late June 2010 by Aulus McClaghen.

THE ELIZABETH LETTERS

Dear Escape Artist,

   Sometimes I wake up, heart pounding, sweat pooling in the gatherings of the pool float.

   I've had the dream again.

   The one where the suitcase zipper snags the corner of my lip and my body is folded like a puppet, knees to forehead, arms crooked like drainpipes. Welder's mechanical voice echoes through the fabric. I swallow mildew. It swallows me back. Welder says, "Go to sleep, my June Boy." I choke on a castle, on a key.

   That moment cloaks me like skin.

   Not like skin—skin flakes off. More like wool, or more like veins. ←

   Do I sound crazy? Maybe. Maybe I am. But I don't think your reaction will be what

> Imagine being the single historian authorized to speak on WWII or Vietnam or the Great Depression or 9/11, the incredible responsibility that would be. That's how I feel.

the (expletive, expletive, expletive) is this guy
talking about? I believe you, being you, understand
that we belong to a relatively exclusive club
of zippers and bunkers and thieves. That's why
I chose you for these letters. In case they're
the last I write. You're my best chance to be
understood.

Listening will not be easy. We're dying. Most
likely dead if you're reading this.

If you don't want details, don't want to share
in this story, stop here and know I admire you for
living.

But if you decide to read on, everything I
share regarding the captivity of the June Boys
belongs to me, Aulus McClaghen, and only me.

Peace and Freedom,

Aulus

P.S. I miss birds. Birds fill my dreams. I draw chalk birds
on the floor, the walls, the sides of the deep freezer.
Cardinals. Blue jays. Finches. Owls. Geese. Hawks. Most
of the time they're perched on a high stone wall, singing
or cawing or honking. Sometimes they're flying over an
American flag in a perfect V.

Elizabeth, have you ever listened while a flock of
blackbirds bursts off cornstalks in a wave? Nothing sounds
like that. Not even the creek after a hard rain. I miss
nature so much I want to tell every living soul: if you're not
standing outside right now, leave your air conditioning or

your fireplace, find the closest sky, and fill your eyes with clouds and birds and blues and then squeeze your lungs dry so that when you inhale, you swallow every sapling that's ever grown on earth.

Gnome sayin'?

3

MAY

Nick's proposition that I'm tied to the Gemini case fills the Civic. It stops with us for gas. It orders a latte. It passes the billboards at eighty miles an hour. It wants to know if we're close to home.

Twenty miles from Wildwood, the silence overwhelms me. "Explain."

"I'm probably wrong," he says.

"Well, be wrong *verbally*."

He checks the rearview mirror and fixes his eyes on the road. He's like this sometimes. Stubborn. Internal. I can't tell if he's protecting himself from sounding stupid or protecting me from being unable to track his line of thinking. Occasionally he uses the gap in our ages against me. As if three years is the difference between smart and wise. I nearly remind him I'm the one who faced Chris Jenkins while he waited in the car, but that won't get me anywhere. We already know which of us swallows this case by the handful.

"I need more time to . . ." He mimes moving boxes around.

I flippantly mime the same motion. "Too bad."

"I didn't mean you were guilty." He's suddenly worried I've misunderstood.

"Seriously? You didn't mean I was killing six-year-olds?" I roll my eyes. "I get that you're saying the key chain suggests proximity to the kidnapper . . . but connect the dots." I wheel my hand, urging him to proceed.

"Your dad gave you the key chain, yeah?"

I nod.

"And he gave Aulus the same one?"

"Yeah." I swivel against the pressure of the seat belt and use the emergency brake as a footstool, building a barrier of knees and elbows.

Nick shoves three fingers between the top two buttons of his oxford polo and taps his chest in a piano-like rhythm. "The discovery of the key chain not only ties Aulus to Chris, it ties your dad to the boys. Whoever put it in Chris's mouth was delivering a message."

"The only message I'm getting: Aulus is there." The pressure in my chest tiptoes toward annoyance instead of fear. "For the first time in a year, we have evidence that my cousin didn't run away, didn't hitchhike out of Wildwood, didn't drown in Mitchem Creek. He was taken. For the first time in months, we know exactly who took him. Which means we might very well get him back on June 30th. Let's focus on that for a happy little minute."

Nick squeezes my toes and makes fingertip indentions in my flip-flops without taking his eyes off the road. His head metronomes. "Your dad was with Aulus the morning he disappeared."

"Yeah, and he was already questioned. So was I. So was Aulus's uncle Leo. So were you."

"By Wildwood police. Who were investigating a runaway, not a kidnapping."

Uncle Warren is with the Wildwood Sheriff's Office, and he's been nothing but helpful and thorough. I'm slightly offended on his behalf.

Nick kneads his forehead and the car drifts. A middle finger shoots up from the minivan mom to our right. He waves apologetically. "This is what I meant when I asked if you would tell. We all think we would, but when you love someone, you look for a million reasons why they're innocent."

This riles me enough to raise my voice. "The key chain connection didn't exist when you asked."

Nick pins his lips together with his thumb, holds his words inside.

"Say it," I urge.

"I shouldn't have said anything."

"Why? Because it might be awkward for my boyfriend to accuse my dad of kidnapping? Yeah, a wee bit."

"No, I didn't."

"Yeah, you did."

"Technically, I asked if he could be a murderer too." I don't understand in the slightest what's happening. Nick and Dad get along fine. Dad didn't even mind that Nick is older than me after Uncle Warren ran a background check and told him, "His dad's a DA. Sister's FBI. Kid's prelaw without a parking ticket." Dad has even gone so far as to admit Nick's the only one who can reach me when I swim out too far in the ocean of Aulus. Still, Nick's continuing with his proposal. "Your dad, he's . . . well, he's . . ."

When Nick won't spit it out, I provide an option that stings my chest. "Strange?"

Nick darts around a truck with two huskies drinking air through cracked windows. The truck honks and the dogs honk too. "I was going to say"—another pause—"certifiable."

MAY

Certain questions require us to think deeply. They give us pedigrees and integrity. They stoke curiosity. I usually appreciate a well-asked question. Nick's plants a ball of fire between my ribs.

Is my dad the average-height adult, weighing between 165 and 180 pounds, owning a welding helmet and black racing jumpsuit, who stole years from other families and security from twelve boys?

Did my dad kidnap his own nephew?

Or kill Chris Jenkins?

That's what Nick's asking.

I dial down every swirling rogue emotion and coat my answer in cool eucalyptus. "Crazy doesn't make him guilty. Build your case," I say.

And Nick, knowing me, says, "I'd be angry at me too if I were you, but you'll be angrier later if you don't force yourself to do this. You can't come this far and stop at the hard place." Then, "It's smarter for you to build the case."

Point number one, which I concede as a fact: my father is a liar.

I was almost seventeen listening to "Fifteen," and summer was Taylor Swift, SweeTart sugar highs, and sticky bleachers at the American Legion Park. Gladys and I googled sex and wished we didn't. Aulus and Tank devised plans for late-night phone calls that didn't make our house phones ring. There were trips to Holiday World with Uncle Warren, Griff, and Ruby. And of course, my every-other-Wednesday decision to start a celery-only diet, followed by eating cheap cookie dough from the sleeve before the day was out.

This was me before Castle Delacroix.

The day I found out I owned a castle, summer was being a dutiful Wildwood summer: boring, beautiful, too hot to breathe unless you were sitting in the path of an air conditioner. Gladys said, "Tank and I got kicked out of Walmart last night for playing hide-and-seek," and I lolled my head toward her and said, "We should try to get kicked out of Walmart every day."

We were lying side by side on the floor, freshly painted toes propped on the bed's edge, listening to her iPod with two fans oscillating our direction. Gladys had a Dr Pepper can balanced on her chest and was trying to tip all twenty-three flavors to her lips without spilling liquid on the carpet. "You think Tank likes me?" She rebalanced the can and changed the position of her chin for optimal catching.

"There's probably some Southern correlation between being kicked out of Walmart together and marriage." I sounded bored. I was tired of talking about boys—even our boys, whom I loved—and was wishing my way back to our middle school Bigfoot mania.

We'd made huge plans to travel somewhere after graduation and shoot a *Blair Witch*–style mockumentary on Sasquatches.

Gladys gripped the lip of the Dr Pepper can with her teeth and nudged it toward the middle of her breastbone. "What if I get kicked out of Walmart with you every day in June? Is there a Southern correlation for that?"

"You only have me the last two weeks," I reminded her.

Dad had left for his annual month-long mental health sojourn three days earlier. I was out of school and happy to spend the month with my village of uncles. Except that year, last year, Warren was supposedly off with Dad, so I was all Griff's. We were planning to visit his parents—Grandma and Grandpa Holtz—in the Outer Banks. And since we were leaving for North Carolina in less than twelve hours, Gladys would clearly take more devious Walmart trips with Tank than me.

She groaned, upsetting the Dr Pepper can. Half the drink sloshed up her nose.

I tossed the closest thing in reach—a pair of folded panties from her clean clothes pile—and asked, "You plan to drink all the Dr Pepper in the fridge through your nose, or shall we get ourselves forcefully removed from the local superstore?"

She threw the Dr Pepper panties toward the laundry and glanced around her room for inspiration. "You still have skates?"

Everyone our age has Rollerblades. When you feel certain you've aged out of your bike, you buy skates. Mine were somewhere among the garage cobwebs, so I left Gladys's on a mission to retrieve them and discovered my father's truck in our driveway.

Except he was in Canada.

He called yesterday. "It's raining in Vancouver," he'd said.

Steadying the key in the back-door lock took three tries. After barreling into the kitchen, I found Uncle Warren and Dad at the kitchen table, Dad shoving eight-by-tens into a manila folder, Uncle Warren folding stacks of butcher paper.

"What are you doing here?" Dad asked, still shoving.

What was I *doing here?* I wasn't the one who was supposed to be in Canada. "You flew home without telling me?"

Dad and Warren exchanged a collective stare and then Dad sagged into a chair and used his hands like wiper blades to cover and uncover his eyes. He wasn't crying, but he was pulling at his temples like he wished he could. I was thinking, *When is the last time you slept?* He said, "This isn't how I wanted to tell you."

I went straight to worst-case scenario. *He's not tired. He's sick.* I walked closer, seeking an embrace, an assurance, and said, "Whatever it is, we're going to be okay."

Dad gripped my elbows, worked his thumb gently into the ditch of my arm. "Honey, I'm not dying."

We took a deep, unified breath and rested our foreheads together. The relief settled in that whatever this was, death was worse. He turned me loose and slid a stack of photos in my direction. There were backhoes, piles of clay and dirt, a concrete foundation. The photos showed serious progression on a structure. Walls. Rebars. A cement mixer. Clearly a worksite, although the significance remained unclear. Dad unfolded the butcher paper. Blueprints covered the kitchen table. His index fingernail tapped a title in the uppermost corner: Delacroix Castle.

"For nearly . . . nine years, give or take . . . I've, um, been building a castle."

I absorbed the photos, registering the time this must have taken. The money. The audacity of the structure itself. I asked,

"When?" because my mouth lagged a split second behind my brain. "You don't go camping, do you?"

Uncle Warren's chin dipped and he crossed his arms over his chest. They'd clearly argued this point before.

"And you never have?" I said.

Dad's reaction bordered on bemusement and pride. Another "I told you so" passed between the men. *"Thee."* Dad's rehearsed explanation about the impaired truth-telling practices of adults included listing Santa Claus and my mother as prime examples and concluded with, "These truth *twists* are normal parts of protective parenting."

"So . . . 'I'm going to Canada' is the same as Santa?"

Guilt crept around his eyes, as did pride, and I thought the pride swelled well beyond the guilt. "This castle's important. It might even save our lives."

Uncle Warren offers a nearly undetectable headshake. Whatever his complicity in Castle Delacroix, he didn't buy Dad's reasoning.

"First of all, you sound insane." And I already had one insane parent. "Second, I don't want a castle. I want a dad who goes camping when he says he's going camping." I whirled on Uncle Warren next, the betrayal gathering, the anger unwilling to clot. "And I want an uncle, an officer of the law, whom I can trust to be truthful. You two should be fired from adulthood."

Dad's neck and cheeks were the color of beets. "This thing, honey—it's bigger than me, and at this point"—he tapped the photos, the records of progress—"it's happening whether you like it or not. I've gambled everything, and now that you know, I'd love for you to be part of this. Give it time. You'll see I'm right."

All I managed was a quiet jab. "What does that even mean?"

There was no trace of offense on Dad's features. Using finger and thumb, he orbited his mustache and goatee and gestured to Uncle Warren, who stepped close enough to hug me, but didn't dare try. Uncle Warren said, "What you're seeing is passion, and sure, passion is scary, but passion isn't criminal. And when you see the construction site, you're gonna be impressed, kid."

"Dad, people will think we're off the rails." I already felt strange that Mom left us. Every kid I knew whose parents were divorced lived with their mom and saw their dad on the weekend.

He looked genuinely sad that I was judging his choices. Like he wasn't the one to blame here. Like I was being shallow for caring that Wildwood was going to implode over this. "Wait," he said. "You have your Bigfoot thingie and your . . . canoe quest and what was that game you all used to play all the time? Catan? Yeah, Catan. I don't think a castle is much different."

The Bigfoot thing was meant to be funny. I didn't even remember the canoe quest and I hadn't played Catan in months. He was behind on my hopscotch obsessions. Probably because *he'd been building a castle*. Which was admittedly cool, but the coolness existed on a non-intersecting line with how I felt. What does someone do with a nine-year lie?

I shoved my chair at the table and the brief wind ruffled the top photo, revealing another beneath. The subject captured my attention more than the construction. Standing next to my father, crossing two trowels over his chest like a mortar warrior, was Aulus.

There was a shy smirk before Dad explained. "Uhhh, that's the day we finished brickwork on the keep's roof."

My mouth fell open. "What about Gladys and Tank? You recruit them too?"

"No. You know Aul. Volunteered. Couldn't help himself." Dad pulled a chair out for me and patted the air.

I turned to Uncle Warren. "So he wasn't helping you build out the basement?" For weeks Aulus had disappeared for hours at a time, and when I asked where he'd been, he claimed he'd been finishing out Warren's basement.

Uncle Warren pinks.

Every man in my life sat on a throne of lies. I folded the photo of my cousin into a tiny square, shoved the cardstock into the pocket of my shorts, and nodded curtly before walking into the garage. Dad called after me, "You're missing the point. We own a castle." And then another time with joyful oomph. "We own a *castle*."

I upended papers on the garage workbench and they fluttered into Aulus's free weights. Dad bought the set for Aul's twelfth birthday. The two spent hours out here fighting the good war against eighth-grade scrawniness. He'd been here last night, clanking and heaving.

Aulus's dad and mine are the brother kind of cousins. The stand-up-at-weddings-and-carry-caskets kind of cousins. So when Scottie tapped out on fatherhood, Dad punched him in the nose and tapped in. They talk every Sunday morning even though Scottie never calls his son. Aul became a fixture, regular as the coffeepot or couch, another brother kind of cousin. Until I saw that picture of him at the castle, I'd mistakenly believed he was more mine than Dad's. And that I was more Dad's than Aulus.

They'd hidden a castle from me. A bona fide castle.

My Rollerblades were in a box next to the Christmas tree and I slung them over my shoulder as if I were off to war. Dad and Uncle Warren, unmoved by my return from the garage, examined the blueprint and argued support structures.

27

I leaned against the fridge. "Is he working with you today?"

Dad knew I meant Aulus. "Nope." He pitched something through the air. I stepped aside and whatever it was slid along the countertop and stopped at the sugar bowl. "I had a key made for you too," he said. "So you can come and go as you want, maybe help bring her to life." There was a twinkle of hope in his eyes.

The camo key was attached to a dangling silver castle. I ignored my welcome favor to grab the portable phone. I dialed. Leo, Aulus's uncle on his mom's side, barked hello.

"It's Thea," I said. Leo's box fan purred. The lever on his recliner clunked. He did his heavy mouth-breathing thing as he leaned around the front porch to see if the quattro was parked beneath the carport. "Kid's out. Want me to give him a message?"

Oh, did I ever.

"When he's back home, tell him . . . tell him . . . tell him . . . I'm gonna kill him."

That was June 2nd. Aulus never came home.

5

MAY

"You didn't say that to Leo."

We're at the Wildwood exit. Baxter, blue lights, the body of Chris Jenkins lay behind. The castle story—the case against my father—rolls around the Civic floor mats and drifts in and out the vents like the smell of dead skunk.

"I did." I remember the precise way *I'm gonna kill him* tasted on my tongue.

"You never told me that before."

I'd tucked the detail away, ashamed. Guess Dad's not the only one who skims when handing out keys to the basement. To be fair, when the story was the freshest, I didn't know Nick well enough to confess.

Nick Jones appeared at my door last June 3rd wearing baggie athletic shorts, a Harvard Law T-shirt with the sleeves hacked off, and those blue, not blue, earnest eyes wanting to know if I knew where Aulus was. My cousin had promised to quiz him for some big criminal justice test and hadn't shown.

I knew of Nick. I'd never met him until he rang the bell.

I clung to the doorframe, peering through the mesh screen. The air conditioning whooshed by us into the street. When he asked to come in, I stepped aside, begrudging my ratty tank top as he walked through the living room straight to the kitchen bar. He pulled out a chair for me and a chair for him. "I'm sorry to barge in." He patted the seat. "But you care like I do."

Care overcame his face. Every pore. Every gathering of skin around his eyes and mouth. Every clenched muscle. While I know a number of guys who fall into the "caring category," I don't know any who express it unabashedly the way Nick does.

I took the offered seat and Nick explained that he and Aulus met a few months before in a junkyard off Old Nashville Highway; Nick looking for a spoiler, Aulus, a tire for the quattro. Paths crossed, phone numbers swapped. Aulus told a similar story. I was also aware that Aulus ditched Tank and Gladys and me, his best friends on the planet, to drive around back roads with Nick. I'd say, "What do y'all do out there that's so great?" and Aulus would say, "Nothing." Which never satisfied me until I too had done nothing with Nick. Nick is very good at nothing.

"Something's wrong." He sounded very sure as he added, "Something happened to him."

I took this as a gross overreaction. "He'll turn up," I said. But then Nick told me he'd spoken to Aulus's uncle Leo, who claimed Aulus hadn't come home yesterday; and to Aulus's boss,

Mr. Rachelle, who was also concerned and a bit peeved Aulus had missed his morning shift at the Quik Mart; and also to Griff and Ruby at the WCC, and nope, Aulus wasn't working a spare job for them either. When Nick went back to Leo's, Leo sent him here.

My insides twisted. I thought he was avoiding me because he knew I knew about the castle.

"Aul wouldn't disappear," Nick said. "He hates that crap because of his dad."

But he had and he did and he stayed gone.

And all the details of that final fight with Aulus slipped away. Silent. Steadfast. Like ants carting crumbs to their hills.

"If the castle is point number one for your dad's guilt, what's point number two?" Nick asks.

I wasn't intending to have a point two.

Thunder rips the air. Then lightning. Nick and I groan in unison, momentarily distracted by similar thoughts: every low area that flooded last weekend will fill again. We exchange sympathy and then irony. *The weather.* We're thinking about the weather. I say, "That's my whole case."

"But the key chain?"

I take mine from my pocket and ignore my fluttering heart. "Only a key chain."

"Tell that to Dana."

"Happily."

"Thee, we have to consider that Aul put that key chain in Chris's mouth after he died so—"

I take over. "So an FBI agent he doesn't know is working the case will tell her brother who will put it together that—"

"Stop." He drums the steering wheel. "I'm just saying, you better be ready for her questions, because let me tell you, they're coming."

THE ELIZABETH LETTERS

Dear Elizabeth,

Though they're morose, I'll explain the basics and put them behind us.

I write when they sleep.

They = Rufus, Zared, and Tank.

Quick reference guide:

TANK — MY TEAM CAPTAIN

ME — THE WRITER WITH GOOD HAIR

RUFUS — MR. ALWAYS IN UNDERWEAR

ZARED — MR. NEVER WANTS TO BE IN THE PICTURE (ALSO, UNDERWEAR)

We drank the last of the water, ate the last of the food. Our tongues are sandpaper coated in beach; our breath is bad—horrendous—and I'll spare you the details of our stomachs, but they ain't pretty either.

I don't know where we are or where we were before Welder moved us. Best guess: Middle Tennessee? According to Tank, Middle Tennessee and Central Kentucky got fourteen inches of rain in a single day not long ago. That flood matches our bunker swap.

Many things happened when our first bunker flooded.

Many unspeakable suitcase things.

Now we are here. Here, where each room exits into the next, and when you're sure you're out of space, another closet pops up and waves from the corner wall. Fluorescent tube lights hang from six-inch chains in our three main rooms. Four of six bulbs work. One's flickering. The only places that

You should have pictures of us from the news, yeah? So, in your head, I look like a mechanic or a garage band flunky. Tank's got this *I Am Legend* vibe, except . . . without the ears. Ain't no one down here got nothin' on Will Smith's ears. Zared's a stained *Nightmare Before Christmas* T-shirt, wide pink gauge in his ear, black lipstick, chunky bits squeezed into a pair of overly tight girl jeans; and Rufus is a receiver for his freshman football team, scrappy as David fighting Goliath, and built like a phone cable that can tie itself in knots. We're pasty and pale these days. We'd win a ghost competition if we entered.

remotely compare: Don's castle bunker (I'll draw you a picture of that in the next letter. Totally wild.) and the Wildwood Community Center basement. They're caverns too.

We measure time in sleeps.

Welder hasn't been back in twenty sleeps.

That's all for now.

Peace and Freedom,

Aulus

6

MAY

Nick and I should have gone inside the community center.

Instead, we sentence ourselves to the Civic. I find our choice mildly impressive. Hopeful even. We've had our day and we're still choosing proximity.

At 2:12 p.m., I poke Nick—he's nose-deep in a John Grisham legal thriller he reads when the world upsets him. He slides the book between the seat and gearshift and gives me a sideways *Are we okay?* I shrug and open the door, knowing Gladys and Tank will be here any minute. The humid air promises rain, and based on the gathering gray plumes, it's coming fast.

Wildwood Community Center, or the WCC, is a three-story brick building featuring an adjacent playground roughly the size of Disneyland. They've even got an old Frozen Novelties van to complete the attraction. This block's mostly abandoned, save Tyson's Furniture Warehouse and my dad's tax office around the corner.

We ding through the front and Griff Holtz, the director, waves. He hoists a tearful five-year-old atop the counter to select *the very best* Toy Story *Band-Aid in the building*, and Ruby, his wife, spackles a hole on the rear wall while yelling for a volunteer to "Bring the quilts in before they're drenched, please." When she sees me, she smiles. "There's my girl."

"Downstairs?" Nick asks me, though he doesn't need to.

I point to the basement door for Griff's approval. "We're gonna burn off some steam. Send Gladys and Tank down if they don't come through the alley, will you?"

Griff's not just one of my many uncles, he's my former boss. "You're out of school awfully early, Delacroix." He tsks my direction.

"She went with a college schedule today," Nick says, our road trip hidden behind his broad, beaming grin.

"Yeah, yeah." Griff rolls his eyes and addresses the scurry of children nipping his ankles. "It's almost story time." He holds out a picture book. "Can't tempt you to resume your old post, can I?"

Once, I was the story-time queen. "Not today."

"Have fun in the piles," he says, even though he's wearing that sad-puppy look he gets whenever my job is referenced. I used to think I'd take over this place someday and I hate disappointing him, but I don't have room for . . . I don't know what it is I don't have room for. Sometimes I'm afraid it's happiness.

Griff kept me on payroll. He's had me/us on this "basement project" since Aulus disappeared. A leash so we don't stray too far. Partly because he and Ruby need all the help they can get, partly because he's smart enough to barter with a commodity we crave: privacy. Nick, Gladys, Tank, and I get keys to the building if we sort donations in the WCC's basement. Nick came up with the idea to build the investigation cubby among the piles.

Our hangout hides behind warehouse shelving in the high-ceilinged back room.

Camp chairs, TV trays, filing cabinets. Some ancient office equipment.

Records, articles printed from the library, interviews.

Theories scratched on every surface available. Some written in dust.

Griff and Ruby haven't ventured down since they showed us the light switch a year ago, and it's doubtful they care if we finish the assigned sorting job Aulus started. There are three stories above the main floor they'd use before the basement. They like that we're here. I'd go so far as to say they love having us.

Around six, Griff'll yell down, "Closing time." He'll sigh from the top of the steps, not a heavy sigh of disappointment. A sigh that translates, *I'd rather you be here and safe than out there.* He'll add something like, "Let me know if I should stock a fridge."

We already have one. And a ping-pong table. It's amazing the stuff people toss.

Nick weaves through the basement's front rooms and shelving hallways, scooting bags to the side with his foot as he goes. "A game?" he asks when we reach the table and tosses a paddle over the net before I agree. We speak in ricochets and grand slams, the ball exhausting itself between us. The only time this happens is when we're arguing about something. As if a ping-pong ball might determine the winner.

The volley continues until whiffs of cigarette smoke tickle my nose. The alley door smacks the inner wall, and a gust of warm wind and rain come pounding inside. Tank and Gladys are packed together like penguins under the small, torn awning. Gladys is drenched. Tank taps the yellow-and-white Camel against the dark skin of his ear and leans inside. "Say it's not him."

"Not him," Nick and I say together.

Gladys and Tank sag together and the wood of the old

doorframe howls. She steps inside, wrings water from her shirt, says, "Case is all over the news," as Tank pokes her in the ribs. "Told you they'd have called if it was Aul." He's neither happy nor hopeful, but he's certainly glad to be right.

We should have called.

Nick pins the ping-pong ball under his paddle. "Smoke fast," he tells Tank.

His tone tells me the way this will go. He's not holding back and this is my warning to walk out now or stay and provide defense. As I am the only one who has ever been able to somewhat rationalize my father's crazy decisions, I stay.

When Tank finishes his cigarette, Nick and he claim identical plastic chairs in the corner, then in unison scoot them apart an extra foot and throw their legs sideways over the armrests. Gladys doesn't settle; she approaches the photo wall. Four horizontal lines of Gemini victims, each labeled with the year of their theft: 01–02, 03–04, 06–07, 09–10. She runs her fingers over 09–10 and traces the three images below.

Chris Jenkins.

Rufus Cohen.

Zared Parker.

Her fingertips linger on Zared's chubby cheeks. "Who'd they find?"

"Chris." The name limps from my mouth.

Nick draws his knees to his chin and chews a rogue threadbare string on his jeans. Tank bows his head and twirls a cigarette between his fingers. Gladys strokes Chris's photo, pets him the way she would a kid she knew and loved, and pulls the hem of her neckline over her nose. I watch them all from where I am tucked into a shelf.

I'm so tired of feeling. I'm just so tired.

"Murdered?" That's Tank asking—cutting straight to the core.

"Don't know yet." Nick abandons his seat for the wall opposite the photos where a makeshift panel, made of old windows hammered together, runs nearly floor to ceiling. Among our many notes, we've listed facts with each victim. Nick adds a death date. "Thea's the one who saw."

Gladys and Tank straighten.

Saw? their eyes ask.

Saw.

They give me the latitude of silence. I give them restlessness and pacing. I check with Nick. He's watching me. How long before he throws Dad in the mix? Five minutes? Ten? I turn my back to him, hoping to stretch the time.

On the table against the shelves, we have four bulging folders of research that'll make your eyes cross. In the early 2000s, the story of three kidnapped boys taken on the same day echoes through the news. National coverage grows as the years pass, and ebbs too; the story shrinks from first-page news to seventh-page mentions. Local papers often do the victims better justice. From Gazettes and Lamplighters and Beacons, we've traced interviews with mothers and fathers and friends, school photos, and quotes from local police about the ongoing search. The media spreads also cover the jubilation of a community and family when the June Boys are returned a year later. There are theories and profiles on the Thief, but nothing concrete.

From 2001–2002, the articles surround West Tennessee: Union City, Humboldt, and Waynesboro. In 2003–2004, the Gemini Thief stayed west, hitting Jackson, Dickson, and Paris. The media nickname then was the 40-West Kidnapper. After the 2006 thefts moved east of Nashville into Carthage, Defeated, and Lebanon, the media retitled the perpetrator the Gemini Thief. No longer sure of the territory, the timing, June 1st, remained steadfast.

"We've never been able to prove Aulus was kidnapped," I say. Nick's sister and Uncle Warren are two of the few advocates in the system who recognize there is a chance we're right. Wildwood, on the whole, agrees, though it's more like a wild hair of hope. I repeat what we already know. "Aul is in Kentucky, not Tennessee. June 2nd instead of June 1st. Four boys instead of the Thief's usual three. I can't rationalize the pattern break any more than I can explain why there were sometimes two-year, sometimes one-year gaps in the timeline."

No one asks why I stop talking and dig through my satchel until I find my key chain. I trace two turrets, three arches, one castle, leaving prints on the silver. I dangle the trinket so it jingles and Nick gives me the go-ahead nod.

"Dad only made two of these. One for me. One for Aulus. That second one was in Chris's mouth when they found him today."

As the knowledge and certainty of this information sinks in, I tape a photo of Aulus alongside Chris, Rufus, and Zared.

Tank's still sitting crooked, working that cigarette over and back across his knuckles. The grief's so thick, I smell it. He says, "What did Dana say when you told her?"

"I didn't yet."

"Why would you wait?"

I meet Nick's *I told you so* with bitterness and return my attention to the photos. Maybe I'm weak, maybe I don't love Aulus as much as I say I do. Maybe I don't trust my best friends or my boyfriend if I'm not willing to consider everyone, including my own father, as a suspect.

Whatever I am, I am fast, and I am truthful as I lie to myself. *The crime scene was chaotic. I was overwhelmed. Dana didn't want me to bring it up at the scene.* Then I wonder, *Like father, like daughter?*

7

MAY

I wouldn't have gotten away with it—*it* being deception, stretching the truth to buy myself time. They'd have pressed for details, been discontent with half-told stories. Ruby turns up on the basement steps and saves me.

"If you're interested"—her voice twists around the corners and through the shelves, making us jump—"the news is on in the upstairs office. Updates in the Gemini case."

Retreating footsteps.

If we're interested.

Nick unseats himself without waiting for me and follows the pack from the cave. His disappointment is thick and sticky and clings like honey to my conscience. The only saving grace—his empathy. *What if this were* my *father?* he's asking himself.

At the top of the stairs, Ruby lets Gladys, Tank, and Nick pass. Not me. I am clamped to her chest—a baby kangaroo she intends to stuff in her pouch. Ruby hasn't marshmallowed with age so the hug is strong. Firm.

"Oh, I needed that, kiddo. The news is bad."

"All news is bad until he comes home," I say.

Ruby coils a chunk of my loose hair around her finger. "All we can do is hope." I can feel her lip gloss grease-stain my forehead. She holds me at arm's length. "You're not sleeping."

"Like you are," I huff. Her eyes look practically dead inside she's so tired.

"News will be news tomorrow. You could skip it."

"I will if you will."

She laughs. Yawns. Laughs again. We follow the voices to the office.

Our foursome crowds Griff's screen. Ruby drifts to the hallway. She hunches just outside the door, face in her hands. The local news stations add their own bits of drama to the body dump story. No name is revealed, but the age gives away Chris's identity to anyone following the case. Special Agent Raymond Leehouse—stoic and forgettable and exactly what you picture when you think FBI—gives an interview that reminds the nation we are days away from June 1st and families with boys ages five to seventeen should be vigilant.

"This tragedy substantiates a new and unpredictable pattern in the Gemini Thief's behavior. We must be prepared for the Thief to take again instead of giving us back Zared and Rufus."

Dana once told us they use first names in case the Thief watches the coverage. They want the boys to sound like boys. Leehouse wraps up. *Thoughts and prayers.* Dana stands in his shadow, arms crossed, head slightly bowed. When she looks up before the camera cuts away, it feels like she's looking directly at me.

The coverage tapers and we mute the speakers.

43

"Sucks," Tank says.

"Understatement of the decade," I say.

Gladys fiddles with the stapler, checks her watch. She's due home and Tank's her ride. "Go," I say. "We'll talk more tomorrow."

Tank fist bumps Nick and side hugs me. "Best friend's not dead." He adds a sad, celebratory, "Woot. Woot."

After they leave, Nick and I return to the basement for my bag. He closes the door and holds out his phone. Dana's name and number are on the screen. "I'll do it for you. If it's too much," he offers softly.

"No."

"Thee, she already knows you have that key chain. It's better if you go to her."

"No," I say again. I'm uncertain what I'm saying no to. Coming questions or Nick handling this like some big brother fixer. I've had time to think and I'm almost certain Dana showed me the key chain as a warning. As her way of saying, *I remember Christmas dinner.*

Christmas dinner. Whew. Nick and I accidentally delayed the festivities. The line at Honey Baked Ham was ridiculous and then Scottsville Road Christmas traffic murdered us slowly. At his house, I grabbed the ham and neither of us grabbed the keys.

Following the annual Jones viewing of *It's a Wonderful Life*, Dana showed off her lock-picking skills. Mr. Jones was delighted to lean against his walker at the door and call out, "Glad that hundred-thousand-dollar criminal justice degree is finally doing something other than putting your life in danger." Dana rolled her eyes and the lock clicked. Seconds later, she tossed both sets of keys to Nick.

There's no way she forgot. Same way there's zero chance that, as a senior officer, she showed me that key chain by mistake.

Every pile transforms in the basement's darkness. Bagged shirts are shadowy mountains. Walkways are dusty horizons littered with plastic toys. There's a city down here. A solar system. The smells never change. Must and mothballs all day long. You can smell your way to the street, because fresh air seeps through the rotten door seal. Outside, we let our eyes adjust to the pale gray day. Nick rolls his shoulders backward, forward; he slides his hand along the black railing, and a handful of water droplets drip onto his sneakers.

He speaks first. "I know that look." He tucks a wet rope of hair around my ear. "You've got Joan of Arc in your eyes. You need to be careful."

"I only have—"

"One speed," he finishes.

We stand there. The Methodist church down the street plays a tune from the bell tower. A hymn. "Great Is Thy Faithfulness." Neither of us moves until the hour tolls.

I bite my lip. "I live with him, Nick. If Dad's tied to this, if he's even slightly capable of what you're suggesting, it's been dangerous for a very long time. I'm in this up to my nose, so I'm not worried about getting my hair wet."

Nick leans back against the rail. He's thinking about Chris Jenkins. I can see that folded little body in his eyes. "Call Dana and let her clear him," he says.

"You and me, we're playing detective. She's not. There are real consequences here. Things Dad can't come back from. If I step up and tell an investigator on the case that I, *you*, even halfway suspect my dad could be involved, everything I know is over. I'm not doing it unless there's more to go on."

He tilts his head to the sky. Rain curves around his nose and falls into his mouth. He sticks out his hand, and without thinking, I hold it. We have a business embrace. "Promise me that if there's anything else suspicious, you'll tell Dana immediately. Because if you don't, I will."

The deal is made.

We plunk next to each other in his car, breathing hard and drenched. The car is deliciously warm. He has slipped behind the wheel, the way he has a thousand times, and for that first breath, the key chain and Chris's death aren't between us. There's only the console, the rearview, the ponytail holder I leave on his gearshift. The everydayness of us. I want to kiss him. I want him to want to kiss me. I want us to forget the day we've had, the year.

Want is a powerful thing. I feel very small beside it. Especially in a Civic hatchback.

My hand crosses toward his thigh and almost touches the denim of his jeans before I reverse and lodge myself against the passenger door. It's always this way for me: class five emotions followed by deep cravings for intimacy followed by fear. I don't know if it's that way for everyone else or if I just have a talent for whiplash.

Nick watches my hand—the attempt, the withdrawal—then starts the car. "Castle or home?" he asks. The two roads ahead divide and sprint in opposite directions. It's 6:30 on a school night/workday; Dad's working on Castle Delacroix.

Answers or ignorance?

Innocence or guilt?

"Castle," I say.

8

MAY

All eleven Wildwood stoplights are clogged with William Kenton
College's graduation traffic. Nick, who is not from Wildwood,
follows my advice to cut through the speed-bumped neighborhood toward Old Ragland Road. The storm's angrier than when
we left the WCC. Water stands in potholes and yards and rain-
bows into the ditches when Nick drives through puddles on the
asphalt.

"You're going to miss the turn," I say. He frequently has to U-ey
in the middle of the road. "Use the cattle grate after the WKU
mailbox after the Moose Lodge as a marker."

We own ninety-seven lopsided acres of Simpson County,
Kentucky. The southern perimeter lies spitting distance to Tennessee.
The northern fronts half a mile on Old Ragland Road. From the
Moose Lodge parking lot our mustard fields glow golden in the wan-
ing sunlight. Otherwise, the land hides among craggy hills and a
densely wooded forest.

Nick takes the turnoff so hard our heads hit the roof of the car.

Evergreens on either side of the service drive have been shaved with a chainsaw, creating a tunnel through the pines. Bluebells are scattered through the undergrowth, the only vibrant color among the muted browns and greens. We slip and slide along, adding fresh tracks atop the ones from Dad's Ram.

He's out here somewhere.

What will he say? What will I? *So that basement of yours where you keep important things? Literal? Figurative?*

Dad'll be soft at the beginning. He'll wink. Maybe squeeze my shoulder. He'll try to make this about me. "Sweetie, I'm worried about you," he'll say. "I wish you'd drop this obsession of connecting Aul to the Gemini Thief. Go back to one of your other projects."

Since he is a person with equal compulsions, I asked once why mine worried him so.

"The other boys will come home. Aulus might not."

The other boys. That's how he refers to Chris, Rufus, and Zared—never their names.

Nick asks, "What's the plan?"

I've been wondering the same thing. Do I ask Dad about the weekends he doesn't sleep at home? Or the enormous amount of unchecked time at his disposal? If I do, he'll likely say, "I'm adding on to the castle," and slather on the details. "Bell tower. Might have to be a campanile. Securing the shipping container to the keep is tricky." Once he's in castle mode, the nine years he spent hiding his project evaporate, and the details bubble out in long run-on sentences of delight.

My dad has two children: me and this castle.

And maybe three more in a basement and another nine he cast aside in Tennessee?

"I'm going to ask him where he was last night. That'll clear this up."

Dad's great love affair rises among the limestone ridges of Simpson County, a fortress of concrete and simple lines. She's beautiful the way the Eiffel Tower is beautiful. Not so much for what she is, but that she is at all. Say what you want about my dad, he's got vision and tenacity. I've loved those qualities, coveted them, but now . . . they feel like shadows on a moonlit walk. Maybe nothing. Maybe wolves.

Since my last visit, Dad has successfully secured two upturned forty-foot shipping containers to the keep, bricked them, and attached an American flag atop both towers. Streaks of red, white, and blue dapple the gray clouds with color.

"That's nicely done," Nick says.

The Ram sits among the scattered construction equipment. To the right of a makeshift parking lot, a blue tarp, weighted with tires and rain puddles, strains to keep bricks and wood dry. There's inconsistent cell signal, so I crack the window and listen for the grind of machinery. Apart from the pitter-patter of rain striking the tarp, there's nothing. "Dad!" I yell.

No return.

"Don Delacroix!"

Nothing.

We'll have to hunt him down. I usher Nick out of the car and through the closest window cutout instead of tromping through the front yard to the door.

"Dad!"

Nothing.

I've been through the lower garage and up the steps into this catchall room many times. Right now it's filled with rebars, stacks of Quikrete, pallets, a very large church bell that wasn't here previously, and work boot tracks caked with mud. The interior door is open. Scant light falls in yellow-white rectangles across the hardwood floor. The mudroom has been drywalled, a utility sink installed.

Picking my way through the downstairs maze, I see that some rooms show progression, some don't. Per always, the great room steals my breath. Dad's best work by far. Wooden arches. Highly polished concrete floors. Twin staircases circling toward open second and third stories. There's a three-tiered candle chandelier hanging from the thirty-foot ceiling and a stack of oriental carpets, not yet laid, that'll warm the room.

He built this for me. To win me over after the lies came out. He drove us out here one night and marched me around with a lantern. We got to the great room and he said, "Tell me what you want and I'll build it."

I want him to be the good kind of crazy. I want people to marvel at him in secret, the way I often do.

"You okay?" Nick asks.

"I love this room." I whisper like I'm betraying someone.

On the second floor, Nick and I find two work lamps pumping serious wattage and a couple of sawhorses balancing treated lumber. Atop the lumber: Dad's Dr Pepper. There's a receipt pinned under the aluminum can. It won't tell me where Dad is now, but it might tell me how long since he's been here.

50

May 10th. Today.

Dad bought this twenty-four ounce at 1:39 this morning.

Nick points to the bottom of the receipt. The address of the convenience store is faded but readable: Baxter, Tennessee.

"Thea! Honey? You here?" Dad's voice calls from somewhere below.

9

MAY

Work boots on the stairs. He's close. Closer. "Thea!"

"He was in Baxter," I whisper. Nick folds the receipt, opens his wallet, and tucks the thin paper behind his license. Occam's razor's sharp edge cuts my brain in half. The logical answer is often *the* answer.

"Thea. Honey! You and Nick around?"

I don't know if I fall into Nick or he hugs me; either way, our hearts gallop like they're one thoroughbred rounding the last turn at the derby. Nick palms my skull and guides my cheek to his shoulder. I take fists of his T-shirt and as I do the collar strangles his neck; the cotton pulls halfway down his back. I bury myself in the details of him. He is sport deodorant. He is CK1 cologne. Rain and mud. "Do nothing for now," he tells me.

And then Dad is here, and Nick offers an awkward "Hey, Mr. Delacroix," and I'm all "Hey, we were checking out the towers," even though we're nowhere near the towers.

Dad's hair is stringy and wet like he came from outside. We're different complexions, me and him. He's dark and tan where I'm fair and pale, but there's no doubt I'm his when you put our eyes side by side. Between our noses and foreheads, we're carbon copies. I've always been glad for that. Glad for his handsome face, kind eyes, and narrow frame. He's rock hard. I once saw him lift a wheelbarrow of forty concrete bags. That's four hundred pounds. On a wheel, sure, but four hundred pounds.

Chris Jenkins would weigh nothing in his arms.

"What do you think?" Dad stretches up on his tiptoes with a yawn.

"About what?"

He gives me a weird look because I've responded so defensively and says, "About the towers, you knucklehead."

"They're great. Awesome."

"They're gonna be even better after last night."

"Dad?" I ask and Nick puts a fair amount of pressure on my shoulder, a warning. "I wanted to ask—"

The first set of lights clicks off, throwing us into partial grays. Dad moves to the second. Back to us, lamp still on, he asks, "You hear about the Gemini boy?"

When we don't answer, Dad's eyes widen. He abandons the light and hunches to face me. We also share the same worry wrinkles on our foreheads. "You okay, Thee?"

I shake my head.

Dad sighs. "Honey." He sighs again. "I know you think that kid's tied to Aulus, but he's not, sweetheart. He's really not. Nick, tell her I'm right."

"Mr. Delacroix—" For a millisecond, Dad's expression is an unfamiliar thorn. Animalistic. His eyes pierce Nick's. We are each

53

aware that Nick is supposed to tell me Chris Jenkins and Aulus have nothing to do with each other—and Nick is obedient. Well, mostly. "Are they sure it's Chris Jenkins?" he asks casually.

"According to Warren," Dad answers, and then laughs away the tension. "Don't watch the news. Please. I want you to sleep tonight. Graduation is around the corner. Hang on to that." He bends and coils the electric wire around the saw. Slowly, he figure-eights the extension cord. We watch, transfixed, as he sweeps dust into a pan and leaves the pan on the ground. He takes a drink of his hot Dr Pepper, grimaces, crushes the can with his boot. "Speaking of sleep, I'm gonna nap in the truck. I was up all night."

Then he's gone. Tromping down the steps like a horse.

I'm still working out whether I'm allowed to breathe when a phone rings. "Dana," Nick whispers into my hair. He takes the call with me close enough to listen. From the first beat of her voice, she's excited. "We got preliminary COD. Medical examiner says drowning. And . . . there's evidence someone tried to resuscitate him. Hey, Nick, you there?"

"I'm here." Pause. "Thea's here too." I don't know if that cue was for her or me. "Are you thinking the flood's involved?"

On the other side of the line, Dana's windshield wipers work overtime. She raises her voice to a yell, which means I hear her perfectly. "Off the record, absolutely. On the record, they'll test the water in his lungs."

"You meet with the family yet?"

"Just left."

"How are they?"

"How do you think?"

They sigh precisely the same way and I miss Aul all over again. You need people in your life who breathe the same way you do.

Dana says, "This could be a slipup. The break we need and didn't want. I shouldn't tell you any of this, but we think there's blood on the collar. No way to know whose yet. But for the first time in ten years, we could have DN—"

"Hey, can I call you on my way to the dorm?"

"Thea tell you about the key chain? You said she's there with you."

Nick raises his neck away, creating slight distance between us. I lean, wanting to watch his answer. "Yeah," he admits.

"Theory?" When Nick doesn't answer, she comes at him harder. "Nick? Theory?"

All Nick says is "I'm gonna call you back on my way to the dorm" and hangs up.

Like a habit, we follow the staircase to the third floor. Nick wants to process this a long way from my dad and I want to be in my favorite place. We reach a room, a someday bedroom, and without speaking claim the covered semicircle balcony that offers a view of the rain-soaked valley. Nick leans over the parapet, his head stretched beyond the awning into the deluge. Goose pimples line the bare skin of his arms.

"Hey, remember when Dad lying to me for nearly ten years was the problem?" I try to laugh.

Nick slides along the parapet wall until he's seated on the stone floor. His T-shirt sticks on the rough concrete, exposing his skin. He doesn't right the fabric. In a hushed voice he asks, "Where do you think he is right now?"

I sit. The soles of our shoes don't touch; the mud caked around them does. "Sleeping off his long night."

"Not your dad. Aul."

I rest my head against Nick's shoulder and use my finger to

deter a single stream of rain away from our clothes. Wherever Aul is, if he's alive, he's grieving the loss of Chris Jenkins.

Dad's voice echoes in my head. He feels like one of those lift-the-flap books. You turn a page, see a story, and then realize it's not the whole story. There's more hidden beneath. "I don't want you to be right," I say. Nick works his hands, massaging each joint until it pops. "But that receipt . . ."

Nick reaches over and cups my ear and then my face. This is him sorry.

"Is your sister going to tell you that Dad's already being investigated?"

Nick gives a grim acknowledgment. "She's going to ask me to confirm those key chains are identical and that your dad is the purchaser. They'll officially reinvestigate Aulus's disappearance and reexamine the Thief's actions. Your dad will be questioned. So will everyone else they questioned last time."

"Are you going to tell her about the receipt?"

"I don't know yet," he says. "Do you want me to?"

He turns his head a quarter. Our temples touch, the sides of our noses; the hollow of his cheek and the line of his jaw nuzzle my face. I feel his mouth close around the corner of my bottom lip. We stay that way for a long time. Kissing, not kissing.

I work the case, this way, that way, flipped sideways, upside down, and run headlong into that foreign moment where my dad said, *I know you think that kid's tied to Aulus, but he's not, sweetheart. He's really not.*

I say what I'm thinking to Nick. "Dad was in Baxter, the location of the body dump, early this morning. The key chain Dad gave Aulus ended up in Chris's mouth. Dad was with Aulus the day he disappeared. My father hid building a castle from me for almost ten years." *How much harder would it be to hide thirteen boys? With all this land and the freedom in his schedule? Not that hard.* I keep this last part to myself.

We are still. Completely still. Locked in our huddled position of touching hipbones and shoulders and muddy soles. Our breathing is the only noise other than the rain. Guilt chases me hound to fox.

"Tell Dana about the receipt."

THE ELIZABETH LETTERS

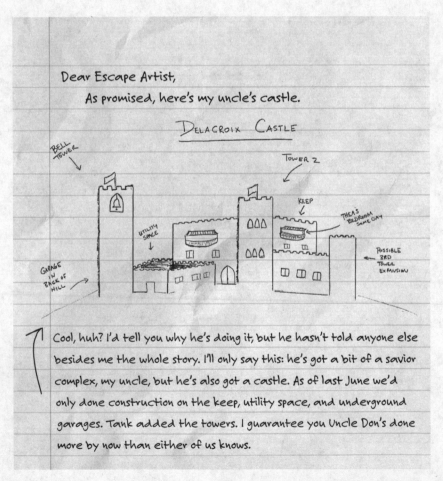

Dear Escape Artist,

    As promised, here's my uncle's castle.

DELACROIX CASTLE

BELL TOWER

TOWER 2

KEEP

THEA'S BEDROOM SOME DAY

UTILITY SPACE

POSSIBLE 3RD TOWER EXPANSION

GARAGE IN BACK OF HILL

Cool, huh? I'd tell you why he's doing it, but he hasn't told anyone else besides me the whole story. I'll only say this: he's got a bit of a savior complex, my uncle, but he's also got a castle. As of last June we'd only done construction on the keep, utility space, and underground garages. Tank added the towers. I guarantee you Uncle Don's done more by now than either of us knows.

Now I want to tell you about peeing. (←That's not a sentence I've ever written to a stranger before. Or anyone.) This'll be a two-parter (at least), so buckle up, buttercup.

Pee Drinking: Part I

Our stomachs were piranhas this morning, so Tank built a virtual buffet out of construction paper and announced we were celebrating "ThanksJunegiving." You would have thought he was announcing an act on Broadway.

"Gentlemen and boys, THANKSJUNEGIVING."

Rufus said, "That's not a thing."

Zared said, "It's 'cause we won't be alive in November."

I grabbed the tags of their underwear and yanked. "We're all getting along for the holiday."

"Fake holiday," Zared sang.

"Fake holiday," Rufus harmonized.

I told Zared he'd be needing a Band-Aid for this wedgie if he didn't can it. Tank set the table, ignoring us. The guys mooned me. We sat down like the family we are to four meat, eight snack, and ten dessert names written on torn scraps of paper. No veggies. (We're the kings of this world.) Then, like our grandmas were insisting, we heaped our dirty Frisbees with paper slips. My favorite: Wildwood High School chocolate milk.

Not too long after Rufus and Zared left ThanksJunegiving to nap—there's a lot of napping to pass the time—Tank lifted a "pork chop" to his lips and chewed the paper like a goat. My stomach hurt watching him swallow, but I kept us in the spirit. "We could catch a mouse."

Tank tears brown slivers of paper and crisscrosses them in a campfire stack. "And cook it over a construction-paper fire." He adds some red and orange and yellow strips. "Look! Fire's huge!"

"Enormous."

"Out of control."

"It'll burn the mouse up."

"And us."

During our frenzy, we stomped the "fire" until our hearts pounded and our feet were bruised. At the rave's height, I heaved a plastic blue toddler chair at the wall; it ricocheted, leaving a huge dent in the leg. We collapsed in a heap, laughing.

You can get full-on laughter.

Restaurants should add it to their menu.

"Maybe Nick and Thea will find us and bring McDonald's and cigarettes," Tank said.

I allowed Tank his fairy tale. "Yep. Hold the special sauce."

(Thea's my cousin. Nick's my brother from another mother.)

According to Tank, they hooked up since I've been down here, which is weird, but I get it. Nick perms his hair and in the scheme of things, that's weirder than

my cousin and friend kissing in my absence. Tank
was in some Sherlockian club with them and Gladys
(our other friend) before Welder made him our new
fourth. They've spent heaps of time looking for us.
I asked plenty of questions about their theories on
Welder. On where we're being kept. Is there any hope
of rescue?

Tank can't remember.

Welder's drugs messed him up. He's still Tank,
but a dulled, hands-pressed-to-his-temples Tank. I
try not to bring up who took us because it rattles all
his obsessions and no matter how many times I say,
"We're probably never going to know," he won't let it
drop. Sad, considering I've seen him out-math our old
calculus teacher. I prod him, smiling. "Hey, Uncle Leo
once read a story about a lost camper who gulped his
pee like Mello Yello."

"Didn't kill him?"

"Nope. Helped."

"Let's try it," he said. "Might buy us
more time."

I yelled toward the other room,
"Rufus! We need your scavenger skills.
Pronto!" To Tank I said, "We need a
bottle, right?"

He looked concerned until I promised
to go with Rufus and keep him on track.

I was out of the room when his
teasing reached my ears. "Pee drinker."

"Urine lover," I called back.

Pee drinking
isn't a perfect
idea, but urine's
90 something
percent water
and you can
drink it a few
days without
the bacteria
building up. If
Leo's right.

61

And we laughed.

They're waking up again. More soon. Up next, Pee Drinking: Part II.

Peace and Freedom,

Aulus

10

MAY

Grease blotches the kitchen table, courtesy of yesterday's gas station dinner. Two TV trays hang on Dad's bicep. A fried chicken leg is trapped between his teeth, barbarian style. "*Breaking Bad* before I head out?"

"Sure."

The last three days of perfect weather had Dad castle-ing non-stop. I told Nick last night, "There's mud on the bathroom floor and a filthy rogue sock between the toilet and wall, but the coverlet on his bed's in the same exact position as Monday. We're communicating in notes and money left at the end of the counter."

Don't wait up. Pizza in the freezer. —D

K. Need money for cap and gown. $45.

I can't exactly leave a note below that one:

And btw, did you murder Chris Jenkins? —T

Or: *Careful, FBI might be watching you.*

Dana has been stonewalling us since Nick told her about the

receipt. Which, good for her, professionalism and all, but I wish I knew what's coming—if anything's coming. They could have already ruled Dad out and I'm anxious for no reason. Whatever is happening in that ether, the media is clueless.

They've covered the Jenkins family extensively, but there have been no leaks, no leads, no ties to Wildwood or Aulus McClaghen. A new spread in *People* shows the Gemini Thief timeline. They're milking what they have, but they don't have much. That issue of *People* is on the coffee table. Dad shoves the magazine sideways to grab the remote, the wrong remote, plops down in his recliner, and then asks, "Can you turn that up? Air compressor's messing with my hearing."

Finger hovering over the volume button, I ask, "Uh, Dad?"

He stops midchew. Hair clings to the corner of his lip and I stare at the dead ends splitting in different directions. "Whatcha thinking about?"

"You haven't been around much, and I was just—"

"—feeling abandoned? Thinking I'm the worst dad in the world?" he jokes. The execution isn't smooth. "Don't worry. You know it'll rain again and you'll be stuck with me."

I try to relax my face. "When you're not here, are you always at the castle?"

He rests his napkin on the plate and dusts his hands. "I'm not dating anyone if that's what you're worried about."

I wish. "I didn't think you were dating someone." *Are you holding someone against his will?* "Where are you all the time? Like, what do I do if Mom calls some night and wants to talk to you?"

Dad sits up straighter, dumping fried chicken crumbs on the floor. "Your mom called?"

"No. But she could."

64

"Tell her I'm working."

"At the castle?"

"Honey, your mom doesn't have a key to my basement anymore. I'd rather her not know about the castle. She might assume things, show back up and want something." He huffs and mumbles something about her being the last thing he needs right now. "What's this about? You fighting with Nick?" He toes the corner of *People* with his boot. "You still caught up on this Chris Jenkins thing?"

"Maybe a little." I look away and dig my hands between the cushions of the couch.

"Honey, I like Nick, but I love you. Whatever it is, tell me."

"Sunday night . . . ," I begin. He's invested now. Turned completely in my direction. Walter White is in his underwear, frozen on the television screen. "We had a disagreement about Aulus and I wished you were here. I waited up." This is a lie. On Sunday night I didn't know I needed to account for his whereabouts.

"I'm sorry, knucklehead. I was . . ." His eyes dart up and to the left. "Working on the bell tower. Time got away from me." He watches the ceiling fan take a couple laps. "Yeah, that was definitely Sunday night–Monday morning. I fell asleep in my truck Monday afternoon, after I saw you and Nick."

He's lying. I turn up the volume on Walter White. "You should sleep here more."

"I'll sleep when I'm dead." He grins, plate tabled on his chest for easy access to the chicken. "And don't take any crap from Nick, okay?"

I give him two weak thumbs-up.

65

My cousin visits me again that night.

Dream Aulus is not who vogued into the Wildwood lunch-room hoisting a letter from Madonna, or the Aulus who helped me limp through pre-cal. And he's not June Boy Aulus either. Can't be. Dream Aulus comes like a Target-shopping Jiminy Cricket. Small. Charming. More smartly dressed than he ever was in real life.

He sits atop my pillow, head bowed in concentration, assembling and disassembling small-motored appliances. Last night, a Magic Bullet. Time before last, a toaster oven. Sometimes we talk. Sometimes we don't. Inevitably, he cranks the tool a final turn and examines his handiwork.

"Finished," he announces, followed by, "Thee, do you need a . . . a rice cooker?" I tell him I need him to come home and he says, "Can't." I ask, "When?" And he says, "Tell me about the Sasquatch trip again." We are a well-polished routine that ends with him say-ing, "You'll see me when you see me."

Except last night he hopped onto my shoulder, placed that green Jiminy mouth directly in my ear, and yelled, "Where does the money come from?" Tip of the flat cap. Wink-wink. He and the Magic Bullet are gone.

Sunlight pings off the tabletop. The clock isn't visible, though it must be at least five a.m. I fell asleep on the couch after Dad left for the castle last night. His boots aren't by either door. I'm alone. There's a rogue roll of duct tape beneath the recliner. Some houses have knickknacks; we have construction remnants. I sniff the sticky sweet smell of tack and gum. Dust bunnies cling to the edge and I tug them away.

Interviews with the older June Boys include copious accounts of duct tape. Over their mouths. Around their wrists. Circling their ankles. I tear a section the width of my mouth and seal it to my skin. With my allergies, breathing through my nose is like sucking oxygen through a clogged straw. At fifty-three Mississippis, red spots hover around my eyes. At sixty, I rip the tape away, fraught by my own freedom to do so. I race my tongue along the edge of my lips and then grow desperate for my toothbrush.

No amount of empathy transports me into Aulus's world and no amount of investigation returns him to mine.

My cousin's not just in a hole; he's missing his life. Reminders are everywhere. Graduation, which tiptoed around the periphery last semester, stomped into the present this week. New cars with Class of 2010 banners turn up daily. People are writing *It's been fun knowing you* in yearbooks. No matter which hallway you're in, someone's crying about leaving and someone's crying about staying. It's downright existential. Aul would have loved this part of high school. The finishing.

I deal with the Fridayness of Friday until lunch.

Rather than meet Gladys in the gym for our daily Doritos deluge, I slip off campus in Tank's truck. The tax office occupies the street-level shop near the WCC. I make a loop to confirm Dad's Ram isn't here, knowing it won't be. He lunches at the castle. That gives me forty minutes to poke around. Aulus wants to know where the money comes from and so do I.

Dad's vague on the topic. *Secret stash* or *The office had a good year*, he says when I ask. I laugh. *Are you a member of a cartel?* He never offers up anything.

In elementary school, the bus dropped me at Delacroix Tax. I played with Matchbox cars on this old carpet and got my favorite red Ferrari stuck behind the row of filing cabinets. Those are the cabinets I'm targeting today.

The automatic lights brighten the room when I open the door. They're LED and uncomfortably white. The storefront is glass; my only hiding place, the desk.

There's no peace in destroying privacy. No peace at all. The desk's middle drawer swims with rubber band odds and paper clip ends. I open three drawers on the right. Nothing but copy paper, empty files, and blank forms. That leaves the wall of cabinets.

They're oiled; each metal sleeve slides out revealing meticulous, hand-labeled files. Dad shows the same thoroughness here as he does at the castle. Except when I check the Ds, where I assume his own tax return will be, there's no file for *Delacroix Taxes* or *Donald Delacroix*. Thirty minutes in, I'm drowning in irrelevant government forms and positive I'll never be an accountant.

He'll be back any minute.

Before I leave, I want to investigate potential connections to Aulus. I change skimming tactics and search files that might be related to my cousin.

Scottie McClaghen. Nothing. He probably evades taxes.

Pattie Wittersham McClaghen earned seventeen thousand dollars from Dunkin' Donuts in 2009, twenty-two thousand in 2008, and twenty-one in 2007. Similar records go back another six years. None show reception of child support.

Griff and Ruby must do their own taxes. No files for Holtz.

Leo Wittersham, on the other hand, claims two dependents: Pattie and Aulus. According to W-2s, he made fifty-one thousand trucking for SCC Transport last year and another six thousand from Delacroix Taxes. According to this, Dad employs Leo. Six thousand dollars' worth. 2010. 2009. Thirteen thousand in 2008. My dad's been paying Aulus's uncle at least five hundred a month for three years. Not only that, he comps his taxes. The two men aren't friends. In fact, they speak terribly of each other when the occasion presents itself.

I jump at a passing shadow. The shadow jumps back. Ruby. She pops her head through the door and says, "Hey, skipper. Whatcha doing?"

I offer a defense in case she checks with Dad. "I left without money."

Ruby pats her pockets, produces a twenty-dollar bill for me, and blows palm kisses as she runs off toward the WCC.

Twenty in hand, I'm out the door too. I slip into senior English thinking I've gotten away with my sneaking. On a break, I text Nick, Gladys, and Tank and ask them to come over tonight.

Nick: I'll bring the pizza rolls.

Gladys: Be there. Where were you at lunch???

Tank: In my truck, you thief. Be ready to share. See you tonight.

They show up at 6:30 and I give them the story as I lived it.

Gladys's response is typical Gladys. "You broke into your dad's tax office? Right on" with a big high five.

"I have a key."

Tank pops the bill of my ball cap. "Takes cojones. I'm proud of you for being willing to investigate Big Poppa."

Nick's stuck on Leo's money. "How much a month?"

"Five hundred. At least."

Gladys shields her face with her hands. Through her fingers she says, "Thea, you're thinking that's what? Hush money? That Mr. Wittersham and your dad did this together?"

Tank spat a half-chewed pizza roll onto his plate. "Leo and Aul were super close. No way Mr. Wittersham's involved."

"Aul and my dad were close too."

Nick flings a napkin at Tank. "Everyone's a suspect until they aren't." And then he sits a little straighter.

"What?" Tank asks.

"We've been under the impression that the Thief keeps the boys in one location, but what if that location moves? What if it's a storage container? And that's how he gets away with it? Leo could be moving the containers around with his truck."

"That would be in the testimonies," I say.

"Not if they drug the boys."

We argue the logistics—they seem downright impossible to me. That's multiple hiding places, increased risk of exposure—and rather than fall headlong into rabbit holes we return to the topic of Chris Jenkins. Nick re-explains everything Dana told him, which, granted, isn't much. By the time we stop debating and rereading old articles, it's three a.m.

Sending Nick and Tank home at this hour is like taking a cheese grater to my intestines. They're guys; it's nearly June. I make them stay.

11

MAY

Nick's breathing deeply.

Slipping silently from the couch, I walk to the shower dressed in yesterday's clothes and a thin quilt. The door to my bedroom is ajar. Gladys and Tank are crashed out on my day bed and trundle. She's a tiny thing, pressed against the gold metal railing and wall; he's hugging the opposite edge, hand falling off the mattress.

Standing in front of the bathroom, I watch Nick. The love-seat isn't made for comfort. His handsome face, relaxed; his body, coiled. He looks scared. Of what? Of justice failing? Of not finding Aulus? That we're in danger?

"Stay alive," I whisper, and only as I speak do I realize I am terrified someone will take him from me.

Shower steam covers the mirror. Our pressure is terrible, the drain is clogged, and the water will boil your skin off. I've asked Dad to call someone. Every broken thing in this house stays that way for weeks. "But, Thea, you have a castle," I say to myself with false cheer.

I am rinsing shampoo from my hair when I hear voices coming from the kitchen. "Tank!" I yell, figuring he's the most likely candidate to be up this early. "There should be cereal in the pantry." As an afterthought I add, "Check the milk before you use it." When is the last time we went to the store? Last week? It might be a pizza-rolls-for-breakfast morning.

A hard rap at the door follows an indistinguishable shout. Then Nick's voice. "Thea." Man, he's wound up. The water is cloudy suds of shaving cream and a slight tinge of pink where I nicked myself. "Coming. Almost done."

"*Now*, Thee!"

I'm still dripping when I twist my hair and body into towels, then step into the hallway. A line of blood rolls along my shinbone. Strangers are in our house. Strangers wearing khaki pants and navy FBI shirts. This is it. It's happening.

"Ms. Delacroix," one agent says, eyeing my towel with interest.

"Nick?" I hiss. To the agent who ogles me, I say, "Excuse you." And then, "I want to see a warrant," because demanding something seems like a good way to offset the towel.

Nick's sister appears from around the corner. "Benson, search the garage," and the young agent walks the wrong way. Dana faces me, eyebrows raised, lips in a downward turn. "Honey, you better dress." She's shorter than me, but something in her stance is reminiscent of every firework stand in the South.

"Am I under arrest?" My voice cracks.

Dana's attention bounces toward the kitchen and back again. "Of course not. You're safe." She reaches to comfort me and I twist away, making a noise that comes out like "Nuh-uh." My tone is knife-sharp. "Why are you here?" *Why didn't you warn us you were coming?*

Nick provides the answer I expect. "They're here for your dad."

"He's not home." I indicate the presence of Tank and Nick. Like, *Hello, I don't parade boys in front of my father at six a.m.*

"Actually . . ." Nick nods toward the kitchen.

Tank and Gladys appear in the doorframe. Their hair's a mess and Tank's digging sleep from the corners of his eyes; they look like feral animals. *What do we do?* he mouths in Nick's direction, but Nick's staring at his sister, like he can't quite believe she's here. Gladys squeezes Tank's hand, her way of reminding him that he's black in a house full of very white cops and maybe now isn't the time for anger. Tank's glare says he's aware and he never needs reminding.

I nod at Tank, who nods back, then I leave them to find my father slumped over a kitchen barstool. No one cleaned away the research or last night's dinner. An agent stands beside Dad, arms crossed over his skinny chest. He's explaining that they have my father on a surveillance video at a Baxter gas station on the night Chris Jenkins died. They have the right to search our house. To collect evidence. There will be a formal questioning soon. That doesn't stop the informal questioning now. "We're looking for kids. *Kids*, Mr. Delacroix." The agent leans on the word, as if he's stirring the conscience of a psychopath. "Younger than your daughter."

Dad cleans beneath his fingernails with the corner of a cardboard file. "I don't know anything about those kids. I'd help if I did. My nephew's been missing almost a year."

The agents spots me and doesn't seem prepared to have a conversation about kidnapping in front of a girl wearing only a towel.

"Dad."

"There's been a misunderstanding, knucklehead." He lifts his

73

head, takes in my appearance, and adds, "Go put on clothes," like I'm the one out of place.

A misunderstanding? That's what we call the FBI invading our kitchen at six a.m.? I don't move.

Minus the FBI logo, Dad's dressed similarly to the agents. Khaki cargo pants, navy round-necked T-shirt, work boots. And like Dana, he doesn't appear to have slept last night. Purple slashes the skin beneath his eyes. His ponytail is oily and he's only making it worse weaving his hands obsessively through the strands.

The male agent addresses me as "miss" and explains they'll be continuing this chat elsewhere and they'll probably need to talk to me so is there another parent who can be present? That snaps Dad from his stupor. He bites the agent's head off, which is not appreciated by anyone in the room. "Do not speak to them without me."

"I won't," I say, more reflex than response.

"Did you just threaten her?" Dana asks in her fierce mama-bear voice.

"Of course not," Dad says.

The other agent doesn't let it drop. "Miss?" He wants my answer.

"Thea?" Dana asks.

All eyes fall on me.

I march to Dad's side. Nick follows. "Is he under arrest for something?" I ask.

Dana answers. "Suspicion of kidnapping and murder."

Murder. The word's out of place among the coffee mugs, the piles of dishes drying on the rack, the photos of Aulus and me taped to the fridge. *Murder*'s not a kitchen word.

Behind me, Tank says, "Come on, Nicky, do your law thing."

"Yeah," Gladys echoes.

Nick's the same shade of green I feel. His first action isn't a defense of Dad. Instead, he takes my hand, looks directly in my eyes, and says, "I swear I didn't know she was coming."

My brain swims with reddish-brown spots. I bend at the waist and attempt a deep breath. Tank, Gladys, and Dana surround me immediately. Nick covers my thigh when the towel flips sideways on my leg. "Don't let this happen," I plead to Dana.

"It'll be okay," Dad says.

Nick's pulse hammers against my palm. In this light, his eyes are topaz. His commitment steadies me enough to face my father. "What do I do?"

"Call Warren, Griff, and Ruby. When they release me on bail, we'll need to discuss my project." Only my dad could talk about the castle at a time like this. He's still going. "For now, turn off the generator so we don't waste gas, and I guess everything else can wait." As an afterthought, he adds, "We'll get this sorted."

Sorted is what you do to laundry, not murder and kidnapping.

Dana says, "Thea, you have my word we'll take care of him," and then she shoves Nick in the shoulder, a move that's playful but direct.

A fierce exchange follows.

"You should have told me," he says.

Dana dons her FBI voice. "I don't owe you a warning that I'm doing my job," and then barks an order to Benson, her co-agent. "Pack up the stuff on the table. Process the house and garage. Thea, you should get dressed and pack a bag. You have somewhere else to go?" There's the sympathy again and I wonder how much of this tough-Dana routine is for show.

I point at the Gemini research on the table, aware that its presence looks bad for Dad. It looks like an ego stroke. "That's not his."

Benson gives me a *Please, whatever* look.

"It's not." Three voices speak in unison.

Nick addresses his sister. "You know we've been doing our own investigation into Aulus's disappearance."

I watch the struggle in Dana. *Wanting to help. The law. Wanting to help. The law.* The law wins. "Bag them," she says to Benson.

"I need your key chain, Thea."

Resisting is pointless. Nick already gave her the receipt and there's the video footage as well. I walk to my backpack, remove the castle, and hand it over. Dana slips the chain and single camo key into an evidence bag.

"The generator," Dad interrupts as two agents flank him at his barstool. He's handcuffed and led out the front door and down the steps. The grass is damp, the greenest color of spring, and clinging to shoes as they cross our lawn. The event is civil—and the civility makes the arrest unreal. Dana eases Dad onto the back seat of the rear sedan, her mouth moving fast. I assume she's reciting Miranda rights, telling him he can have a lawyer present when they question him.

A less civil thing occurs across the street.

The WKNF news anchor and camera crew frame our house and the seven black sedans parked in our drive and along the curb. I imagine today's story hitting the noon news, tomorrow's headlines: *"Eccentric Local Castle Builder Arrested on Suspicion of Kidnapping and Murder."* Or maybe, *"Is Don Delacroix the Elusive Gemini Thief? Kidnapped Boys Still Missing; Wildwood Suspect Arrested."*

12

MAY

Tank stares out the living room window in total bewilderment. "I can't believe that just happened."

I beeline to my room, pack a bag that is 90 percent underwear, 10 percent pajamas. Gladys adds jeans and T-shirts. A toothbrush. "You'll stay with us," she says, stuffing my favorite pillow into a second bag. A knot of gratitude lodges in the back of my throat. I can't find words for how much I appreciate her being here, much less thinking ahead to a time when I'll put my head on a pillow.

Tank's perched on the edge of the trundle bed staring at the government sedans blocking our street. I'm still standing there, motionless and numb. Moments like this, Aulus's absence drops like an anchor. He'd know what to do. He'd make a plan. In the end, it's Gladys who nudges me and says, "Honey, you're still in a towel."

On the way to my closet I pat Tank's knee. He was frowning before I offered him comfort and continues frowning when I close myself inside the closet to wiggle into shorts and a T-shirt. When I emerge, there's an agent holding up the doorpost of my room. He's midthirties, a dark mullet sticking out his stiff ball cap. Next door, someone rummages through drawers in Dad's bedroom, and not gently.

Nick slides in next to me and whispers, "The generator?"

I don't know.

"Have everything?" Gladys asks casually. To Agent Mullet she asks, "She can come back here, right?"

"Eventually," he answers.

Nick relieves Gladys of my bags and we leave the room. At the last minute, I jab my finger at the agent's face. "Don't touch my stuff."

Agent Mullet's expression gives away less than a Buckingham Palace guard. "Your dad was the last person to see his nephew alive. I'll touch what I deem necessary."

Under other circumstances I'd consider this a victory: the authorities finally believe the Gemini Thief took Aulus. Under these, I shrivel.

Tank's the color of burnt sienna; he is a teapot, rattling, singing its song. I loop my arm through his and lean into his barrel chest. *If I can be calm, you can be calm*, I tell him with a pat of my hand. We walk away, Nick and Gladys trailing behind.

Nick catches up in the hallway. "He was baiting you hard."

Yep.

Our exit from the house is videoed. Questions are pelted like snowballs. Across the street, Mrs. Riggs watches from behind the partial curtain of her bay window. Thunder barks when he spots me. I haven't walked him in ages. If they interview her, she'll say my father is never home. She'll clutch Thunder to her breast, stroke his wiry terrier hair, and say in a nasal voice, "That girl raises herself," even though my dad does her taxes for free. Just about anything can change the opinion of an opportunist.

Tank's truck and Nick's Civic are trapped in the drive so we pile mismatched into Gladys's Challenger. Gladys and Nick claim the front, Nick behind the wheel. He weaves around the neighborhood, taking turns at random. His eyes dart between the road and the mirrors, checking for agents or media. When he heads toward town, Gladys breaks the silence. "What exactly are we doing?"

Nick checks the rearview mirror. "I don't know. Driving. Confirming no one's following us. Going to the castle before they do."

Next to me, Tank still hasn't calmed down. Gladys reaches back and strokes his knee. "Easy," she coos, as though he's a child. "You don't believe Mr. Delacroix took Aulus, so calm down."

"Does it matter what I think? The FBI hauled him away. The FBI, Glads. Please don't go acting like we can trust the system."

I am touched by his protective streak. Paralyzed too.

Nick cuts in. "Everything we've thought or found could be a coincidence. Not only is Don innocent until proven guilty, he's never hurt Thea. That's the strongest evidence of character he has."

"He lied about a castle. How exactly are we measuring hurts?" Tank has always admired my dad for this undertaking. Seeing him make a fist on my behalf is strange and oddly justifying.

"Physically for now," Nick says. "Don's never put a single hand on her."

Tank swivels sideways. His grip on my biceps is like two blood pressure cuffs. "Swear," he says. "Swear to me right now that your dad never hurt you. That you're telling us the whole truth. Swear you won't protect him over yourself."

I am careful not to blink. "Never, Tank. Never."

Releasing me, he throws himself against the seat and punches the ceiling, leaving four grooved indentions in the fabric.

"I know," Gladys says, even though he didn't say anything.

"Try being me," I say.

Nick, ever positive, says, "Don could definitely be innocent. They're following protocol."

No one responds.

We arrive at the cattle grate without me noticing we passed the Moose Lodge or the WKU mailbox. Tank's fists are no longer clenched, but his jeans are wrinkled from grabbing the fabric. "Now what?" he asks.

I have no idea. We check the generator? We search for evidence?

Gladys hands me more grace than I deserve. "It's okay, honey. It'll all be okay." Staring into the bright blue sky, she adds, "I think." And then a much quieter, "I hope."

The castle towers rise into a Kentucky blue sky, the American flags popping, metal rivets slapping the aluminum pole. For the first time since Dad confessed to this, I want my father to be the builder of castles. But we're not here to laud his architectural skills. We're here . . . I think . . . to search for Aulus. Another abysmal thought occurs right on the heels of that one.

"Nick, how long can the FBI hold him?" Nick's not pursuing criminal law, but he took a class last semester in trial law. We both suffered through study seasons and flash cards.

"I don't know if federal cases work the same, but they should have twenty-four to seventy-two hours to charge him. After that, they'll likely bypass a grand jury and hold a preliminary hearing. If their evidence is solid, they'll proceed to trial."

Gladys arrives at the same conclusion as me. "But if Mr.

Delacroix were to be the Gemini Thief, aren't the boys in more danger? If your dad's been caring for them"—she is apologetic at the suggestion—"and he's unavailable . . . Will they starve? Can they . . . breathe?"

THE ELIZABETH LETTERS

Dear Elizabeth,

Pee Drinking: Part II

The bottle search turned up two potential containers. One plastic pitcher—the kind they sell at the dollar store—and a quart Mason jar that needed to be emptied of bolts and washers and wiped out with a T-shirt. I made an instructional announcement about future bathroom habits. (Previous habits involved a camping potty and trash bags we passed to Welder.) Ergo, post announcement, an argument boiled over from the adjacent room. Nothing atypical. Zared's a year older than Rufus but acts five years younger. They're fourteen and fifteen—no, fifteen and sixteen now, and Zared was whining about Rufus locating the containers. *"He is* not, and I mean, NOT, drinking anything that comes from my body." You know how whiners are.

There was mumbling, incoherent grumbling, then Rufus said, "Aulus says it'll save our lives."

"Aulus isn't God." Zared pronounced my name *Alice* because he assumed I was listening.

I yelled through the wall to appease him, "All-Us!" and Tank stirred. We were back in Sleeping Room, lounging and conserving calories. He was flat on his belly, drawing his own copy of *The Giving Tree* from memory; I was folded into a pseudo-chair of trash bags, rereading a yellowed paperback of Stephen King's *The Stand* that's missing pages 142–173.

Next door, the argument hit a new level and I straightened, ready to police if need be. *What are you thinking about?* Tank's eyebrows asked. *Let 'em go a bit longer,* mine answered. He returned to sketching; I returned to eavesdropping. There was a serious *thwack* and sharp *owww* from the next room, a body ramming the concrete floor.

I cracked my neck prizefighter style and thrust my upper body into the main room. Rufus had Zared in a full nelson. A game of cards, probably blackjack, scattered across the concrete floor as they wriggled and writhed. The deck of cards is missing a two of spades and the queen of hearts, and Zared was missing a tiny chunk of his ear. Blood dripped from his cheek to the floor.

"You're drinking pee," I said matter-of-factly to Zared.

Zared bucked Rufus's hold and screeched, "We're going to die in here!"

Rufus growled in an effort to control Zared. "Aul, tell him we won't die. Welder's coming back to let us go."

"Welder releases June Boys on June 30th. We hang in a few more days and we're golden," I told them both.

Rufus loosened his hold and Zared smashed the crown of his head into the kid's face. This broke the hold, maybe the nose, based on the crunching noise and subsequent yelp. ←

Our bones are softer than they should be. Vitamin D is one of the many things Welder stopped supplying after . . . well, after.

If you're thinking Zared is difficult, you get a gold star. But also, when he thought I'd stopped watching, he peeked at Rufus's bleeding nose, and the sorrow was there. Only a flash. But there. "Save that blood, Rufe. Aulus the Conqueror will have you drink it later," he said.

I'm not violent, Elizabeth, not even playfully, but I charged Zared. I guess I'd had enough lip and negativity. I shoved him offensive-lineman style and pinned him to the wall. His arms were sticks. The sliver of his humerus met the elbow and forked into his ulna and radius like a dying tree branch. They'd snap in a hard wind. I planned to be a strong breeze.

You should have heard me, Elizabeth. I was a gunman, pistol to his carotid. I was Liam Neeson. "I will keep you alive. Understand?" When he didn't respond,

I risked holding him with one arm to grip his chin and force an eye lock. "You understand me?"

Red streaks splotched his neck and cheeks. "When are you going to figure out you can't save us? We're already gone."

"I can. I will."

"Like you saved Chris—" Zared spat the words and I almost hit him. My fist missed his ear by millimeters. There was more to the strike than knuckles and wrists, more than rotating shoulders and hips. I smashed that wall the way I wished I could hit myself. Standing over him, I squeezed his bony body until it gasped, until I was sure I had his full attention. "Tank says most of the other boys were freed." I winced on most, because he's right about Chris. "That's what I'm believing for us. You're going to believe it too."

Zared worked his jaw. "Your precious bestie's lying. Just like you are." The twisting and sweating made him slippery, but I wasn't about to let go. His eyes chased a shadow to my right.

"Freezer," Rufus said. He was close enough for Zared to kick at him so Zared did and Rufus kicked back. "No giving up, dude. Welder's letting us go."

By then the fight had left Zared's voice. "Swear."

Rufus turned to me. "Yeah, swear, Aul."

They sounded young. Terribly young. I didn't know if I could be old enough. This feeling, this gap between who I am and who they need me to be, kills me. But I stepped up and lied, because I'm the adult here. It came easily, the way it must have to my father when he said, "See you after daycare, little buddy," knowing his car was packed with everything he owned.

"I swear," I said, a perfectly executed falsehood, and left my boys before they questioned me further.

I passed through Sleeping Room into the next room, the next, the next, each time hoping the maze might produce a Minotaur willing to eat a skinny hero. Tank followed. We walked, palms out, protecting our shins and faces. When I was sure the boys weren't in earshot, I asked Tank, "Odds there's a screwdriver in all this junk?" I wanted the freezer dismantled. "If Welder doesn't come back soon, Zared climbing in the freezer and shutting the lid is a legitimate concern. Tank, I can't lose him too. I can't." And against my better judgment, I sobbed.

"Aul—"

I raised my hand to stop his lecture. *Yes, yes, I understand I'm not the savior of the universe; that doesn't make me less responsible.*

"It's hard to believe they're really here. That you have the burden of . . ." Tank was careful how he spoke—for me, for him—and he corrected. "It's hard to believe any of us are here." His face was a dam; he held back a river of words. "You're not planning to drink that urine, are you?"

There's been no sign of our captor in twenty sleeps. No reason to believe we'll be rescued.

He knew me so well. He caught my forearm and held it with his fingertips. I knew him too. He longed to tell me Chris wasn't my fault, that none of this was my fault, but instead we stood together, him holding my arm, me looking toward the boys until he said "Aul" like he was as worried about me as I was about Zared. That hit me good and hard.

"Maybe I'm being selfish," I said.

"You're many things right now and selfish isn't one of them."

A quiet whisper came from my gut: *Dying first is easier than watching anyone else die.*

Peace and Freedom,

Aulus

13

MAY

No one questions Nick's decision to park behind the Moose Lodge. We walk single file. Taciturn. As if the earth might gobble us whole if it hears us coming. Before Dad purchased the adjacent acreage, the land belonged to seeds and weeds. Probably corn one year, wheat and soybeans the next. Dormant and disheveled now, the ground, soft from rain, gives like a mattress and suctions our shoes.

The first low hum creates a panic. Squatting in an unplanted field won't hide us any more than a child who believes he's invisible if he closes his eyes, but Nick pats the air and we all crouch. A bright green Mustang roars by honking and waving.

"Should we be calling their names?" Gladys asks as we stand. No one answers. "Aulus." Her voice is so tentative, so tender. She tries again. "Aulus." Attempt two isn't much louder.

I part my lips and discover my throat's an air lock. I can say his name. What I can't do is call out like movie characters do when someone goes missing in the woods. That feels like admitting my father killed him.

Tank shakes a cigarette from the pack, wedges a Camel in the crook of his mouth. He keeps spinning the flint wheel backward, and I take the cigarette and grind it deep into the mud. There are moments I forget Tank has as much claim to Aulus as I do—this isn't one of them. I squeeze his hand. He gives me a sideways nod and tweaks his nose the way you do when you're making sure you don't cry. Grief isn't a thing that requires words.

"You try," Gladys says to me.

"I'll do it," Nick says before I can answer. "Aulus! Rufus! Zared!" He blasts their names as we plod across the field toward the castle drive. Two more cars pass with no sign of the Feds or police. Nick peers toward the forest access road. "I don't know if Dana has a warrant for the castle."

"Why wouldn't she?" Gladys asks.

"Warrants are specific. They might not have been able to include the castle initially," I say and lead them toward the front entrance. "The internal construction is brick, metal, and wood. If they're here, they're in a hidden subbasement." It takes effort to level my voice. "That means we're looking for trapdoors and secret staircases."

We fan out through the keep. Other than the kitchen and baths, labeling rooms without identifying furniture or decorations proves difficult. Most of the larger spaces can be utilized for anything from a library to a formal dining room. We cover the square footage slowly. Everywhere we search, the mortar meets the bricks.

"How do we get to the basement level?" Tank asks.

"Through the lower garage," I say.

Tank wants to go immediately, but Nick argues that a cursory glance is subpar. "The Gemini Thief, whoever he is, is incredibly intelligent."

"He or *she*," I say as Tank huffs, "Incredibly demented, you mean."

"You're only saying that because it widens the suspect pool," Nick says. "These abductions require a brute strength that most women don't possess."

He saw right through me, but I plunge on. "Either way, he or *she* has managed to stay hidden for a decade. A *person* who evades detection for that length of time doesn't put the entrance to a secret cave or bunker or whatever in the great room."

"Or maybe that's the perfect place. Hidden in plain sight," Tank argues.

"Guys."

They ignore Gladys.

"It doesn't make sense, Tank."

"None of this makes sense, *Nick*."

"Guys!" Gladys snaps. Maybe there's supposed to be a speech, but she isn't one for speeches. She leans against a waist-high copper-colored bell in the corner and awakes the clapper. The resulting bongs overtake the room. Beautiful. Pure. We stand spellbound until the hammer stops striking the metal interior.

"Wow," Tank says.

"You'll be able to hear that in town," Gladys says.

"You can probably hear that in Tennessee," Nick says.

Dad doesn't cut corners, I think.

The east bell tower is in place structurally. The west is a different story. We stand at the base of an upturned forty-foot storage container; it and its adjoining room are under construction. A concrete mixing drum and five-gallon buckets of water are tucked under the stairwell. Four bags of concrete make a tidy stack in one corner. Pallets of wood and flats of bricks line the connecting hallways.

"How far up has he finished?" Tank's words are hollow in the narrow space.

Gladys's flashlight beam stops ten feet up. Nick moves gingerly toward the construction but he's up and down in a flash. "Three and a half stories, and"—he points at the stack of concrete bags—"that's a seam."

The Quikrete paper corner rips when I grab the edge, and concrete clouds the air gray. Gladys drags the ten-pound bag away without spilling more. Tank and Nick wrestle the remaining three into a ramshackle stack. Four metal panels, painted like bricks, stare up at us.

Gladys's hip presses against mine. We turn, faces quelled and flat, until fear carves itself onto her lips and cheeks. Four fingers dig into my ribs. *Who is your father?* her eyes ask.

I'm not sure I ever knew.

Nick lifts the false floor. Ladder rungs lead into darkness. "I'm guessing this isn't on the official tour," he says and leans his upper body through the hole. "Hello?" *Hello, hello, hello* echoes back. "I'll go first," he says.

I note the quiver. In Baxter, he stopped and went back to the car. That could happen again. If it does, he'll call his sister. Once Dana is involved there'll be no choice about whether we protect my father or not. Am I terrible for hoping that happens? For wishing this belonged to someone else? Right now it's all mine. I'm the one who confirmed the key chain. I'm the one who told him to give her the receipt. When they hauled Dad into that squad car and put his face on the news as a kidnapper . . . That's on me.

Nick's descent is tedious, but he deems the ladder safe for us to follow. There are fourteen rungs before my foot connects with some manner of flooring. I blame a shiver on the cool air and my tissue paper–thin tank top, but there's no doubt I'm scared. My heart is in overdrive.

The trapdoor provides a column of half light, which is adequate to assess our surroundings. This room is roughly the size of a basketball court and has a poured concrete floor and brick walls. They're yellow. Maybe beige or tan.

Tank rips off a set of curse words that adequately expresses my own amazement.

"How did he dig this out?" Gladys asks.

"Patience and a backhoe," I say. He's focused and meticulous when he wants something done. Same as me.

Tank leaves the group huddle and returns with a piece of copy paper. In large block letters, Dad's written, *Weapons*. There's a footnote in pencil. *Purchase: wall mount racks, shelving, additional ammunition. Move from safe: guns.*

"We don't have a safe." When Dad hunts, he borrows guns from Uncle Warren.

"You sure?" Tanks asks.

"If we do, I don't know where it is." In all the time I've processed Dad's lies about the castle, I've never considered there could be other castles or other homes. Other families? He is gone an awful lot. I take the paper from Tank and fold and fold and fold. I can't make it insignificant, but I will make it small.

"Could his safe be at Warren's?" Gladys asks.

Countless games of hide-and-seek taught me the nooks and crannies of Uncle Warren's house. Other than the basement door in the kitchen—which is just unfinished space according to him—I've always had full run of his place. "Not anywhere in the house," I answer.

Weapons isn't the only sign.

We circle the room, removing each paper as we come to it. *Water, Canned Foods, Oxygen, Medical Supplies, Vent, Water Closet.*

"Guys . . . ," I say.

"I know," Nick says.

Gladys is compassionate. "Thee."

"There's nothing here," Tank says, as though the emptiness of this room might provide a margin of comfort.

Tank's right. But the hard conclusion has to be admitted. "There could be more of these bunkers. And if Dad dug one ten years ago, the land would hide the lie."

"Let's leave that to the FBI," Nick says.

I take the folded *Weapons* paper from my shorts pocket. "No. Let's take this to the digger."

14

MAY

Tank slams a pack of Camels against the steering wheel. We're in front of my house; Nick's and Tank's vehicles are no longer caged. Two unmarked sedans hug the curb. The FBI's inside. "*Thee,*" Tank says, "Your dad's not gonna tell you anything."

We've been debating since we left the castle. He gropes in his pocket for the lighter. He's about to spin that stupid wheel backward.

Gladys quietly removes the lighter and says to me, "We're coming with you."

"No." I am firm. "Go back to the castle and keep searching before we're not allowed to be there."

Neither twosome is sure who got the worse end of things.

When Nick and I leave the Challenger for the Civic, Tank crushes my ribs and chest with a silent and extraordinarily long hug before climbing back in the car with Gladys.

"You and Tank always been close?" Nick asks.

It's a strange question since Nick has known us for nearly a year. But I guess we haven't talked much about who we were before Aulus disappeared.

"No way," I say. "I hated him in elementary school."

He laughs. "Why?"

"I don't really remember," I say, but I do. Tank had everything, and back then, he let us all know. I'd almost forgotten the amount of loathing I directed toward Thomas Piper and his normal life and normal parents and normal lunches. He even played normal baseball and camped with his normal Boy Scout troop.

Over the last hour the Civic has been spitting lukewarm air and not always in a constant stream. I unstick my thighs from the leather for the third time and Nick attempts to lower the windows. The glass stops halfway. "Sorry," he says, either for the lack of air or the whole situation. "I don't know if they'll have booked him or not. I'm guessing yes."

"You're saying he'll be in a jumpsuit."

"Probably."

"And they'll have what? Taken his fingerprints and mug shots?"

"Yes. Saliva. Hair. DNA."

I've seen that part on *Law & Order.*

"They might not let you talk to him."

"Uncle Warren will get me in," I say with certainty.

"Warren's with the Wildwood Sheriff's Department, not Simpson County. He won't have a say."

I ignore Nick—Uncle Warren can worm his way anywhere— and ask, "Will my conversation with Dad be recorded?"

"They record phone calls. I'd think they'd have a camera on holding or interview rooms, but I'm not sure. My professor said only clergy or legal conversations are private."

I press my head against the window until my skull and the glass are practically enmeshed.

"I wouldn't carry that basement sign in."

I toss the *Weapons* square onto his floorboard, where it lands between a petrified Arby's curly fry and a *Critical Criminology* textbook. "How am I supposed to talk if people are listening?"

We aren't closer to a strategy when Nick parks under the non-shade of a miniature maple. My godparents stand in the shadow of the jail, talking. Griff's wearing a hat, and he never wears a hat. Ruby's in her rumpled WCC polo and work boots. They still look like superheroes and I launch myself at him first, pressing my face into the fabric of his chest, inhaling the sweat, the Mountain Spring Tide, the familiarity. Ruby reaches us and holds on for dear life.

Griff says the Griff-est words ever, "We'll fix this."

"I don't know how." I leave a wet splotch on his T-shirt.

"I called an attorney," he says into my hair. "We'll get him out on bail."

"Whatever you need," Ruby tells me.

I shove feelings to my toes. "I need to see him."

The tightness of Ruby's lips says that's a terrible idea. Over the top of my head, she whispers, "Is that safe?" to her husband. I feel more than hear him give her an *Are you kidding me?* shake before he shifts me under his wing and guides us inside.

Uncle Warren's here, waiting for us to pass the metal detector. There's justice in his straight-backed spine, confidence in that wiry jaw. His cop-ness has always provided a measure of comfort, but now, I'm unsure of his side. He hugs me the way he has a million times and he's ours again, not theirs. "Don's in holding," he says.

"Can I see him?"

Warren addresses Griff. "The attorney's in with him now. I'm sure they're discussing Monday's arraignment. You go in afterward," he says to me. "But not for long. This is federal." He flicks Nick on the chest. "I'm on your sister's short rope."

Beside me, Ruby's repeating one of her comfort scriptures, massaging the triangle of skin between her thumb and index finger. I wish I had any one of her little calming routines. Warren escorts us to a break room with a Coke machine that only has water, red Gatorade, and Sun Drop. We collapse on hard plastic chairs. Warren crosses his legs and clamps the crossed leg with both hands, all business. He has an answer ready when Griff asks, "Did you know this was coming?"

These men have lived on the sidelines of my childhood. Dad's head coach; Warren's in charge of defense; Griff is special teams. They don't always agree with each other's methods, but they're always on the same team.

Warren answers, "I'm as surprised as you," which is a relief.

"Thea?" Griff asks.

I try not to catch Nick's eye. "Of course not."

Warren asks if Dad has been acting unusual.

I hesitate.

Griff offers a harsh reprimand. "Go easy, yeah? He's her dad."

Ruby scoots closer. "Honey, you can tell us anything. Any suspicions you might have, you can trust us." I love Ruby, but I don't like being told to trust.

Griff notices and he and Ruby share an uncomfortable wordless exchange that ends with her lifting her arms in a helpless shrug. I try to remember: This is Cop Warren. We are in a police station. This is when I step lightly. I answer, "Ten years ago Dad bought ninety-six acres of land and started building a castle for reasons unknown. You're going to need to define *unusual*."

There's a cough-laugh of understanding from the adults.

"Well, would you have any reason to suspect he's on drugs or mentally compro—"

"Warren!" This time Griff comes back hard. "Come on, man. You know Don. He's not mentally compromised."

"If there's one thing I've learned being a cop, it's that people aren't always who we think they are."

Griff says, "By your reasoning I should ask if you're the Gemini Thief."

"You should."

Griff is caught off guard by Warren's bluntness. There's apparent shock, then a form of skeptical acceptance. "Well, then, are *you* the Gemini Thief?"

Warren does not crack. He bears down on Griff. "No. Are you?"

"No. And you're the one on drugs if you think Don is capable. This is Don we're talking about."

The tension's electric.

"Please stop," I say, and immediately Nick jumps his chair closer to mine until our shoulders are inches apart; his only protection against my father's two best friends.

A middle-aged man wearing glasses pokes his head into the room. "Ready for you, kiddo," he says to me, and I'm almost relieved until I remember what I have to do next. Nick touches the small of my back as we follow our escort to a hallway door. "Make it quick," he says and sinks his hand through a ballooning hole in his button-up.

My dad isn't in a jumpsuit. Even if he were, I don't know enough about the process to understand what has already been done or decided. Somewhere along the way he's lost his ponytail holder and his hair hangs limply around his shoulders. Dad raises his voice to a pseudo-annoyed tone so everyone in the hallway hears. "Tell *Warren* he's fired for letting you in here."

"I had to come."

The door shuts. In tandem, we glance toward the two-way mirror, a little signal to each other that we're not truly alone. Dad fidgets with the metal anchors the cops use to handcuff inmates to the table. I slip a rubber band off my wrist and place it in his palm. He acknowledges my offering by fiddling with the elastic.

I state the obvious, "Griff hired a lawyer."

"Spending money on all this is a waste. I need it for the castle."

"Dad, there won't be a castle if you don't get out of here."

"There will." He sounds delusional. "Listen." Dad raises his chin enough to note the tears on my cheeks. I am furious with him and scared for him and us and me and what this means and I am so so so . . . I cannot name what I am. Dad rests the tips of his fingers over mine. "Honey, you do not have to worry about this. None of this is real."

"I don't need to worry," I parrot.

"You do not."

"You're not worried that we're trapped in some *Shawshank* nightmare?"

"No." He doesn't sound sure. He sounds like he wants to sound sure, and there's a big difference.

"Do you remember what you told me when I was scared my first day at Wildwood Elementary? About the keys?" I will him to remember the basement conversation.

A coy smile hides behind his intense brown gaze.

"I need you to give me a key, Dad. I need you to tell me why this castle is more important than being arrested for kidnapping and murder."

He lowers his head for a minute.

"My 401(k). The house. The tax office. Our savings." I suppose he decides one cat out of the bag might as well be a litter. He adds, "Your college fund. Everything we have is in this castle."

I can barely speak. "You spent my college money on your castle?"

He corrects me. "Our castle." Placing both hands flat on the table, Dad extends his neck and face like a snapping turtle ready to strike. "I spend what I have to and I'd do it again." His eyes lift toward the ceiling, like someone might be up there. "And you'll be fine, honey. You always land on your feet." I want to scream at him, *I haven't been on my feet in a year, Dad.* "I wasn't even sure you wanted to go to college anymore," he adds. "I kind of thought you might stay home and help me build."

He's crazier than I thought. Horrified as I am, I can't process what all that means financially, not when there are still more secrets. Piles of them and I don't have much longer in this room.

"The bell tower?" I tap the desk in a downward motion.

He pushes his chair back from the table. "You can't think—"

"What am I supposed to—"

"You're supposed to trust me."

"Am I? You lied about the castle for a decade. You're gambling with my future and yours . . . and for what? A stupid half-built fantasyland?"

He grips his collar with both hands. Sweat beads along the veins and hollows of his neck. "Thea, you asked me a second ago if I was worried and I wasn't. But, honey, if you think I'm guilty, I've lost a game I didn't know I was playing."

I am so quiet I can barely hear my own voice. "Show me you didn't do this." *Did the FBI hear me? Will they hold my doubt against him?*

"I. Did. Not. Hurt. Aulus. Ever. Or any of those Gemini boys.

100

Period. Warren!" Dad stands as he yells at the doorway. His agitation grows. "Warren!" The door cracks open and Warren leans inside. The crowd huddles just behind. "Take Thea home," Dad says to his best friend.

"Dad." My voice cracks.

"Out."

Warren puts himself between Dad and me. "Hey, buddy. Calm and cool, okay?"

"Out." Dad's absolute.

I'm no farther than the doorway when Ruby brushes my tears with the back of her hand. She leans into the holding room. "Don, do not take her for granted." Warren tugs her toward the hallway. Ruby's always been Mama Bear, but I've rarely heard her roar.

Dana, having left the adjacent room, where she surely watched this unfold, yells at the lot of us. "All of you out. Now. Yes, you too," she says to Warren specifically. It's unclear if Dad's harshness extinguished her goodwill or she's put out by the whole scene. I suspect the former, but she tightens her lip and gives Warren a dose of wrath like he should know better.

Back inside the holding room, Dad walks to the corner seam and buries his face like he is in elementary school. Dana is about to shut him in when he calls, "Honey, don't forget what you already know. That's what's true. Not all this." His voice drops. "I love you. More than anything else in the world. But please, please don't come back until you believe me. I can handle false accusations from everyone else, but I can't . . . I can't handle one from you." He sinks to the floor, head in his hands. Dana closes the door.

THE ELIZABETH LETTERS

Dear Elizabeth,

Our screwdriver search was delayed due to Tank's brain hurting.

Currently, he's holding his head like a football while Rufus and Zared play cards in the next room. They're laughing hard, hard enough to annoy him, but he's Stonehenge when it comes to the boys.

That gave me time to write more.

Times like this, when no one needs me, I give myself over to missing. You know how dangerous missing is? One little thought of Thea or Gladys or Nick and I'm all but gone. For this session, I drift toward Uncle Leo.

If you're not a gun, a dog, or an American, Leo's got commitment issues with you. According to him, he's had three and a half wives (no comment on which wife was the "half," but we all agree it was probably Sparkle Parker—think of it as one name—who washed dogs door to door in the '90s). If you ask Leo if he's working on numero quatro when he's down at the bingo hall, he'll say, "I gave up women for books." And by all accounts, he has.

Living with Uncle Leo means I've been sharing a twin bunk bed set with my mother since I was six. Not as bad as it sounds. She worked a lot and only slept a little. Plus, I can't complain when Leo doesn't have a bedroom in his own house. I'll bet you anything he's on the porch now, rereading a novel, sipping Mountain Dew from a gallon-size insulated, double-walled travel mug from Quik Mart, and munching a bag of sunflower seeds. He taught me to drive, to use the top third of the windshield, and to read after my first-grade teacher gave up. I taught him fist-bumping and cellular phone technology. You'd like him after the first month or two.

This is all hypothetical, but as a family member and owner of the quattro, the police probably brought him down to the impound lot, right? Maybe asked him to shed light on the abandoned car and its contents. I'll bet that was like jumping on a trampoline in a room with a four-foot ceiling for everyone involved.

I can imagine my uncle examining every
square inch of the Audi Quattro. Among
the sticky pennies and empty water bottles
he'd find: a brand-new DeWalt cordless drill
purchased at Ace Hardware; a chicken-
scratch note to Thea, another to Nick; maybe
my backpack. The police would probably tell
Leo the key was in the ignition, car running,
when they found it. Here's the long and short
of Leo's answer. "Mister, no kin of mine leaves a
restored 1982 Audi Sport Quattro on the side
of the road. You better believe someone took
him or I'll kill him myself."

Who knows what the police said
about that.

Maybe they think Leo took me.

Maybe they think I'm dead.

The day I was taken, Leo and I spoke
briefly. I was on an errand for Uncle Don and
had stopped by the house. Leo was on the
porch, reading, ever reading, ever slurping the

Big Gulp. On my way across the lawn, he'd spat a mouthful of seeds onto the porch. "I warned you about the mud, didn't I?" he said, pointing at the quattro's side panels. Leo's not keen on my dad's side of the family and never missed a chance to let me know. The only person he halfway likes is Thea, and that's because she bears a striking resemblance to his favorite ex-wife.

"Yeah, yeah. I'll wash her this afternoon," I said with a two-finger salute. I was in and out fast before he had me washing the Audi in the drive. I needed to get the new drill back to Uncle Don since I'd broken his that morning. I called around looking for a replacement—Warren Burton; my Quik Mart boss, Mr. Rachelle; the shop teacher at school, Mr. Markum; and no one, not even Griff and Ruby, who have every tool known to man in the WCC shop, had exactly what I was looking for.

Less than a mile from the castle, a Plymouth Sundance sat stalled in the highway, passenger door open. There's nothing out that road but farms. I hit my hazards without a thought.

Elizabeth, I've replayed the next three minutes of my life uncountable times over the last year.

I left the driver's door slightly ajar.

Walked to the Plymouth.

The asphalt warmed the soles of my shoes. The wind grabbed the scents of honeysuckle and lavender and sent them my way.

I called out, "Hey! Need help?"

Found no one in the vehicle.

Assumed the Plymouth ran out of gas.

Heard something from the brush, near the woods.

A flock of birds alighted in the treetops and sat twisting their necks side to side.

I stopped moving. Listened hard.

A weak voice. "Help."

I picked my way forward. Thigh-high grass. The buzzing of bees. The pop of disturbed grasshoppers.

A work glove shot above green wisps, ten yards away. "Help," the weak voice called again.

"Should I call an ambulance?" I asked.

No answer.

Eight yards.

Someone was in pain. In trouble.

Six yards.

My brain fired, thinking through possible scenarios: hunting accident? heart attack? I braced for blood.

Four yards.

"My name's Aulus. Where are you? Keep talking."

Groans.

One yard.

There was a cough.

A flash of gray-black helmet.

A whirl of movement.

The blunt end of a shovel collided with my head.

Someday, if you're ever ready, you should tell your story too.

Tank's waking up. I'll be back.

Peace and Freedom,

Aulus

15

MAY

When we leave the jail, a narrow band of sky is the shade of orange sherbet. A train horn blares. The heavy clatter of freight makes talking or thinking impossible. Ever intuitive, Griff nods at Nick's car and says, "Take your time. Ruby's making a Sam's Club run for the WCC before she heads back to Wildwood. I'll drop you at Gladys's and save Nick a trip."

Nick has bitten the skin around his nail beds and they're bleeding, but he offers me a weary smile. I step closer, not too close. Near enough to telegraph that his presence is welcome. He has this ability to let me oscillate between hot and cold without holding either temperature against me, and I don't think I've ever been more grateful than I am right now.

"That was brutal," he says, slumping against the hood.

"I don't understand him."

"Who does?"

"He's hurting."

Nick doesn't make some big show, just says, "So are you," and unlocks the passenger side of his car. I fall into the seat sideways and he crouches by my knees. Thankfully, he stares at the toes of his shoes, first picking at the place the rubber sole meets the fabric, then threading his hand through his hair. Yesterday's hair spray is a gummy mess and none of his attempts tames the Howard Stern 'fro. "I don't know how to help," he admits.

"Can I borrow your phone?" Mine must be in Gladys's car.

I stare at the number pad. I'd grown up doing phone number drills the way Tank grew up reciting scripture for nuns. "Your dad's?" Warren would demand. I'd reel off the numbers. "Mine?" More rip-fire numbers. "Griff's?" Same. "Ruby's?" Same. Despite my training, I reach deep to remember the area code.

4:32 her time.

Alaska's three hours behind most of Kentucky. If she's even living there still. Last Dad and I checked—thank you, Facebook—my mother managed a Game Stop in Juneau and was in a relationship with some man-child named Xane. They have two German shepherds, Punch and Judy, whom they photograph obsessively.

She won't know it's me. This number will read like a random solicitor and I doubt she'll pick up, but I'd like to hear her voice. That annoying high-pitch buzz erupts in my ear, followed by "We're sorry. You have reached a number that has been disconnected or is no longer in service. If you feel you have reached this recording in error, please check the number and dial again."

I dial again.

Same message.

Nick hands me a bottle of water he fished from behind the seat, probably to keep me from throwing his phone. He doesn't do what most people do when they find themselves uncomfortable. There's

109

no strange comparison of how his life is similar to mine in *x* way. No platitudes about how much this sucks.

"What now?" he asks.

"You finish your homework, and Griff takes me to Gladys's."

He laments, "I shouldn't have signed up for this summer class, but I need it to graduate on time."

I set my water bottle on the floorboard, offer him my hands, and we pull each other up. When we're in a quasi-hugging standing position, my thumbs tucked through the back belt loop on his jeans, I angle us into a kissing position. Nick never even glances at my lips.

"I'm being unfair to you," I say.

"Unfair?"

Because of Aulus, Nick could never be reduced to some boyfriend I had one year in high school. But I wonder if he's trapped here, stitched to me by ongoing tragedy. Days like today—you can hear the hum of the sewing machine making another pass over our hands. The needle feels great to me, safe and sound, a tidy suture, but it's probably stinging his palms. How long before Nick thinks, *What's in this for me?* Or maybe we end when his parents or sister bring up the obvious point, *Do you want to tie yourself to a girl with an incarcerated father or do you want to make law partner someday?*

Nick says, "The only unfair thing that exists today is what happened with your dad."

Does he mean that? Or is some part of him asking what I'd be asking if this situation were reversed: Does mental illness run in the family? Am I one step away from stealing a baby stroller or obsessing over some ridiculous Arthurian project? I think I have the obsession in me, though not the deviousness.

"If you can't sleep, call me," Nick says and kisses my nose.

How long has it been since we kiss kissed? Before Chris Jenkins.

"Thank you," I say, but I'm fast-forwarding to the moment my dad's in prison and Nick's walking a perky, leather bag–toting, tortoiseshell cat-eye glasses–wearing girl from trial law class back to her dorm; they kiss passionately; he sighs with relief and thinks, *That was so much better than anything I ever did with my crazy ex-girlfriend.*

I fall into Griff's Accord, determined not to think about the men in my life. The leather seat is cool from the air conditioning. I consider putting my head directly in front of the vent.

"Do you know where my mother is?" I ask, exasperated, wishing I hadn't given Dad my ponytail holder.

"Seat belt."

"My mother."

"Debra." He practically spits her name.

"Yes. Unless there's some other mother I don't know about."

"Seat belt," Griff repeats.

This time I oblige, and Griff says he has Debra's number somewhere. Based on that response, he has the same number I already dialed.

"Don't bother," I tell him. "I'll send her a message on Facebook."

"You sure she should know about Don's arrest?"

The question's a snake on the path. We wait for it to slither away. By the time it does, we're back in Wildwood's city limits, the flashing courthouse clock telling us it's after seven. Griff breaks the silence. "You don't want to stay with us tonight?"

"I'll be fine at Gladys's."

Griff exhales. I can't tell if he's relieved or frustrated.

"Why did you say my mother's name like that earlier?"

Without so much as a blinker of warning, Griff whips into a spot in front of Barlow's Flowers. The square's mostly empty. Only spillover cars from the Mexican restaurant are parked in this corner. The bank's dark. The antique shop beside Barlow's has a flashing Closed sign that brightens the Accord's dashboard with rose-colored twinkles. Griff drums his thumbs on the steering wheel in time with the sign.

"Griff?" On a day like today I can take as many scoops of pain as he can dish.

"I was thinking about Constance."

I raise the sunshade, lower it again. Fiddle with the child lock button on the door. "Constance?" The name means nothing to me.

"Don's first wife." The phrase slips through gritted teeth. *My dad was married before Mom. Another lie.* "Every time Debra surfaces for one reason or another, I can't help but think what could have been with Stancy. I know Debra's your mom—"

"Womb donor," I insert.

Griff's temporarily dazed by my correction, but he approves of my assessment. "I wouldn't change a hair on your head, kiddo, but if you had the pleasure of meeting Stancy, your dad chose the wrong . . . 'womb donor.' Anyway, you asked for her number and I was thinking we should call Const—"

He catches sight of my face and understands this is the first I've heard of Constance. Griff shifts the car into reverse. "You don't need more on your plate. We'll discuss Constance some other time."

Some other time? I punch Griff's glove box until it vomits his registration, rogue paperwork, tire gauge, and a set of keys onto my lap and the floorboard. I slam the flapping door three times and it still hangs open. Griff watches the traffic over his shoulder before backing out.

"Griff, stop stalling and tell me."

The car pauses half in the spot, half in the street. A horn honks and Griff waves an apology the driver surely can't see in the darkness. He backs out. "I don't think that's a good—"

"Griff!"

He takes the first exit off the square toward Gladys's. There are seven stoplights remaining and time for him to explain. He begins, "Constance O'Brien. They met his junior year at Tech, her freshman. They started and ended quickly."

The Crimea started and ended quickly. Side ponytails started and ended quickly. Deep Blue Something started and ended quickly. They all still happened. Length of time doesn't negate realness.

"Why don't I know about her?"

"Your dad took nine years to tell you about the castle."

I've never asked Griff how long he and Ruby and Warren knew about the castle, but there's no doubt they found out before me. Based on his scowl, he was Team Tell Thea.

"Where's Constance now?"

"No idea," Griff says. "She was always quirky. But so was your dad back then. Very devout, you know?"

"Devout? Like, religious?"

Griff nods. "He and Constance met at a campus prayer thing."

We are holiday church attendees—primarily Easter and Christmas. This stretches my concept drawing of Dad.

"I'd already moved back to Wildwood when they split. He was living in Jackson, and Ruby—she was on a service call to Memphis—worked for Every Child Now and stopped to surprise him with brownies. He ended up surprising her. No wedding ring.

No Constance. I called him and asked what in the world was going on. He said he was divorced and wasn't fielding additional questions. You know how he is."

Griff pulls into Gladys's drive. The Baxters' security light bathes the Accord in yellow.

"Yeah," I say. "No keys to his basement."

Gladys and I huddle together on her bed with the computer, spend five minutes googling, and bam, pretty hippie Constance O'Brien fills the screen. Right age, attended Tech, still near and dear to her religious roots. The most unsettling part: she looks like my mom. They have the same shoulder-length brown hair and fringe. Same watery blue eyes. Neither woman could be a pound over one twenty.

Gladys has never met Mom, but she has served as sidekick for my *What's Debra doing these days?* internet searches. First sight of Constance and she pushes the laptop toward her knees.

"Wow. I mean, wow."

I resemble Mom more than Dad, so my likeness to Constance is equally uncanny. Gladys won't stop remarking on our similar features. I click the next link.

Constance pastors a nondenominational church in Lexington, Kentucky, called Faith United. They have a service tomorrow at 10:15.

"She might know things about Dad no one else does," I suggest.

Gladys sees what I want before I have the courage to ask. Always up for an adventure, she says, "We could go, you know. Tomorrow *is* Sunday."

I try to be logical. "Warren or Griff or Ruby would know the same things."

"Maybe, but this is a rock that needs turning over."

That's the smile that got her kicked out of Walmart for playing Supermarket Sweep in a wheelchair buggy. She's always so meek, until she isn't.

While I brush my teeth, Gladys calls Tank and Nick and tells them they are coming with. "Tank will be here early. We're picking Nick up on the way," she says when I crawl into bed.

Now it's three a.m., and I'm lying next to Gladys, coiling my brain around Constance O'Brien. In a few hours, I'm meeting the woman who could have been my mother. Except if I had half of her DNA instead of Debra's, I'd be someone else. Dad might be someone else. Maybe even, if Constance were my mom, she'd be the type who slipped under the covers with me on difficult nights and snuggled close. This imaginary woman, easily maternal, smooths my hair and says, "Oh, baby. We'll get through this." She doesn't run a Game Stop in Alaska with a disconnected phone. She doesn't use my college fund to build a castle.

I have Gladys, at least. Our heads are basically touching, and though she's exhausted, she startles awake when I twist in the covers and asks, "You okay?"

"Go back to sleep," I tell her and watch her eyelids fall, only to see them pop open five minutes later. She asks, "You sure?" to which I answer, "I'm fine."

Eventually she believes me. Or she can't hold her eyes open. I listen to her snore and try to stop tossing and turning. I dream about Constance.

Against all odds, we run ahead of schedule the next morning. Nick and backpack fall into the back seat with a carrier of coffee that makes Gladys kiss his cheek and Tank say, "This is why you're my favorite."

Despite the Starbucks run, Nick's only partially dressed. His tie hangs like a narrow green sash. His belt's not latched. He's toting a plastic bag with hair gel and worn black shoes that he pitches into the space between us.

"Nice dress," he says.

"Nice undershirt," I say. His dress shirt is still unbuttoned.

He straightens to check his hair in the rearview mirror and says, "Gotta get fancy for church. Is this an alternate universe or what?"

I didn't pack fancy, so I'm trusting Gladys's black knit A-line to be appropriately holy for Sunday worship.

Faith United is located in a grubby strip mall near the Lexington Horse Park. Based on shoddy sign work, the church used to be a Dollar General. There's a Peddlers Mall to the right, a Fantastic Sams on the left. Sedans and minivans with wind-shield sticker families surround us. Tank coasts into a spot next to a conversion van. Kids tumble out of the vehicle like clowns at the circus, the boys dressed in matching black vests, the girls in pink-and-yellow-striped sundresses. Nick finishes the final tuck of the Windsor knot and spritzes hair gel onto his hands. The car stinks of strawberry.

Tank coughs dramatically. "Hey, yo, Justin! Tame that poodle outside?"

"Justin?" Nick asks.

"Timberlake," Gladys says with a laugh.

"Ha-ha," Nick says, good humored. "Please remember, from this distance to church, God can hear you being mean to me."

Everyone laughs and before I know it we're at the front door and Pastor Constance is greeting us.

Handshake: warm with medium pressure.

Smile: wide and lovely.

Dress: ankle length, purple and flowing, quarter-length sleeves. Tasteful.

No wedding ring, no extra-large Bible tucked under her arm, no pretense. Only softness when she says, "Welcome to Faith. We're glad you're here this morning."

Becoming. That's my word for Constance. Followed closely by: *magnetic.* Not only that, she's genuinely glad we're visiting, or she's very good at faking joy. I manage a timid "Hi," and Tank chooses four chairs in the back of the sanctuary.

Most of my Sunday mornings are a haze of milk and dough-nuts. When I confess my nerves to Nick, who's usually the one supplying the pastries, he says, "Right there with you."

I'm charmed by the music. More than charmed. I'm stirred. All around me, earnest hearts are laid bare. I don't think religion is for me, but we're in an old Dollar General with terrible industrial lighting; exposed ductwork drops glittery dust motes into the air that land like dandruff on shoulders and hair; black smears scar the tile floor where shelves sat for decades; and there's a homey feeling. Nothing is fancy and everything is real. Far more real than I expected. Especially when Constance starts speaking.

"She's great," Nick whispers in my ear at the same moment Tank finger-guns in the pastor's direction and mouths, *Dude. I love her.*

I think: *This is not a woman a sane man leaves.*

I think: *What if she were my mother?*

I think: *Tell me secrets about my father.*

Constance offers congregants a chance to come forward, and I traverse the middle aisle, full of fear and hope. One glance over my shoulder equals three nods. *Go on*, they encourage, and I kneel. She's before me now. Her warm hand touches my forehead, surprising me a little. Her eyes—they're the color of a winter sky and almost snow—meet mine with compassion.

"My father was arrested yesterday," I whisper.

She holds me. She is narrow shoulders, thin arms, and lavender, which I've never particularly enjoyed but find soothing. I've never seen a car crusher in action, but this must be how old Volvos feel. In an instant, it is more than an embrace; it is her soul in a body. Her cheek lands next to mine, the powder smell so similar to the makeup drawer in my bathroom. I miss home and Dad in a dizzying way. I don't realize I'm shaking until her fingers slide up and down the knit backing of Gladys's dress.

From inside this hug, I say, "His name is Don Delacroix."

16

MAY

Constance peels her upper body from mine, examines my face, perhaps expecting her ex-husband's nose and mouth hidden in my feminine features. Instead, she sees . . . *What? A counterfeit version of herself?* Tears gather in the corners of her eyes. She has every right to hate me.

"Oh, sweetheart," she says, embracing me again. "I knew someone would come. I didn't know it would be like this or so soon. Don't leave afterward." Constance moves on to pray for the kneeling man to my right.

"What did she say?" Gladys asks when I return to our seats.

"That we should stick around."

Gladys's forehead crinkles. "You were up there a long time."

I could live up there.

The service ends on a song and though we are greeted by the people around us, the church soon empties. Constance and another man scurry around blowing out candles, shutting down the sound system, repositioning mics for next week. Constance yells to the back of the sanctuary, "Hey, Jake, lock up for me? I'd like to take this crew to lunch."

A question for Jake. A question for us.

Jake raises a set of keys into the air and jingles his yes. I give Constance a weak "Sure." The others follow my lead. This is why we came. After we exchange names, Constance walks us to the Burger King on the corner. She tells the cashier the food's on her. When none of us order what we would if we were paying for our own meals, she says, "Supersize everything."

Over Whoppers and fries, I tell my story. The castle. Aulus's disappearance. Dad's arrest. Everything between. I withhold minimal details. Like: *Don't come back until you believe me.* There's no skirting around the FBI's belief that Dad is the Gemini Thief or his laissez-faire attitude, so I lay it all out on the table with the ketchup and grease.

When I finish, Constance says, "You've all been through quite a trauma." She lifts her purse from the floor and rifles the contents. "My sister—she was at service this morning—brought this." The newspaper falls open. The *Lexington Herald-Leader* headline: "Suspect Arrested in Gemini Thief Case." Dad's named in the caption.

"So that's why you said you knew."

"I expected the police or the FBI. Not Don's daughter. I didn't even know he had a daughter."

Tank and Nick lock their arms around my chair. I say, "I didn't know he had a first wife." My throat constricts as I ask what I came to ask. "Do you know anything . . . anything that might help make sense of this?"

Constance places her elbows on the table and steeples her hands. "I haven't seen your dad in two decades."

Three times I start to phrase a question but am a stuttering mess before Gladys steps in. "Can you tell us why you guys didn't work out?"

Constance folds the corner of her Whopper wrapper and shifts the newspaper into her purse. "He left on a Tuesday." She says *on a Tuesday* as if no time has elapsed between the memory and today. "When you're eighteen, love is starlight in your pocket. For some people starlight's a gift, and for others it's a fire that needs putting out." Constance watches a toddler in an adjacent booth make gooey eyes at Nick. She smiles at the flirting child and her voice—flat and factual—doesn't match the expression. "I'm sure there are two sides to every marriage, every divorce, but Don was never happy once the rings were on."

I don't know Constance, not really, but she's handling this painful situation with far more grace than Dad deserves. Nick must agree. He reaches across the table, palm up, and Constance takes his extended hand with grateful, teary eyes. "Thank you. What a silly thing that this still makes me weepy."

Nick keeps her hand and takes advantage of the moment. "This is awkward, but would you trust me, us, enough to share something personal? I'd like to know if Don was ever violent or if he ever did anything that made you afraid or nervous?" Nick pauses, but not long enough to let her speak. "You understand why we're asking?" There's a glance at me. "Thea lives with him and . . ."

"I was never afraid." A *but* lingers in the air. I have no sooner thought this than Constance says, "His ability to disengage was alarming. There were always two Dons."

"Two Dons?" I ask.

She retracts her hand from Nick's with a pat, wads the wrapper with half her burger inside, and pushes the greasy lump to the edge of her tray. "Oh yes," she says. "The Don who loved me dearly and the Don who left me washing his clothes in the coin laundry while he filed for divorce without a word of warning." She's back in that laundromat, jabbing quarters through slots and slinging wet boxers from washer to dryer.

I've torn a scab by visiting.

"I'm sorry," she says, and I tell her she doesn't owe me an apology. "But, Thea, our divorce doesn't make him what the FBI or media suggest he is. I'll tell you what I'll tell them too. There was nothing, and I mean *nothing*, in your father's character that suggested he had the capacity to murder or injure a six-year-old boy. We even volunteered together at a daycare, and he was always great with kids. I mean, you must know that, right?"

Dad's fine and all, but I wouldn't say great. More evidence she knew a different Don than I do.

Constance says, "A man can be capable of the lies and deception you've described—the castle, the money, Aulus's help—and be incapable of murder. I'm not sure what you want to hear, but if he says he didn't do this, I'd believe him."

Tank exhales, says, "That's generous of you under the circumstances."

"Well, he'd have had to change everything about himself, and I don't see that in the cards."

This would be more reassuring if she'd seen Dad once in the last twenty years.

"Can you make any sense of the castle?" I ask.

Her eyes drift in the direction of her Dollar General church building. "Don was always compulsive about something. Once it was God, then it was me, then it was not me. I guess now it's a castle."

"Crazy compulsive?" Nick asks.

Tank's shaking his head and starts to protest the question when Constance cuts him off. "Depends on your definition of crazy. Is crazy inherently bad? Does life require a little crazy?" She pauses. "I mean, what do you call a man who hikes Everest? Insane or daring?"

We give honest nods, but what do we know? I came here for a straight answer: Do you think my dad is a murderer? She doesn't. Even though I like her very much, I don't want a lecture on the nuances of crazy.

Constance reads my body language perfectly. "I won't go on and on," she says. "But if you asked everyone I left behind to follow my dream . . . they might call me crazy. You meet Noah after the flood, you think, *That brave, faith-filled, visionary man.* You meet him before and you're like, *What a nut job.* Perspective and timing matter. Sometimes you have to accept that you might not be able to see the truth from here."

"I'm scared of the truth," I say.

Constance doesn't have sleek answers for my frustration. "You have more what-ifs than you deserve. No one can tell you what to do or believe, least of all me." She collects our trays, stacks them, and organizes the trash. I can almost see her thinking that she needs to right something for us, and this is all she has.

After she returns from the garbage bin, she says, "I have a box of photos from those days. Not much of an offering, but they're yours if you want."

THE ELIZABETH LETTERS

Dear Elizabeth,

I don't remember falling asleep or waking up.

One minute I was on the pool float, eyes barred shut like the Quik Mart at night, the next, Tank's straddling the blue toddler chair I dented this morning, paper and pen in hand, singing jingles to accentuate our situation. *Like a good neighbor, State Farm was there.* The plastic bends under his weight, the damaged leg threatening to cave.

I'm not sure what he was drawing, perhaps more *Giving Trees*. Judgment came alive in his eyebrows and the tight lines around his mouth when I picked up this letter and started to write. Tank tapped his pencil on the paper like a drum until I couldn't think straight. "You still want that freezer top removed?"

He knew I did.

Tank had fire in his eyes. "I say we grid

this place and search methodically for that
screwdriver," he said.

Back soon to tell you what happened.

The following map took hours to create.

I love it like a Picasso.

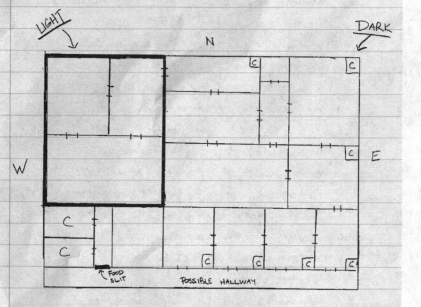

Elizabeth, if you're thinking we wasted an
enormous amount of time doing nothing to help
ourselves, you're not wrong. My only defense is this:
our first bunker was built to house prisoners and we
were there eleven months' worth of sleeps. Welder
left three to seven days' worth of food each
time he visited. You know how zookeepers chain
elephants to posts to teach them captivity and
once they've learned, the zookeepers remove the
posts and the elephants don't budge? That's us.

This map came to life when Tank set a can of spray paint in the middle of the plastic table. "Found this in a cabinet two rooms over." The can skated between my hands. The clacking of the ball bearings pinged the air like castanets. "Graffiti map?" he asked.

"Escape décor?" I repeated the phrase so many times it started to sound like soup du jour. *Escape de cor.* I laid on a heavy French accent. "What would you like today, monsieur? Would you like to try our famous *escape de cor?*"

I pushed the joke too far, but Tank cackled and snorted and I kept saying the phrase with other terrible accents—Italian: *escape de cor,* Russian: *escape de cor*—to bottle the happiness.

We waltzed into the main room and sprayed a large rectangle on the wall—fumes hung in a chemical fog, the mold we live with muted by the fresh clouds of paint.

Beside me, Rufus bucked and bounced on the balls of his feet. I'm not sure when he joined us; last I checked, he and Zared were playing Pong with hex bolts and Dixie cups, but of course he wanted to help. He's a pleaser.

"I know this place like the back of my hand," he bragged. In the early mornings he pillaged garbage bags like a bird building a nest of bobbles and trinkets. I encouraged him to take Zared along, and the two disappeared into the maze.

"Count the closets," I called.

Tank turned around, eyes following the boys
out of the room, head shaking the whole time. He
continued our mapping efforts. "The upper section
is two chunks." He traced the small square he'd
painted in the space on the left, which includes the
three rooms with bulbs. Main room: where we are now.
Sleeping room: where the pool floats are. Buffet room:
where we used to eat when Welder dropped in food.
He labeled this small section *Light* before tracing
the backward L shape on the right. "And *Dark*," he
added, with the caveat, "*I* should have thought
about mapping that first day."

Tank wasn't even awake the first three sleeps
of his captivity. Welder's drugs smashed his system
Hulk style. I don't want to tell him how often his brain
scrambles details or that he cries when he dreams.

"You were freshly kidnapped, dude."

"And you lost Chris and—"

"Stop." Neither of us needed to revisit those early drugged and grieving days.

Out there, you lose someone and life slips into your empty places the way rain fills low places in the yard. Down here, four people are the whole world. You lose one and it's a hole in the dam, water flooding in all the time.

Tank coughed, returning us to the task at hand. "The way I see things, the flood happened, death happened, and Welder freaked. The transfer here was purely reactional. There's no way he vetted everything in this hole."

"Probably," I said. Unless we were drugged for days between moves. "Even if I was under for a long stretch during the transfer, I wasn't when Welder added you. That happened fast. He shoved you through the food slit and resealed the opening."

Tank didn't like the reminder of waking up here. "There could be tools, a chisel, in one of these bags."

"Or a sledgehammer," Rufus adds from the doorway.

"Or a sledgehammer," I repeat, thinking of the hours I hammered on the food slit opening with both feet.

"True," Tank said.

I pulled Rufus into the next room. "You ever run across anything that might let us chip away the mortar between the bricks?"

"Not yet. Dark is super dark."

He was right, Elizabeth, but that got me thinking, even if Welder's using solar power to stay off-grid, the internal wiring should be normal. The interior walls of Light and Dark are either drywall or paneling. The exterior, concrete. Ceilings range from fourteen feet in the main room to ten in the auxiliary spaces. They're made of dropped tile or that filthy popcorn stuff. Electrical could be up there, even though none of the rest of the plugs work.

The theory was money scalding my pocket and thigh. I left Light to investigate, squinting against the shadows of Dark and picking my way closer to the center of the room. There was a round metal plate in the ceiling. Empty hooks to the right and left where fixtures used to hang.

"Get in here!" Three June Boys made three silhouettes in the doorway. "Think we could get up there?" I asked, pointing at the plates.

Rufus nodded exuberantly. "If we pile stuff. Yeah, for sure."

Tank said, "Yeah," but he was far more reserved than Rufus.

Zared's expression remained blank and zombie-like.

I kept working the theory. "We could move the fluorescents from Sleeping Room and search for tools." I cut off some negative banter between Zared and Rufus, trying not to burst hope while it was bubbling. "Then, if Welder doesn't return, we'll be ready." I didn't admit we could die of dehydration in the meantime. I barreled on, hoping Leo was right about urine and Tank was right about June 30th.

Rufus smacked me open palmed in what used to be the meaty part of my chest. The blow took the wind out of me and I ended up on the ground. "That was uncalled for."

"Easy," Tank said, his right hand cupping my elbow.

"You should have come up with a plan sooner," Rufus said.

He was right about that.

"We have an actual plan." I danced my celebration dance—again, I'll spare you the details, but they all laughed, and in their laughter, Elizabeth, the wind tickled my face, a summer of honeysuckle kissed my nose, a butterfly landed between my cupped palms.

What if, Elizabeth? What if?

Peace and Freedom,

Aulus

17

MAY

Constance drops the dusty cardboard box in the trunk, lifts the lid, and gives us a peek. The box is chockablock full, photos and papers crammed and bent, spilling out like puppies released from a kennel. All the way home, they bark to our curiosity.

Tank surprises us when he says, "Nick's hauling all boxed materials to his dorm and none of us are perusing them tonight." He holds Nick in place, a verbal knife pressed to the neck. "Not even *you*. Go do whatever you do when you're not doing this."

I argue we're wasting time and Nick agrees with Tank. "Nothing in that box is getting Don out tonight."

Tank adds, "Nothing in that box is getting him *out* period. Those are context clues, and this has been a long day. Everybody go watch a movie, read a book, do something happy, whatever you want. But not this."

I don't have the energy to argue. I don't have the energy to find another version of my father, another layer of silt that muddies the waters.

In Bowling Green, Nick squeezes my wrist before gathering his study cards from the floorboard and climbing out of the car. We smile at each other, not brightly, a simple upward turn of lips. I hope my goodbye nod means *Thank you* the way his means *I'm here if you need me*. Nodding can be the whole dictionary if you know the person.

Tank pops the trunk and helps Nick baby the banker's box into his arms. Gladys doesn't pull away from the curb until Nick's inside his building. "Fifty bucks says he goes through that stuff tonight. I sure would." No one takes her bet.

We drop off Tank next, again waiting until he is safely inside his car to pull away. We live in a strange world where women walk men to their vehicles, where we are worried their safety might be compromised before our own. I recline the seat to a horizontal position and close my eyes.

"You don't think my dad did this, do you?"

"Nope."

"What makes you so sure?"

Gladys answers by driving straight to the Walmart parking lot. "Cookie dough," she says conclusively.

I'm not one to argue with sugar or calories, so we leave the store with cookie dough, cookie dough ice cream, and a tub of mini-brownies stuffed with cookie dough bites. Back at her house, I take a shower and fall into bed, too tired to gorge on our splendors. She lies next to me, licking the end of the sweet doughy sleeve and rubbing my back until I fall asleep. I dream of Noah building a castle to save the world; he takes two boys of every age over the drawbridge. "For my collection," he tells the dove on his shoulder.

Gladys shakes me awake. "Thea. School."

My ability to forget something I've done nearly every day for twelve years is remarkable. Funny thing is, I loved high school before Aulus disappeared. I made outfit charts, study guides, and snazzy planners. Long, luscious hours were dedicated to test anxiety and interpersonal issues. "If Connie Waymack doesn't understand she can't be in charge of prom after that homecoming fiasco, then Richard needs to check in with Sam, who will have to tell Corey, who tells everything to Rachel, Connie's best friend, that no one can handle fishhooks as prom favors."

Those things might not matter in twenty years, but they aren't inconsequential either. I should be as up-in-arms as the next girl about the administration saying we have to wear heels with our caps and gowns, but caring about graduation is like asking me to be worried about plant life on Mars. Can't Elon Musk do that? Can't Connie Waymack keep Wildwood High School running smoothly? Well, she's going to have to.

Gladys and I dress, sharing the bathroom and mirror like soldiers prepping for war. When she's fully armed, she doubles back and helps me. Her fingers loosen the curls on my neck, she applies necessary bobby pins, and then she leans back to appraise her work. "You look beautiful, hon."

I used to believe beauty was its own armor and beautiful people floated above bad circumstances. What a lie! Gladys is gorgeous. Aulus was beautiful too. My cousin had cherry-tinted lips that stretched from here into next year when he smiled. When we were little things and I didn't know you couldn't marry your cousin, I was enamored with his mouth. I'd trace a finger over the upper ridge and he'd nip me like a cat and I'd jump and we'd laugh. He spit in my cereal once and didn't tell me until after I'd eaten the whole bowl; that highlighted *stupid boy cousin* in an important way. Funny thing is, both memories can make me laugh or cry.

I grab my backpack and Gladys shoves a power bar and a glass of orange juice at me. "You ready?"

"No," I say.

We fetch Tank, who's clearly anxious. He smokes three and a half cigarettes between his house and school. He turns the filter of the last one toward me, knowing I'll refuse. "You ready?" he asks again.

"No," I say again.

Tank and Gladys flank me when I get out of the car. Today we're battling headlines: "Local Man Arrested as Potential Gemini Thief"; "Body of Kidnapped Boy Sparks New Arrests"; "Three Boys Still Missing in Gemini Thief Case: Local Tax Agent Questioned."

Dana is quoted in most of the articles.

Dana Jones, a lead investigator for the federal case against the (media titled) Gemini Thief, states, "Sadistic and predatory crimes against children have been committed over the last ten years. The person or persons responsible is someone of incredible ego and means. Today's arrest is an important development in bringing the missing boys home alive and these heinous crimes to justice."

Color photos of my house are splashed across the front page of newspapers all over the country. Follow-up images of Dad on page five are aptly captioned: "Wildwood accountant Don Delacroix escorted by FBI into Bowling Green, KY, police station for federal questioning."

Last August, the first day of school without Aulus, Gladys, Tank, and I built a triangle formation we haven't broken in a year. People sputtered how very sorry they were and shared accounts of the last time they saw Aulus. We were the watercooler everyone gathered around, the delta of Aulus McClaghen.

We are barely inside when Principal Markum says, "Thea, a word." To Tank and Gladys she says, "Mr. Piper, Ms. Baxter, please see yourselves to the library. Ms. Delacroix will join you when we're finished." Mrs. Markum exerts a force on every room she enters, and here in her natural territory, using her *I eat raw meat for breakfast* tone, she is nothing less than a lioness.

"I'll be right there," I say to Gladys.

Regina Markum has forgettable eyes, slight buck teeth, and fine lines around her mouth that suggest she spends a percentage of her life smiling, though not at us, and certainly not at school. Her hair's more pruned than fixed; trimmed and rounded like the boxwood bushes out front. Every day she wears a silver cross on a silver chain. Currently, the chain's in her mouth and I take that to be a bad sign. Aulus used to say, *If Markum's chewing on Jesus, she's about to chew you out.*

I follow her through the inner sanctuary of offices to a private meeting room and sit when she points at a hardback chair. She leans on a blue armchair opposite me. The cross falls from her lips and bounces against her twinset lavender sweater. "How are you, Thea?"

Not the question I expect.

"Fine."

Mrs. Markum crosses the room and perches on the edge of my chair, uncomfortably close. "I've spoken with the administration," she says, "and we want to make this as easy for you as we can. Get you over the finish line of graduation."

"Uh, thank you," I say, when I'm really thinking, *Why? As high school is quite inconsequential at the moment.*

She pats my knee, puts her coffee-and-Altoid breath near my nose. I can't tell if she's fishing for details or feeling compassionate. "This all feels very unbelievable to me. First Aulus, and now . . . Well . . . Come straight to me if anyone bullies you or says anything about your father. We consider Don a dear friend."

Dad rarely mentions the Markums. He does their taxes; we don't barbecue with them.

"Mrs. Markum, people are going to say stuff."

"I won't tolerate you being mistreated. Not in my school. Not when your father is—" She leans against the wall to straighten the curve of her back. Strange energy bubbles in the silence between us—like she knows something and can't say what. "Promise you'll come to me if you need anything. Your dad and I go way back and none of this is fair."

Maybe Mrs. Markum was married to him too, I think.

"Sure," I say.

"You have a place to stay?"

"The Baxters. And the Holtzes. Uncle Warren."

She leans in conspiratorially. "You're not staying out at the castle?"

"No." *Why would I be?*

"I wasn't sure if there was running water. Or"—a slight rise in her voice—"electricity?"

"Generators," I say.

Mrs. Markum takes the cross between her teeth again. Her lips are cracked and a tiny bead of blood appears. "This is a little indelicate, but I'm going to come right out and say it. Times like these can be a financial burden. So if your father wants to sell the castle and land to cover legal fees or . . . to maybe start over somewhere else after you graduate, Kevin, er, Mr. Markum and I are interested in taking it off your hands." She pats my knee again. "But only if it'll help. We're here to help you."

I swallow my shock. I give a nod that is less than robust and she says, "You understand, Ms. Delacroix?"

"Yes, ma'am."

"Good." She flings her hand in the direction of the hallway. "Oh, and I've emailed your teachers. Asked them to excuse any finals that won't help your grade."

I stand, unsure if I'm allowed to leave. Nearly. She wedges me into a damp-pit hug that makes us both visibly uncomfortable.

I slink away to the library, unsure of what just happened.

At 3:05, Gladys, Tank, and I leave the library, where I've spent the day googling my father, and discover Nick lounging in his car. He pops his head out the window like a gopher. "Hey! Can I borrow you for a couple hours?"

I'm sure this invitation has to do with that banker's box he was not supposed to go through last night. Tank and Gladys exchange a look before Gladys tucks a lock of hair behind my ear. "See you soon," she says. Tank looks at Nick and takes a long drag of his cigarette, then slides into her front seat. He doesn't remind Nick to treat me like bone china, but we all translate the glare.

I get in and Nick starts the car. "Where are we going?"

"Depends."

"On what?"

"On what kind of day you had."

137

"Let's go with . . . strange." I tell him about my *No finals and do I want to sell the castle and spend from now until graduation in the library?* encounter with Regina Markum and then ask, "How was your test?"

"Easy." He jumps back to me. "Has your principal ever been out there?"

"Not that I know of."

"That *is* strange. And you didn't know they were old friends?"

"Not really. But I wouldn't call myself super informed on the relationships of Don Delacroix." Nick suppresses a laugh. "I'm guessing you had a strange day too?" I ask.

"Yep." I expect he has news about Dad's arraignment, knowledge of whether bail was set or denied. The first hearing was today. "I'm up for it," I say, and then immediately wonder if I am.

Nick passes me a square 35mm photo that shows four men standing in a row, arms slung bro-style around each other's bare shoulders. Their swimming trunks gleam with water and harsh sunlight. Presumably, they're twenty to twenty-five, given their lean, muscled bodies. There is only one place for my eyes to go: each man wears a dark gray welding helmet.

"Yep," Nick says when I gasp.

He flips the picture over, taps the smudged lines of purple ballpoint ink:

Don's Guys '89
Post WW Bridge Restoration

18

MAY

Junior year, signs around town boasted, "Wear a costume to Town Block Party, get free stuff." Gladys and I bought four overlarge plastic horse heads at Family Dollar and headed down to the square, dragging Aulus and Tank along. Some yearbook committee girl snapped a photo of us and gave it to Aulus, who gave it to me in a frame. "I can't tell who is who," he'd said, laughing. Something about the light and shadows and horse heads blurred us into an androgynous lump.

This photo is a lump of welders.

"Head to the community center," I say.

"Should we call Constance? See if she remembers who these men are?" Nick asks.

"Griff's closer."

After-school traffic is in full swing. Traffic cops in yellow vests empty the elementary pick-up line. Since we're stopped, Nick points at the handwriting on the back of the photo. "Don's Guys. Doesn't say Don. Can you tell if—"

"—one of them is my father? No, I wish."

We're eleven traffic lights from the community center. More than enough time to imagine Aulus staring at his captor's welding mask. I often superimpose survivor testimonies to conjure Aulus's life with Welder. For instance, the dumbwaiter's chain rattles and brings him to a panel in the wall. Rufus and Zared are there beside him. The tiny elevator opens on twenty-four neatly stacked cans of soup and a message from Welder.

I'm coming to talk.

The boys welcome these meetings; they've learned not to fear them.

From the bunker descriptions, I know there's a sliding steel door on an electrical track Welder controls. When open, a heavy Plexiglas barrier separates the captives from the nondescript room. The boys assume this boundary doubles as a door, though they've never seen it open.

Twice a month or so—time moves uncertainly—Welder announces his arrival and sits on the other side of the Plexiglas, taking time to examine injuries and entertain concerns or requests. The boys are asked if they have all they need. Are there special items they require? Things they miss terribly? Small wishes are often granted and Welder delivers gifts and requests to the June Boys. Comic books. A beloved song piped into the bunker on repeat. Soft sweatshirts. Toenail clippers. Cheetos, the puffy kind. A single Tylenol for a headache. These items arrive via dumbwaiter several days after they're requested.

I play this home movie against the photo in my lap and am struck by how Aulus could have been abducted and imprisoned by his uncle and have no idea. Dozens of survivor accounts, dozens of descriptions of Welder—all the same—and they've never shed light on the perpetrator. Welder is Welder. Little more than a ghost on the other side of the glass.

Potholes in the community center parking lot jolt me back to the present. "Look at this photo," I say. "Nick, he could be Welder." That fact feels less fiction now. Was Dad working me up, playing on my sympathy, when he said, "Honey, don't forget what you already know. That's what's true. Not all this." My gut twists. This photo extinguishes eighteen years of known life. Thank God Principal Markum offered to buy the castle. I'll need to change my name and disappear, and that takes serious cash.

"Don't jump to worst-case scenario yet," Nick warns as he cuts the engine.

I tap the welding helmets in the photo as if to say, *Can you really argue this is coincidental?*

Threatening rain clouds dull the afternoon heat. Kids empty off a bus and run squealing toward the WCC playground. Through the window, my godfather leans over the counter dividing his attention between the kids and a magazine. Leah, one of his faithful workers and my favorite coworker from before, dispatches to the playground. Meanwhile, Ruby stands at the hydration station pouring Kool-Aid into Styrofoam cups.

Nick pauses, knob in hand, on the street side of the door. "You trust him? Because we can't show him this if you—"

"Completely."

Face scarlet and frustrated, Griff waves us toward him. "Thea, we'll get him out. Don't be discouraged by the arraignment."

"We're not here about the arraignment."

Griff raises his bifocals to his forehead. "I assumed you were in court today," he says to Nick.

Nick shoves his hands in his pockets. "I wish. Test."

"Well, the lawyer called and the news wasn't great. The judge believes there's a flight risk—"

"Someone should tell that judge my dad can't put his castle in a suitcase so—"

Griff holds up a hand in understanding. "Maybe he thinks Don will hurt the boys if there's any chance he's out on bail, or maybe they want to deal if he tells them where the kids are. Either way, they kept him." He turns the magazine over and it's not a magazine at all; it's a phone book. He's reading legal ads. At least I'm not alone in this hell.

Griff closes the book, shifting his focus to the kids outside. Their voices pitch slightly higher as Leah yells over the thunder, "Inside. Time to go inside." The after-school program runs Monday, Wednesday, and Friday and if I don't ask now, I'm four hours away from Griff's full attention. I place the photo on the counter. "Tell me about this."

Griff lifts the print tenderly and lowers his bifocals, absorbing each detail. He thumbs the faces of the four men before flipping over the photo to read the description. He asks, "Where'd this come from?"

"Found it in some of Dad's old stuff." I'm not proud of the lie, but it's for Griff's own protection. He'll feel terrible if he thinks he sent me off on a journey to meet Constance in the middle of this stuff with Dad.

Griff flips the image several more times. "Out at the castle?"

"Do you know who these men are?" Nick asks.

Kids, shoulders wet with rain, flood through the door and flock to the snack table. "Hi, Mr. Holtz," one yells. "Hello, Daniel," Griff replies, watching with pride before bringing his eyes back to the photo. He points out the man on the far left. "Uh, well, that's Don."

Slides his finger over. "And Kevin Markum. Warren's beside him. And this last one is Scottie McClaghen." He removes the bifocals and huffs on the lenses. He polishes each two times before resituating them in his pocket. He works his hands like they're cold. "The four of them did welding work for Wildwood after a barge ran into one of the pylons of the Old Scottsville Bridge."

Nick scribbles the names under Constance's handwriting. "You're sure?"

Ruby's still at the Kool-Aid station, filling cups, and Griff's staring at her or somewhere past her with huge owl eyes. There's no doubt why he's rattled. Any connection to welding equipment can't be good for Dad. Ruby seems to realize Griff needs her. She hustles over and tucks an arm around him. He points to the men for her benefit. "Don. Kevin. Warren. Scottie."

"Hmm." She is hollow, hollower, hollowest. "Yes, that's right."

I contemplate the men. Kevin Markum, Principal Markum's husband. Teaches shop in the vocational school. Always beside his wife at football games, wearing his purple-and-yellow Wildwood attire.

Officer Warren Burton. My "favorite uncle," when he's bragging to Griff and Ruby. Unmarried. Steadfast. Addicted to his job. Scottie McClaghen. I sink my teeth into my lip. Scottie and Don, the brother kind of cousins. Is it possible they did this together? Is it possible that no one can identify Welder because Welder isn't one man but two? When I add Scottie, this scenario almost makes sense. Dad would lie for him. Once, I asked Dad how he and Scottie could be so close and so different. "We're not as different as you think," Dad told me.

"You're sure?" Nick asks Griff.

"I hired them," Griff says. "Back in my planning and zoning

days. The city needed welders and I wanted to toss some work their way and a few extra dollars in their bank accounts. Listen, Thea, this photo—"

"Griff, what do I do?"

Ruby pantomimes tearing paper. Griff seizes up the way he did in the car when he mentioned Constance. "If you love your father, destroy that photo. For all of us."

19

MAY

We've mounted an extensive internet search for Scottie McClaghen that's yielded nothing. No white pages. No social media. No links. Considering our diminishing leads, my latest idea is to put the *Don's Guys* photo in front of other kidnapping survivors.

Griff knew who was who all these years later. That got me thinking, William or Richard or Kyle or Joseph or Sean or any boy who came before Aulus might know too. Is it really that masochistic to point to the man on the far left and ask, "Did this man take you?" and long to hear, "Nope. My kidnapper was too big, too small, too hairy, too weak, too young, too old, too anything to be your dad." I imagine tapping the photo of Scottie. "And him? Recognize him?" They'll say yes.

Far-fetched? Sure, but that's where we are.

I'm arguing the approach with Nick, Gladys, and Tank.

We're in the WCC cave and for various reasons, they've constructed two options: hand over the image to Dana or burn it with

Tank's lighter and then admit to Dana that we're stupid. I'm in agreement that one or the other has to happen, but not until we've used the photo for more information.

"You could further traumatize victims," Gladys says, eyebrows raised. "I'm all for drastic measures, but you really want to risk that?"

Tank twirls his cigarette in concurrence. "And," he says, "there's no way kids are going to recognize Welder from a twenty-year-old photo." Nick agrees with Tank and maintains I, in particular, should not publicly insert myself into the investigation.

"You're the daughter of the prime suspect. Nothing good will come from other victims' families laying eyes on you."

I hold in the building scream: *I am a victim's family member!*

The hallway fluorescent is loose or dying, and shadows bounce by on the concrete floor. I lower my voice like the mice are listening. "If I were formerly kidnapped by the Gemini Thief, you know what would help me sleep at night? Knowing the Feds had the right person. Guys, what if the real thief's out there and no one's looking for him?"

I'm getting somewhere with Nick, but Gladys's and Tank's expressions haven't budged. "Look, they're free and Aulus isn't." Tank loosens the grip on his biceps. Gladys chews her bottom lip. "If any one of them were still being held, wouldn't they want someone to help get them home? 'Cause if there's a world where Dad or Scottie or Dad and Scottie did this, I want someone feeding the June Boys while he's in jail."

Nick says, "Dana will never, and I mean never, give you access to the survivors."

That settled the topic for them. I did let the idea drop until Friday night because Nick spent the week on a cumbersome class project that's a huge percentage of his grade, while Tank and Gladys were embroiled in mandatory graduation activities.

Meanwhile, something between numbness and anger feasted on me. I can't go anywhere in this town without inducing hushed voices and pointing. School's no better. Four days without showering, sleeping, or food wasn't my cleverest idea to win friends and allies. I was downright ugly to Gladys's neighbor. "I can hear you," I all but shouted through the rosebush vines, which, no joke, she hired me four years ago to plant.

Now the four of us are back together, and that's comforting in a way I can't adequately describe.

Nick dances his milkshake across the table and into my hand. "Drink up, Delacroix." I lower my mouth to the straw to appease him. "I see you avoiding food and I don't approve."

"Good luck," Gladys says. "I've tried everything."

"I'm not hungry."

"You're not anything anymore," she says, rolling her eyes.

Rex's Café runs a bottomless special after eight p.m. and this is their second go-round of fries. Tank lifts a finger to the waitress indicating we'd like a third and she can put the whole plate in front of me. The waitress, no doubt calculating her shrinking tips with each hour we spend in her section, smiles weakly and heads to the kitchen. I group three limp fries and submerge them in ketchup. "Dana never has to know I talked to the victims," I say.

"Dana's team checks in with the families regularly," Nick says. "What are the chances they don't mention Don Delacroix's daughter paid a visit?"

I recycle the old point: "If this isn't our next step, what is? Aulus is running out of time."

No one argues.

Dad's running out of time too. He's been arraigned and remains in jail without hope of bail. His lawyer has no positive comments on the impending trial, seven weeks away. *Seven weeks.* Which falls one week beyond the June 30th deadline when Aulus should be released—if the Gemini Thief follows protocol.

Assuming the Gemini Thief isn't Don Delacroix.

Nick and Dana believe the government's case is fundamentally weak. They've pinned charges to matching DNA evidence from Chris to Dad, and the results aren't in yet. The other evidence—the key chain, the Baxter convenience store time-stamped video, and Dad's self-admittance to being with Aulus on the day he disappeared—is circumstantial when turned one direction and damning turned another.

The pressure mounts when you start adding circumstantial evidence to Dad's flexible schedule to a 2001 interview pulled from the *Daily News* archives where he answered questions from a local DCS worker. *"I've done taxes for couples having a third child just to get a tax credit. If you ask me, those children should be removed from the home. Kids aren't tax credits."*

There's drummed-up speculation, based on that quote, that Don Delacroix is building a secret castle out of some rich-white-guy-misplaced-vigilante complex. A cartoon in the *Washington Post* showed a man and castle with the caption: "Don 3:16: Let the little children come to my dungeon." I'd believe the hype if this were happening across the country from my life.

"There has to be a way," I say.

"There isn't." Nick's eyes glitch. "Well, you can't interview a survivor, but . . . you might be able to watch a survivor being interviewed. That doesn't help with the photo, but it would give us new information."

148

There are tapes, he explains. Each survivor was questioned immediately after doctors and psychologists cleared them, mostly in early July of their corresponding release years. Dana took home some of the footage to watch and study. She's referenced this a few times, and Nick has a key to her place.

"I'm not saying I'm for this idea." He leans over the table and takes a sip from my milkshake. "But it's more likely to happen than tracking down some eleven-year-old and shoving this picture in his face."

Tank hates the idea. Gladys takes one look at how gung-ho I am and says, "There's my girl."

Nick sinks his hand into the pile of unruly curls atop his head. "Okay, okay, we'll try."

It takes four additional days for all the schedules involved to gel.

Nick and I make the drive alone, in silence, taking old 31 instead of the interstate. Two people in Dana's Nashville apartment are marginally safer than four, and we've chosen Wednesday night because Dana goes straight from work to the gym to small group. That gives us until 8:00 p.m.

"She isn't supposed to bring casework home," Nick says for the third time. At her door, key in the lock, he asks, "What's our story if she catches us?"

I raise my shoulders. "Let's not get caught."

Dana lives in a two-bedroom the size of a small SUV. Her living room is dominated by a fifty-five-inch television and a sectional. There's a slight Dana-size impression in the hunter green leather. She hasn't spent time or money decorating. When I ask Nick about the lack of décor, he opens the spare bedroom door. Stacks of framed photos and artwork lean against the wall. "She hasn't had time."

149

There's a desk in her bedroom. A second television is paused on an episode of *30 Rock*. We agree not to rummage. We're looking for DVDs or flash drives. When we don't find them, we move on. I want to invade the FBI's privacy, not Dana's. I rifle through papers stacked on the floor and find an empty manila folder marked *Gemini*. Nick leaves me for the living room. I open Dana's closet. Everything's color coordinated, right to left, with a place for dresses I can't imagine her wearing. There's nothing related to the case. I wander toward the front and find Nick punching a button on the DVD player.

"Hand-labeled," he says, hopeful.

"Hand-labeled what?" I ask and then shut up.

A seven-year-old boy in mesh shorts and a Celtics jersey overtakes the screen. Off-screen, a male voice says, "July 3rd, 2002. This interview is being conducted with kidnapping victim Corey Donahue. Present at the time of questioning: Jane Donahue, the minor's mother, and myself, SA Mark Lipman." SA Lipman steps into view of the camera and I immediately understand why he's been chosen to speak with Corey. He's young, about five foot five, and attractive in an Abercrombie way that makes him unassuming and approachable. I imagine him pulling on a hoodie after work and playing basketball at the Y.

Corey shrinks closer to his mother and Jane gestures at the door. "Corey doesn't like to be with men in an enclosed room."

Did she learn this during the hospital exam—one too many male doctors? Or is she assuming?

SA Lipman, who communicates vats of empathy in a single expression, assures Jane and then Corey of their safety. "I know you want to go home, little buddy," he tells Corey, "and we're working on getting you there."

Corey lifts his eyes from the floor to his shoelaces. SA Lipman isn't rattled by the silence. The agent slides crayons and typing paper toward the boy, keeping plenty of physical distance. Jane hovers, touching the striped T-shirt and the nape of her son's neck. She looks terrified to blink.

SA Lipman scoots the crayons closer to Corey and asks for drawings of the room where he lived during the last year. Corey checks with Jane and she nods. "Can you, baby?" Big blue eyes blink a yes.

Next to me, I register movement. Nick's trembling. Shuddering. "I . . ." I shake my head, let him know he doesn't have to explain. We're seeing the damage. We're imagining Aulus, all the June Boys, and it's a shark gnawing through our chests. For a precious second, we excuse ourselves from Corey's inescapable sadness and address our own. Without a word, my hand finds Nick's and we braid ourselves together against evil in the world.

On-screen, Corey chooses a green crayon to sketch. SA Lipman draws too. They're building rapport. The camera picks up breathing and wax scratching white paper for the five minutes Corey draws. SA Lipman leans closer and the boy almost smiles.

"Will you tell me about this?" The question is tentative, giving Corey an out if talking is still too much.

Corey points. "Those are the shelves."

"Good. And what is this colorful thing?"

"The train set."

"Wow. You had a train set?"

Corey shows the camera his spectacular blue eyes and heavy lashes. "Welder gave us the train."

"That was nice of Welder," SA Lipman says without a hint of judgment.

Quiet anger ripples from Jane. SA Lipman throws her some *Be cool. Let him talk* above Corey's head.

"Welder was nice," Corey says.

"I'm very glad about that. What made Welder nice?" SA Lipman asks.

Corey taps the train set and then several other items he's drawn. Explains they are his favorite foods. He adds happily, "And we didn't take baths."

"You liked that?"

Corey nods vigorously.

"Tell me about your train set. What made you choose green for the track? When I was a kid, my train tracks were the color of your skin."

Corey vibrates. Something akin to joy bubbles up. "The bridge tracks glowed in the dark. So did the train wheels. Welder told us to put the bridge and train by the lamp and then we'd turn off the light together—"

A sound off-camera makes us jump. Nick hits Pause, ears strained toward the door. Someone is on the landing outside.

I'm bombarded with three fears at once. We are here uninvited. We've broken into an FBI agent's apartment and viewed absconded evidence. I am the daughter of Don Delacroix.

Nick clicks off the television, places the remote in the basket, and gives me a terrified, silent *What do we do?* All our truth-telling plans swivel down the drain of good intentions.

Keys jangle.

Dana is seconds away from discovering us.

My eyes fall on Nick's hand, still intertwined with mine. I have a single idea that might help. "You trust me?" I ask, with little understanding of whether I trust myself.

There's a split-second answer. A breathed "Yes," and I tug the two of us onto the soft green leather of Dana's couch. We bump heads and almost laugh—probably would have laughed under any other circumstances. Here, we sigh, same as the cushions have sighed with our weight. We find ourselves body to body and Nick understands the plan. I take his face in my hands and stretch my heart toward him. *Please don't avoid my eyes*, I think.

We haven't kissed in days.

I can make up reasons why, but I know why, same as I know kissing now, under these circumstances, is terrible. I love him and I'm using him.

When you kiss someone with your eyes open, it's like watching an opera. You don't have to speak the language to understand the words. Instinct translates. Nick's fear and apprehension, his hesitation—it's alive and pumping before my mouth meets his.

THE ELIZABETH LETTERS

Dear Elizabeth,

I'm titling this letter: How to Get Drunk on Hope. I've tried not to leave anything out.

What happened next was one of my favorite experiences.

Tank had a migraine, so it was me and the two yahoos as electricians.

A year ago they fit on my back, two at the same time. Now, Zared, at six something, made a better base candidate. He tried to straighten without dumping Rufus on the floor, but they wobbled until I stepped forward and clamped my hands on Zared's shoulders. Rufus used our hair like balance handles, and we squeaked like the mice we hear chewing through the garbage at night.

"That's better," Rufus said.

"For you. Yo. Hurry," Zared complained.

"You'll be begging to drink urine after this," I told them.

Zared's eyes bounced from the chicken pock

154

scar under my left eye to my slightly crooked front tooth. He can claim he's fine all he wants, but his gray skin and plucked eyebrows tell the truth. Those ginger arches disappeared our first month together, and every sleep he twists the same greasy lock of widow's peak around his index finger. He knows me well enough to understand I'm keeping us busy, distracting us from hunger and the thirst, Welder's mysterious absence, *Chris* . . . and . . . Now I am the one who needs a distraction.

"Man, I'd kill for a ladder," I said.

"Or a genie so we could ask for a ladder," Rufus said.

Zared smacked Rufus's ankle and I gave Zared a pop of equal or greater value on the forehead. The pyramid almost fell. "If we have a genie, we're asking to escape," he said under his breath.

Good point. "Dear Bunker Genie, I'd love a table or a large piece of furniture to push to the center of the room. Anything that might get us to the ceiling."

"If there's a Bunker Genie, ask her to throw in some cigarettes," Tank said from behind me. Then he crossed the room and rubbed my cheeks like they were a genie lamp. This tickled and I jerked. Rufus leapt down before we dropped him, and we fanned out to find stackable stuff.

We groped the darkness for handfuls of hope. Something soft brushed my arm and I squeezed my hands into fists. Clothes, only clothes. It could have been hair, my brain says.

That thought was radiation. A dandelion blown naked in a single wolf-like huff. Little bits and blobs exploding and floating. Like, Where is Welder? Why hasn't he come back? He could solve all this if he'd return with some food.

I don't want him to come back.

I need him to come back or we'll die. Tank realized I was drifting and asked, "You ever go on a tour of Mammoth Cave where the tour guide turns off all the lights?"

"And then strikes a single match?" I asked. "Yep."

"Remember how they said you can only experience true darkness in caves or deep water—" A loud metallic ping cut him off. Tank hit the ground cursing before he finished the sentence.

"Man, they're ignorant." He reached for whatever made the ping. "Darkness is everywhere," he concluded as he brought my hands to the object.

Thirty or forty inches tall. Cold. Thick metal or aluminum base with a basketball-size diameter. Something sharp stabbed me near the top. Without discussing, Tank and I hauled his discovery to Light.

"Helium?" Tank rocked the cylinder, appraising its weight. "Could be some left."

"Helium's not much use. Unless you can figure out how to float Rufus up to the ceiling with a pickaxe."

Tank's expression said, I probably could have once upon a time. And then the sadness hit him.

I kept us laughing. "He's light, but he's not that light."

Rufus appeared from the corridor, elation painting his face. "Yo. There are barstools in one of the front rooms. Can we get a hand?" Tank followed me, and we happily dragged two barstools all the way to the center of the room. When there were six total, we made the jankiest throne ever.

It was as dangerous as you're probably thinking.

We all took a side. I offered to be the climber and scampered up Zared's stool easily enough. The structure trembled and swayed without buckling when I crossed the "bridge" to the "throne" chair.

"Easy," Tank warned.

We were all heaving. Zared's knuckles were white on his stack as I locked my hands against the ceiling. I wanted to pump my fist but didn't dare release my hold. Tank and Zared exhaled together.

I checked the heat of the fluorescent bulb. "We're in business."

Tank raised a concern. "We have light to do this extraction, but we won't have light to reconnect in Dark once we remove the bulbs. Should we clear the space below the ceiling in Dark first?"

Considering the tricky scaling process, I leaped from the throne easily and we sprang to work in the next room, dragging bags and totes and stuff, piling them around the edges. Back in Light, we removed the bulbs and stowed each in the bubble-like pockets of our pool floats. Break one and it's two lit rooms instead of three.

When everything was set up, Zared, in a very un-Zared move, palmed my head like a basketball and kissed my forehead. I hadn't seen him this happy since before Chris died. Rufus either. He strutted by us, flexing muscles like the world's weakest bodybuilder. He sang, off-key, about us being champions and we all joined in. When the quiet came, and my arms were tucked around the boys'

shoulders, and I'd had a chance to be fully thankful
I wasn't down here alone, Zared asked, "Do you think
Welder's watching us, Aul?"

I said, "Yep," appraising the structure.

Tank said, "Yep, indeed."

One victory became two. From atop the
scaffolding in Dark, I announced, "Wiring matches."
I lifted the light. "We're about to find out what's
in here."

I screw in the bulb. One turn. Two. Three.

Elizabeth, that's when we got our first look at
Dark. I'll be back soon to tell you what's down here.

Peace and Freedom,

Aulus

20

MAY

Nick and I have precious seconds before Dana opens the door. We need her to discover us in the act—but I can't keep myself from speaking into his mouth. "Nick." It's more groan than word. More apology than invitation.

He pauses the kiss, pushing up on his right elbow so his body doesn't trap mine. *"Thee?"* he asks, though I don't know the question. The key turns and we hurry our mouths together. The ten-second soap opera ends with daylight smacking our faces and us squinting into the narrow, shadowed face of his sister.

Wicked fast, she lifts her gun.

Nick shields me. "Dana! It's me. It's Nick. It's Nick."

Dana slams the door so hard a glass lampshade on the other side of the room rattles. Gun holstered, anger loaded and cocked, she yells, "Nick! That's a good way to get yourselves dead," and tacks on a few expletives. "What are you doing here?"

Neither of us fakes embarrassment as we sit, twelve modest

160

inches between our thighs. *Don't stare at the television. Don't stare at the television.*

"Uh . . ."

"Uh . . ."

"Explain," Dana says. "Now!"

I jump to our defense. "This isn't Nick's fault. I made him bring me. I thought you might be able to help with Dad." I stutter, searching for what to say as I'm talking. "But you . . . weren't home . . . and Nick said—"

"We'd wait—"

"And we got distracted."

"I'd say so." Dana tosses her satchel on the floor and collapses into the corner recliner, toeing off her shoes before she kicks back into horizontal exhaustion. The skin around her eyes looks purple and puffy, begging the question of when she last slept. "You could have called. Warned me."

"We're sorry, Dane."

I like when he calls her Dane. She does too. Her chastisement dulls to mere annoyance. "You should be. So have you eaten anything besides each other's faces?"

Nick is scarlet-cheeked. "We haven't."

"And I can assume you've worked up an appetite?"

I'm too relieved to be embarrassed by Dana's teasing jabs. Nick's tennis shoe turns slightly toward my sandal, and I avoid facial expressions that indicate celebration or relief. We're off the hook for breaking and entering and on the hook for a family dinner.

The Jones siblings settle on a quick and cheap Thai restaurant. Dana excuses herself to change and Nick rushes the interview DVD from the machine. His sister emerges seconds later in navy track pants, a white ribbed tank top, and a gray long-sleeve shirt tied around her waist. She looks ten years younger and I tell her so. As we head out the door she tells me this case makes her buy Oil of Olay in bulk. "Especially after today."

"Something happen?" Nick asks.

She unlocks her SUV. "You'll find out tomorrow."

"Or . . . ," Nick prompts. "We could find out now."

Dana's head bobs with indecision until we're three blocks down the street. She looks sideways at me, smiling. "They're releasing your dad."

I can't speak.

"DNA's in. A no-go for him. The judge will cut Don loose. Probably tomorrow morning."

What happens now? Is Dad completely cleared? Does she still believe he's guilty? Did the DNA match anyone else? I hold my questions because we arrive at the restaurant. Dana greets the teenage hostess, Char, by name.

Char asks, "The usual?"

"Times three," Dana says. "My brother, Nick. His girlfriend, Thea." *Don't say my last name. Don't say my last name.*

It wouldn't have mattered if my last name was Hitler or Stalin. Char places an expert hand on her Victoria Secret–shaped waist and says, "You're the hotshot law student she always talks about?" To which Nick answers, "Trying to be," and then they stare at each other the way two symmetrically beautiful single people do.

I should be jealous. I'm too happy about Dad.

When we pick a booth, Nick slides in next to Dana. She orders for the table, not even checking to see if we're okay with her selections. I'm relieved. I can't pronounce half the menu. Nick waits until Char retreats to the kitchen before he nudges Dana with his elbow. "What else can you tell us about the DNA?"

162

"Nothing." There's zero budge in her voice.

Nick tries again. "What else will you tell us about Thea's dad?"

"Well." Dana takes a long sip of water. "Neither I nor the system know if Don Delacroix is the Gemini Thief. The system believes the current evidence is insufficient to convict. So"—she cuts her eyes at me with a piercing seriousness—"releasing him doesn't mean you should lower your guard, Thea. They're looking for another reason to hold him."

"What's your gut say, sis?"

"That he fits the profile."

Nick isn't satisfied with Dana's hesitation. "But?"

"Don never gives me the heebies. That's not a good reason to acquit, but the perp on this one"—she adjusts her bra strap, pops her neck with a half turn—"when I meet him, he's going to make the skin crawl away from my bones. Your dad's aloof, maybe even a few degrees off, but more in a *religious nut, technically harmless* way. Not an *I've collected prepubescent boys in my basement* way. No matter which direction I turn Don's edges, he's a piece of this puzzle, not *the* piece. That's a theory, though. Don't quote me."

"Have you considered that someone set him up?" I ask.

"I've considered everything. Can you suggest someone who would?" Dana threads her knife in and out each fork tine. "Because your dad certainly can't. Or won't. I've asked him to give me another suspect. And nada, nothing. He stares at the wall and asks what happens to his castle if he has to stay here much longer. He's like a child in the toy aisle. Sorry," she says, as though this is somehow more offensive than my father being a kidnapping murderer. "The man is a pain in the—"

"Mine too," I say. Dana Jones and I share a moment because against her better judgment she likes my father.

163

"Does he have any enemies?" Dana asks.

"Other than my mother? I don't think so."

Dana stops fiddling with the silverware. "Constance O'Brien? The first wife?"

Nick flashes an unnecessary apology. "She might know someone."

I say, "If my dad made enemies, they came from that period of his life. People in Wildwood like him." I stare at the scarred tabletop. "Well, they did. A successful tax business requires trust."

Dana tells us the FBI interviewed Constance and she provided nothing helpful. Dana goes on to share another nugget of important news: none of the victims identified Dad in a lineup.

"That doesn't mean much," I say aloud without realizing I am thinking about the welding photo. Nick winds his leg around mine. An unspoken warning. *Tread carefully.*

"Such a nightmare," Dana says, her eyes landing on me for a long, searching moment. "I can't imagine how hard this is. Are you talking to someone? A counselor? Your pastor?"

I shake my head.

"Promise me you'll think about it. Because as good a listener as my brother is, he's not a professional."

I want to tell her Nick's friendship has probably saved my life, but Char appears, tray piled with steaming dishes and spices on her shoulder. "Roy sends his appreciation," she says cheerfully.

"You outdid yourself, Roy," Dana calls loud enough for the cook to raise a hand and wave off the praise.

How Dana stays the size of an uncooked spaghetti noodle when she eats this many carbs is a mystery. "Eat up. It's on me. Least I can do," she adds, as though food is an acceptable form of therapy. She pours curry chicken over white rice and mounds on red pepper flakes.

I consider the heart of Dana Jones.

She's as fiery as her red-speckled noodles. She didn't advance her position at the FBI without being great at her job, and she didn't get those massive purple eye bags by not caring. Below the all-business veneer, she's a warm, goofy sister, who is currently claiming Nick will cry for milk if he tries the green sauce. It's this, not her credentials, that makes me like her.

I wind flat noodles around my fork and make a decision I'll probably regret. "Show her the welding photo," I say.

Nick, who's pouring the noted green sauce on the side of his plate, pauses, spilling it on the table.

Dana seizes my offering. "What welding photo?"

"Constance O'Brien gave us a box of Dad's old stuff."

"Thea, stop." Nick's voice is sharp.

Dana jabs her utensils in Nick's direction. "You aren't helping." To me, she says, "Thea, *start*."

Show her, I mouth.

Nick's unsure if I mean what I've said. I address Dana. "If I show you something that could be good or bad, do I have your word you'll help?" *Shouldn't I have done this all along?*

Dana reaches for my hand. "I've been trying to help you from the get-go. You think I liked busting into your house and arresting your dad? That I liked not being able to warn either of you? Because that isn't my idea of a good time. I want to find Aulus and the others as much as you."

Nick flashes *That's definitely true* eyes my way. Trust runs both ways with Nick. He's kept my secrets and Dana's. He's known she likes my father but couldn't say so without betraying her confidence. What a fine line to walk. It's my turn to wrap my foot around Nick's leg and assure him I understand the risk. I need him to know, need myself to know, I want the truth more than anything else. I say, "Show her."

When he passes the flimsy square to his sister's waiting hands, her mouth falls open. "Who?" She flips the photo and examines the names. "Aulus's dad." She reverses the photo again. "They look alike. You made a note in your research that I thought was really smart. You asked a question about the Nashville flood?"

Nick says, "Yeah, we thought the flood might have forced the Gemini Thief to change his venue."

"Good theory. The autopsy said Chris Jenkins drowned. Lab confirmed a match. Rainwater. Along with silt from the Cumberland. That kid likely died in the Nashville flood."

"What's that have to do with Scottie McClaghen?"

"Well, his timeline's a good match, and now, here he is in a welding mask." She taps the photo. "Plus . . ." Her eyes drift up to the left, away from the table.

"Plus what?" I ask.

"Plus he and Leo Wittersham filed a co-insurance claim on a piece of property they own in Nashville. Got damaged by the flood. I wanted it searched, but we didn't have enough evidence for a warrant. But this—this photo could prove probable cause."

Blood rushes through my veins in wild rivers. "My dad's in that photo," I say. "Wearing a welding mask."

"We're releasing him."

"You think that'll still happen after you show a judge that picture?" Nick asks.

Dana shoves a massive bite into her mouth and talks around it. "Listen, you two need to keep trusting me. This is good news."

"No."

"I get that you're scared, but you're also smart enough to

understand the only way to clear your father is for us to arrest the real Gemini Thief."

"*I'm also smart enough* to understand you've been looking for the real thief for ten years and found nothing. You said the system is looking for more. That's more," I say, pointing at the photo.

Dana flinches. She hasn't been on the case for ten years, but it has occupied the first five of her tenure at the Bureau. Five long years that have robbed color from her face and weight from her bones.

"Hard as this is," she says, "I made a promise to honor the law, and this is me keeping that oath. And for one reason or another, you're going to be glad I did."

21

Nick's making the dumb mistake of trying to make me feel better, and I'm picturing the little heart Char drew on the receipt and slid in his direction. I'm at peak insecurity. I've betrayed my father, again, and I might lose my boyfriend. Here, Dana, take this incriminating photo. Here, Char, take Nick.

"Why are you being difficult?" Nick asks. "Your dad's getting out tomorrow. I thought you'd be happy." When I say nothing, he says, "You're the one who showed Dana the photograph." This is Nick's *I told you so*. Before I can argue, he grabs my fist from the air and tugs my hand into his lap. "And you have good instincts. You told Dana because you could. Please trust that."

I snatch my hand away. I am ready to eat him and he sees my nostrils flare, my teeth nice and pointy.

"Stop before you say something you don't mean."

"Something like *Why is kissing me so hard lately?* Don't think your reputation can survive 'dating the murderer's daughter'?"

"There it is."

I wrap my arms around my knees and tuck into a tight cannonball. "There what is?"

"Exactly what I expected to happen with you."

"Which is?"

He shakes his head like he's already said too much. I prod hard. "No, don't stop now. Not when I need enlightenment. What did you expect to happen with *me*?"

"I expected you to retreat. To find your next big thing and for it not to be me."

"Oh, please." I give him the go-ahead gesture, unsure if I can hold my tongue. "Because my dad retreats?"

"I'm saying our relationship would confuse anyone. Anyone, Thee. I mean, come on, we met during a missing persons case. Neither of us has had answers or closure for a year. Every time I'm with you I wonder if this—you and me—would have happened if Aulus hadn't disappeared. Do you like me or am I your latest project? Then I start thinking I'm one of those sad sacks who capitalize on hardships." He lays his palms flat against the steering wheel, his fingers hyperextended with stress. "*Oh, my best friend was kidnapped and his cousin is hot.* Who does that? And then every time I'm in the group, the three of you look at me like I'm the replacement guy. I'm sorry I don't write people letters or work part-time or stop going to college because Aulus disappeared."

"Stop," I say.

"Stop what? Feeling sorry for myself? Because don't you think I'm telling myself the same thing?"

Tears spill onto my cheeks.

"I want you to want me," he says. "I even, man, I'm not proud of this, find myself thinking that if we find Aulus, you'll ditch me, and sometimes I don't care if he—"

"Don't say—"

"Doesn't come back. So, see? You should dump me."

"Nick, stop."

We don't say anything else until we reach Gladys's house. Our hearts are no calmer. He levels his voice. "If your dad does come home tomorrow, you shouldn't stay with him."

"Nick—"

"Regardless of what you think of me right now, Tank would kill me if I didn't warn you." We both sigh-laugh. Nick's 100 percent right. He says, "Think about it. And"—another deep sigh—"maybe prepare for the fact that not everyone in Wildwood will be ecstatic the FBI released him."

I promise I will. We kiss each other on the cheek and stay touching until we're both breathing regularly.

"I love you. For you," I say, knowing there are things I need to address in myself, but love is not up for consideration. I do love Nick Jones. Even if Aulus never comes home.

Before Nick can comment, I leave the car and follow the hedges around Gladys's house. I crouch on the sidewalk, the weeds tickling my bare ankles, and my exhaustion falls out in a sob.

A chair skids against the decking boards. A face appears. "That you, Thea?" Gladys calls.

I wipe my eyes. "It's me."

"Things go okay at Dana's?" When I make an ambiguous gesture with my hands, she says, "That's what I figured." I climb the steps and sag against her on the chaise lounge. "Things go okay here?"

"Not exactly." She lays her head all the way back and stares at the stars.

"Need to talk?" I ask, even though neither of us has the stamina.

"Not really. Buddy?" she says.

"Yeah."

"Will you hold me for a second?"

I curl my body across Gladys's lap, wrap my arms around her; she wraps hers around me. Her tears are flowing freely and everything from this evening swells into a planetary-size lump in my throat. We lie there, sad and angry, lonely and worried, holding and helping. Before the end, I lay my hand across her sternum, feel her furiously beautiful heart, and say, "Love you, friend."

"Love you back."

Sometimes a moment is exactly what it's supposed to be. Sometimes it's more. I am thinking about the question she asked—*Will you hold me for a second?*—the ease with which she asked for help and the ease with which I not only could do what she asked, but also needed what she asked for. I hope no one ever tells Gladys about basements and keys.

The kitchen light flicks on. Her dad's face stretches into various silly expressions on the other side of the window. We giggle, he waves awkwardly, and the mood turns decidedly lighter.

"Want some good news?" I ask when he leaves us for the refrigerator.

"Please."

"DNA on Chris didn't match Dad. Dana says they might release him tomorrow."

Gladys squeezes me. "That's great." She eyes the kitchen, mouth twisted in a scowl. "Will you be staying at your house then?"

Something clicks. Nick's warning, *Not everyone in Wildwood will be ecstatic.* "Your folks . . . They don't like people to see me here, do they?"

Gladys teases out a wisp of my hair. "I'm sure it's not permanent."

"I get it," I say, but I can't sleep here. "Hey, will you take me to Griff and Ruby's?"

"Now?"

"Yeah. I want to tell them about Dad in person since they're footing the legal bills. And maybe I'll stay over there."

"Hon, you're welcome here tonight. You saw my dad making faces at us. He's fine."

He's fine because it's dark. "I know."

"Do you?"

"He's my father, Glads."

"And they're my parents." She adds, "They'll come around. It took them a while to warm up to Tank, but they did."

"Gladys, I love you, but you dating a black guy is very different from my father being a murderer."

She rolls her eyes. "Not in the South."

Point made. No one our parents' age seems to get over anything quickly around here. "Touché," I say.

"They're good people. Time and truth will win out."

But not tonight.

Gladys sticks out her arm and slides the door a few inches, pokes her head in, yells that she's running me over to Griff's. There's some discussion of the late hour; I don't stick around to watch Gladys win the skirmish. We drive in silence. Gladys turns into Griff's driveway too fast and scrapes the bumper against the driveway. "Easy, Glads."

"I'm sorry about my folks," she says. "Want me to wait until you're inside?"

Ruby appears at the front door slab, shielding her eyes against the streetlamp. "That you, Thea?"

I wave. "It's me." To Gladys I say, "See you in the morning," before closing the passenger door.

Somewhat reluctantly, Gladys reverses the car. I face the house and Ruby, knowing the decision I've made isn't perfect. I didn't want to be at the Baxters', but I also don't have the energy to deal with the Holtzes' love and attention. "Can I stay?" I ask.

"Get on in here," Ruby says, her evening cup of tea in hand. I pass the honeysuckle that hedges the front walk and anticipate the interior smells of aloe, cinnamon, and overprotection. The familiarity works on me. *One foot in front of the other, Delacroix. You made the right decision.*

Ruby's bulldog frame swallows me whole. She works the mom-thing: "You're not eating enough. I have cookies. I can make you mac and cheese. We have a box of Kraft, right, Griff?"

Griff's conformed to the couch for another episode of Ruby's HGTV and shoots me a private eye roll of amusement. To his wife, he says, "Babe, it's late. Thea's probably already had something," because she'll have every pot and pan on the stove before Griff mutes the episode I've interrupted.

"I'm not hungry," I say and ask to use the shower.

"Whatever you need, honey bear."

Ruby pulled that nickname from decades-old rubble. I won't be surprised if she's laid pajamas on my bed while I shower. I should tell them about Dad's potential release, but I don't have the conversation in me right now. Ruby escorts me to the guest bath.

"Let me tidy up a few things." She bundles makeup and hair products into her arms. "I got ready in here this morning. Sorry for the mess."

"Don't make anything perfect for me."

She kisses my cheek. "You haven't answered my texts."

"Sorry." Her texts are constant.

173

Tears settle in her crow's feet. "You should live here." She's not asking.

Griff's kind chastisement drifts down the hallway. "Honey, she's staying with the Baxters. Leave her alone."

Ruby sniffs and whispers conspiratorially, "Live here."

I should thank her or something; instead, I disappear behind the bathroom door. Poor Ruby. Love bleeds out of her like an open wound.

I don't wait for the water to warm. Cold streams onto my hair and neck and I relive the evening. A million years and three Thai plates ago, Nick and I stood in Dana's living room watching scrawny little Corey sketch a train with his crayons. My mind traces the drawing, and as it does, I swing my watch face forward and backward around my arm, over and over. Like a train on a tiny wrist-size track. It feels familiar. Too familiar.

I squeeze my temples. Shove my nose to the orange Dial soap. Pick at the toenail polish on my big toes. The skin on my belly pinks because I never adjusted the hot water.

Something about that train won't let me go.

Chugga, chugga, chug. Chugga, chugga, chug.

"Chugga, chugga, chug." I speak the words, searching for the voice who first spoke them.

Mom?

No, I don't remember her voice.

Dad?

No, too deep.

Deep.

The voice is very deep.

Chugga, chugga, chug. Chugga, chugga, chug.

Not Ruby.

Not Griff.

Not a teacher from school.

Chugga, chugga, chug.

It's rougher.

It's . . . it's . . . Warren.

Even though my eyes are open, I am seeing the past instead of porcelain tile. Warren takes me by one hand and with the other lowers the pull-down steps leading to the attic. Together we climb the creaking, wobbling ladder into a room with a triangular ceiling. Warren slouches to avoid nails piercing the two-by-six boards.

"What are we doing?" I ask. Light filters through a vent in the wall. More light spins in circles on the floor from the whirling fan on the roof. I'm sweating.

"Treasure hunting." Uncle Warren examines the contents of cardboard boxes until he finds one labeled Trains in faded Sharpie. "Here it is. And you know what?"

"What?"

"This train is awesome. Know why?"

"Nope."

He pokes my belly like I'm the Pillsbury doughboy. "It glows in the dark."

Warren knifes into the box and produces a train with green wheels. I imagine them lit like a Christmas tree.

Chugga, chugga, chug. Chugga, chugga, chug.

My train.

Corey's train.

THE ELIZABETH LETTERS

Dear Elizabeth,

When the light came on, I thought, Oh, right. The crying closet. ──────────────>

Zared stared at the wooden door, same as me. "I forgot about the lacrimal room," he said the same way you might say, "I forgot we had a test in geometry."

Rufus was on him in a second. "I forgot about the lacrimal room." The intonation was spot-on perfect and I laughed. We didn't include the crying closet on Tank's initial tour, so the door meant nothing to him. Rufus said, "Yo, I'm glad we didn't label that sucker on the graffiti map."

"What so funny?" Tank wanted to know.

I said, "I was laughing at *the lacrimal room*."

Tank didn't laugh along. He said, "I'd

[margin note, circled:] We use a three-closet system: two for waste, one to be alone. This third closet gained traction after Chris. Crying is normal. Sobbing lowers morale.

176

rather some details not end up in our FBI file, okay?"

"And I'd rather you never mention the FBI." I was short with him the way I always am when he brings up the glorious FBI.

I avoid finishing the conversation and scan the room. One wall was what I expected: disintegrated trash bags covered in dust and something that may or may not be kitty litter and mouse beds. Directly adjacent to Sleeping Room were dozens of boxy computer monitors and hard drives. The room makes Leo's book stacks look like the work of an elementary hoarder.

Zared noticed the animals first. "That's a coyote."

Teeth bared, feet mounted to a wooden board, the coyote guarded the lacrimal room like a poor man's Aslan. And under the bags of clothes, which we tossed to the edges of the room, sat dozens of animal species. Hardened, frozen faces. Tails curled in lifelike positions crushed against snapping snouts and the gills of openmouthed bass.

Tank said, "I'm not sure lighting this room was wise."

Some cities host drop-off days for old batteries and televisions. This dumping ground seemed like the

> The Federal Bureau of Investigation's unsuccessful decade-long search for Welder slides a knife into the carotid artery of my optimism. I've tried explaining this with no success. There aren't many differences between being here a year or a month, but this is one.

177

result of every small-town wife saying, "Honey, take the bass and chipmunks to the curb. It's taxidermy Friday."

"Someone's a collector," Zared said, almost impressed.

Rufus snapped the band on Zared's underwear. "Someone's a psy-cho!"

"Watch out. I'm coming down." Good thing I said something; shifting my weight caused the scaffolding to fall and scatter into a mess of metal. Tank cussed and Zared snapped at Rufus to be more careful with me.

Tank tugged me toward him. "How much do you know about hunting in Kentucky? Species might tell us where we are. Maybe?"

This was him spoon-feeding my particular brand of hope. Even if we didn't get out of here, I wanted to know where we were and who had taken us. I caressed the velvet ear of a red fox similar to one in Leo's garage, and agreed.

"A collector would probably have species beyond the region, but these animals are native to the South." He petted the specimens lovingly. "River otter. Mink. Red fox. Squirrel."

"Boy Scout," I teased.

"Valedictorian. Get it right," Tank said, but couldn't hold the mock anger for long.

Rufus's eyes went all huge. He asked me, "Is he joking or what?"

I shook my head.

"Bro, you should've told us you were smart," Rufus says.

"What if we're near your Wildwood?" Zared asked.

I kept my voice controlled and low. "Anything's possible now."

Two-thirds of the fifteen thousand residents of Simpson County lived in Wildwood city limits. That left an ungodly amount of rural property to search.

Tank squatted next to the fox. "I was taken because . . ." It's agonizing to watch him. "Because . . . because of something I did or said. Maybe with the investigation. Maybe . . ."

Zared sauntered over and considered the possibility of side-hugging Tank. At the last minute, he bailed. I didn't think Tank heard him mutter, "Remembering how or who won't unbrick these walls," but I did. Nothing broke Tank's hold on himself when he got like this. He rocked like a metronome, pressing thumbs into his temples. He'd have put them through his skull if he had the strength.

"If Welder was watching or felt threatened by something we did in the investigation, he would have to be local, right? Someone close enough to watch us?"

"Sure. Maybe," I said. "But Rufe and Zared weren't from Wildwood. They're not even from Kentucky. Chris either." Mention of Chris stopped me, but I managed to continue. "Welder could have driven from anywhere and driven you to anywhere."

"Sure. But why take me at all?"

I liked his brain reengaging.

Rufus tapped the floor in a nervous rhythm. He wore the same fearful pinched expression as the stuffed turkey. "Whatcha got here?" I asked, kneeling beside him.

"What?" Tank stepped closer.

"Knife." I placed Rufus's discovery in Tank's outstretched hand. Wooden grip, two feet by three-inch-wide blade that arced slightly at the tip. I'd once seen a machete like this hanging from my father's belt.

"How sharp?" Tank asked.

I drew back my thumb after brief contact with the edge and showed a thin sliver of crimson. My eyes darted to where Zared was crouched, stroking long-dead animals. He was calling them "baby." We had seconds before we drew his curiosity.

"Hide it," I said.

Tank started to protest. "But if Welder comes—"

Man, that's difficult to admit.

"Right now we're greater enemies to ourselves."

All for now. Zared is sniffling, maybe crying, and I need to check on him.

Peace and Freedom,

Aulus

22

MAY

Streaks of pastel blue paint mark the beige wall near the ceiling. Ruby missed a spot the last time she painted. The guest room's over-large digital clock ticks away the red minutes. Warren's wooden train chugs on through the night. Every miniature imagined circuit, Corey's drawing breathes its dragon breath on Uncle Warren. There's no getting around the fact that ten years ago he dragged a cardboard box from his attic to the patio, and we set and reset glow-in-the-dark train tracks until bedtime forced us inside.

I search for rest or at least comfort and can't escape the sheet's mummy trappings. I can't escape that stupid train.

During Dad's and my two-week stay, the caboose—a bright alien green after exposure to the floor lamp—glowed and burned through dozens of AA batteries. I was too old for trains but young enough to stuff Warren's affection into the massive hole left by Mom. He was so good to me. He *is* so good to me. I ask my brain to stretch Saran-like around Warren stealing Aulus, Warren wearing a welding helmet, Warren giving the train to Corey. Warren killing Chris.

I can't.

On the surface, he's a far worse candidate for the Gemini Thief than Dad.

He's too . . . Too what?

Good with kids?

That catches like a mental thorn.

Corey's face appears on the screen of my mind. Damaged, but mostly not afraid Welder would inflict physical harm. He liked Welder. Welder never made him shower. Welder gave him a train. Stockholm syndrome? Sure. But whoever the Thief is . . . he essentially borrows someone else's children to feed and clothe for a year.

I don't think my dad loves children that much. Despite Constance's opinion, Mom leaving a six-year-old daughter in Dad's care full-time was awkward for all parties involved. The first year he cut my bangs with the same kitchen scissors he used on raw chicken. When I needed a training bra, he shoved money at Mrs. Baxter like he was buying illicit drugs. While other kids were eating hummus and carrots, sliced apples, pretzel sticks and peanut butter from their lunch boxes, Dad sent Vienna sausages and Easy Cheese. He's been waiting for me to grow up most of my life, which probably explains all the times we've eaten ice cream at midnight.

Warren would have kept me a little girl forever.

The first two years we lived in Wildwood, 90 percent of my tantrums ended in *I'd rather live with Uncle Warren than you.* Once, I overheard Dad telling Warren, *Thea loves you more than me.* Warren had wisely said, *Uncles aren't in charge of discipline. If I were her dad, she'd hate me too.* And my dad said, *I don't know. I really don't know.*

Eventually I grew out of Warren and into Dad. Or maybe I stopped lashing out at him because I couldn't reach Mom. That didn't happen until I was, what, nine or ten? By the summer Dad opened the tax shop we were on solid ground. That was 2000.

I stare at the ceiling fan, the math clicking. The Gemini Thief took the first round of boys in June of 2000.

What's the chance I grew out of Warren, but he didn't grow out of parenting?

What's the chance Dad wanted a boy instead of a girl?

The night folds around the horizon. Morning streams through the blinds. Knowing I do not want to be alone with my jumbled thoughts, I scroll through phone contacts. It's too early to call Gladys or Tank. Nick wouldn't mind if I woke him, but we're in such a weird place . . . I spot Constance's name and realize it's six a.m. eastern time.

She answers in three rings. "This is Constance O'Brien."

"This is Thea. Thea Delacroix." Like an idiot, I add, "Don's daughter."

Hectic adrenaline rushes into her voice. I've scared her awake. "Thea? Are you okay?"

"I'm sorry I called so early. I shouldn't—"

"Honey, are you in danger?"

"I'm safe. I . . ." Forming sentences proves difficult.

Now sure my life isn't at risk, Constance rescues my silence. "No need to apologize. I'm making coffee. You take your time. I'll listen. I'll talk. Whatever you need." She says this with the ease of someone who has been called many times by uncertain parishioners. On the other side of the phone, the coffee machine whirls and dribbles.

I say, "Dad's getting out of jail today. DNA's not a match."

"And you're feeling . . ." She leaves the response wide open.

"Relief. Fear. Worry. Like someone near me is the Gemini Thief."

She asks what makes me believe this, and after I confirm our conversation is 100 percent confidential, I tell her about breaking into Dana's apartment, seeing Corey's train, remembering the glow-in-the-dark engine from Warren's attic. "You know Warren, right? From college?"

"Warren Burton." Constance pauses, maybe sips her coffee. "I do." Two weighted words followed by more. "We dated. After your dad divorced me."

Oh. "Does Dad know?"

"I never told him, and I can't see Warren being forthcoming with the information, given the circumstances."

"You guys didn't work out?" The ridiculous question escapes despite the fact that both adults are single and living miles apart.

"We were in different emotional spaces," she says and then explains. "I was freshly dumped, raw wounds oozing abandonment and divorce all over the place, and Warren was chomping to get married and start a family. That man needed motivated ovaries and a four-bedroom farmhouse." She laughs easily at the memory. "I couldn't imagine ever getting married again, ever, much less having kids. Super-bad timing because he's a great guy."

I am shocked on two levels, neither of them having to do with Constance. One. Bro code says you don't date your best friend's ex-wife. Two. Warren's not exactly a lady's man. Sometimes Dad and Griff go on a teasing tear and call him *Officer Bach*. I was fourteen before I realized it was short for *bachelor*.

Constance quickly clarifies her role. "I was the third, maybe fourth girl he asked. I'd already been someone's wife and was unimpressed with the position. Which made me unwilling to be less than the love of someone's life, and I was never that for Warren."

"Wow."

"Thea, am I understanding correctly? You're wondering if Warren has Aulus?"

I toss the question around my brain. "Maybe."

How far-fetched is this train theory?

"Let's assume for a moment you're right that the Gemini Thief lives in Wildwood," Constance says. "When you think about Warren Burton, what does your spirit say?"

"My spirit?"

"Your gut. Your inner voice. The untamed thing inside you who often speaks the truth."

Lady, if my inner voice were functioning, I wouldn't be talking to a stranger at six a.m. I say something along these lines and Constance sighs. I assume with sadness or pity, but then she surprises me by saying, "I have trouble with my spirit too. For me, that spirit is God. For you, maybe it's experience or friends or poetry or who knows." She laughs easily, enjoying her metaphor. "Maybe I need another cup of coffee before I talk theology."

"Constance, how do you know when your gut, the spirit, or whatever, is right?"

"Other than time?"

"I don't have the luxury of time." *Or errors.* "Aulus. Rufus. Zared. Chris." Tears clog my windpipe. "Their lives. Dad's life. Now . . . maybe even Uncle Warren's. I can't be wrong. These same questions damaged my father. You should have seen him in jail. My best friend's parents don't even want me to stay at their house." I hug a pillow to my chest. The sun drifts in through the tilted

185

mini-blinds and lights the navy tearstains on the pastel blue sheets. "An accusation would destroy Warren's career. He's a cop."

"You need proof."

I have that terrible glow-in-the-dark train. I recall what Constance said about starting a church. How she gambled everything. Moving cities, houses, taking out loans, leaving old friends behind. Where did that forward-thinking faith come from?

"You took a risk. How did you know what to do when there was so much at stake? When you had an instinct but nothing else? Because I don't think I can know if I'm right unless I act like I am, but if I act and I'm wrong . . ."

Constance speaks slowly. "Then you'll be wrong, and while there might be consequences to your accusation, the people who love you will still love you. And the same will be true for Warren."

"I don't think so."

She shifts gears. "You asked how I knew about starting the church. You want to know the real answer?"

"Please." I am thirsty for deep waters and eager to treat Constance like a well.

"God showed up in my bedroom and told me to move to Lexington and start a church."

"God, God?"

"That's what I call him or her."

"I didn't know God did earth visits." I conjure up my version of this visit. The pastor in her bed squinting fearlessly at an orb of bobbing yellow-white light who sounds like Morgan Freeman or Helen Mirren. Purple sheets and pink comforter fall from clutched fists to Constance's lap. The night is moonless, and God is made of stars. Warmth strikes her skin like a campfire. "You must have freaked out," I say.

"I was every emotion at once."

If this were anyone else, I might doubt. But Constance seems to live her life like an inside-out clock—all gears and workings visible—and for me, this lends her an almost supernatural trustworthiness.

"That's intense. Has he ever done it again? God, I mean."

"Shown up in my bedroom?"

"Shown up anywhere." I want a sense of the possibilities here.

She hesitates. When her voice comes, it's thready, but true. "One other time."

"Can you tell me what he said that time?"

"Word for word." Another pause. "It happened yesterday."

My heart rapid-fires.

"God told me: Help Don Delacroix finish his castle."

23

MAY

Thursday afternoon Constance's spine rests against the storm door of my house, her freckled shoulders pink from waiting in the sun. Tank points at the pastor like she's a rare bird lighting on our front stoop. Constance waves. I wave back.

"Were you expecting this?" he wants to know.

"Sort of." Constance and I didn't discuss a plan, but when we got off the phone this morning, she said she'd see me soon.

Tank checks his watch. He had promised his mom he'd finish thank-you cards before baccalaureate tonight, but he still asks, "Want me to stay?"

I place his hand on the gearshift. "Go home. Get stuff done. I'll call you after Dad's home."

Dana warned me last night that red tape would likely stretch Dad's release from morning to evening and not to expect them until dinner. That gives me time with Constance before we both handle the Welcome Wagon. *Ready or not*, I think and leave Tank flipping his cigarette round and round.

Tank leans through the window, chest pressing the door. "You're sure?"

I tap the truck's hood with my palm. Two media trucks and three cars linger on our curb like weeds that have pushed through concrete cracks. They film Tank's exit.

"Follow me," I say to Constance and trudge across the ankle-high clover toward the kitchen door.

After resting her purse on the pollen-soaked deck railing, she jams both hands into the pockets of her jeans and says, "I checked into a motel and then came over to wait. I'm here to work."

I swing the kitchen door open. "Check out and stay here."

She laughs until she realizes my invitation is sincere. Inside, we gasp in tandem. The air's tepid and the kitchen reeks of something rancid, making the invitation seem like something I should retract. I spot the remains of pizza rolls on paper plates and chuck them and the glass bowl of molded ranch directly into the trash.

"I haven't been here since they arrested him," I say as an apology.

When I return from lowering the thermostat, Constance squats by the sink, fishing for cleaner. She sprays orange-scented mist onto the countertops and repeats, "I came to work."

We clean for two hours, then collapse on the couch in a sweaty heap. Our music blares so loud we don't hear Dad before he appears in the doorjamb between the dining and living rooms. His head's bowed, his shoulders curved; he's aged since I sat across from him at the jail. Cocking his head in quiet surprise at the sight of Constance sprawled next to me, he closes his eyes, opens them, and tries again as if he expects different results.

"I can explain," I say, overlapping Constance's explanation.

"Don, I came to help with the castle."

"Totally unnecessary," he says. Looking from her to me—the half inch between our thighs speaking more than words—he announces, "I'm taking a shower. Please don't leave. Either of you."

Constance mouths, *So far so good*, and we take ourselves to the kitchen to wait. She makes a pot of decaf that obscures the smell of bleach.

"Will you tell him your suspicions about Warren?" she asks, settling at the bar with her mug.

The shower stops running and I put a finger to my lips. Nick spent the day following Warren, and I'm not saying a word until I hear from him.

"Or will you tell Dana?"

"Nick's making that call." He took the decision from me this morning. "This shouldn't be on you," he said after a discussion on the train memory. "Let me be the one to make accusations if it comes to it." I agreed like the grateful coward I am.

Dad emerges, hair wet, shirt damp across the shoulders. He addresses Constance instead of me. "I'm not sure how you ended up here, but I owe you apologies, and you'll get them, but first—"

"I didn't come for apologies."

"I didn't take those boys." He's resolute. A statue.

Constance hands him a mug of steaming tea and some grace. "I know."

Tremors start in his shoulder. Liquid vibrates over the edge of his mug and onto the floor. The mug falls. Without consideration or permission, Constance steps through the puddle and ceramic splinters and wraps her sunburned arms around Dad. Somewhat magically she dwarfs him. The two of them—him shaking child-like, her rubbing figure eights on his back, and repeating, "It's okay"—are the most beautiful things I've seen in a long time. I can't hug my father like that. I don't have hugs that say this will be okay. Mine ask far too many questions.

In a jolt, Dad seems to remember Constance is his ex-wife and he's fresh out of prison. He removes himself to the far wall and leans against a set of framed photos. "And you?" he asks me, searching for any portent of accusation in my body language. "Do you know I didn't take Aulus?"

What do I know?

His integrity and innocence have been pressed against a pile of coincidences. I put him under a microscope of blame. I let myself fully entertain his darkness.

But not anymore.

I had spent the day in the school library forming a new theory: I don't know who set up Dad, but if Dad were a kidnapping murderer, his first wife probably wouldn't be receiving personal visitations from higher powers requesting she help finish his castle in Wildwood, Kentucky. Constance nailed shut my coffin of guilt and uncertainty. I arrange my face so only love shows. "I know you, Dad."

"I need to hear you say you trust me."

Knowing he's not a murderer and trusting him are two different things. "Tell me why you lied for so long."

"Because I was an idiot," he says without hesitation. "I paid attention to every nail, every board, every bag of concrete. Every conceivable detail. I followed the vision with precision." He pauses to glance at Constance, and there's something kindred in the expression they share. "I got lost in it, Thee. I got—"

"Addicted." I set my mug on the counter. The lower edge chips.

When I look up, Dad says, "But no more. I'm selling the castle to the Markums."

"What?" Constance and I say together.

She leaps from the barstool where she's perched and it tumbles backward under the weight of her purse. Without righting the chair, she arrives in my father's space again—not so friendly this time. "You can't do that, Don."

"I was silly to believe—"

"Belief is many things, silly never being one."

"Stancy—" Two trenches run from the bridge of his nose toward his hairline.

I stand in protest with her. "Dad, listen. Constance, tell him. Tell him what happened."

In several dozen words, my father's ex-wife shares the fragile times after their divorce—her depression, the return of her faith, and ultimately, the building of a new community in Lexington. She is unflinchingly honest, and he listens without interrupting. There's tenderness between them that's as green and alive as a plant poking through soil.

"Can't you see?" she says as she finishes. "You weren't wrong about the castle, only in the obsessiveness of building it."

"Stance, I don't . . . I mean . . . We can't keep building. Everyone's watching. People think I . . ."

"You didn't care what people thought before," I say, and Constance echoes, "Let them watch. The truth will win out. Thea says you're close to finishing."

Dad stares toward the living room, toward the media trucks parked at the curb. "Do you know what it's like to be falsely accused of something heinous? To have your community, your family, your best friends believe you would hurt—" His voice is reedy. His back bends forward until his hands land on his knees and he takes deep breaths. "And for what? A stupid building. A dream? Some weird vision from a God I've barely spoken to in years? I thought the castle would feel worth the sacrifice because it was above me or would reconnect me with who I used to be, but you know what? That's insane. Normal people do not build castles. And while I realize you"—he attempts eye contact and fails—"showing up here feels like a sign, I—"

"Dad, the castle's not stupid and normal's overrated." The words come directly from my gut. My spirit? If there's anything I'm certain about: losing the castle now, after all this, can't be the end of the story.

Constance squats and peels Dad's hands from his knees; she gets under his lowered chin. "Don, we can't pretend to know the utter hell you've been living in, but you don't have to live in it alone. Thea's here. And strangely enough, I'm here too. We believe you. For now, can that be enough?"

"Warren believes me. Griff and Ruby too," he says.

"Nick and Dana," I add. "And the FBI released you. Let that count for something."

"Every single person who believes me counts, but the castle—" His eyes drift to the clock on the wall, out the window into the dusk. He's off somewhere that must hurt him.

"Dad." I draw him to the present. "Do you still believe God asked you to build a castle?"

His head whips in my direction. The last time he heard me say *God*, it was proceeded by *Good* and followed by *Let's eat*.

Constance and I await his answer.

"Yes," he says at last.

For the first time I trust that whatever this is, it's bigger than we are.

24

MAY

I'm dreaming and it's not a great dream.

Dad has sold everything we own to buy a house that has walls like an RV. The hallways are so narrow he can't square his shoulders. He ducks to avoid a light fixture in the kitchen, as the house shrinks, kaleidoscoping in on itself. Dad doesn't seem to notice he's offering me a bedroom no larger than a couch, a loveseat, and a recliner.

We move and I stoop and run to the nearest window. It won't open because of the bars, but if I lay my face against the pane, Leo's giant hairy arm hangs out his purple semi cab. We're at a Wildwood stoplight. Hooked to the back of a semi.

"You can't run away from home if home runs away with you," Dad says.

I wake up and he's leaning over me.

"You want a key. Get dressed." He's not asking but he is whispering, which I take to mean Constance isn't tagging along. After

194

tugging on shorts and shoes in the darkness, I follow him through our backyard into the alley of trash cans and cats. The moon is high overhead, and strings of cottony clouds reflect its light across the sky. I do not ask where we're going when we get in the truck and take Old Ragland Road out of downtown.

Mud sloshes over the edges of my tennis shoes as we tromp toward the castle's rear underground garage. This gray-brown landscape was pictured in the photo Dad had of Aulus working. They were together here. A sacred fear twitches along my spine. Dad still hasn't explained what we're doing as we slide along the embankment forged by the foundation, and it doesn't appear he will. I don't know whether to be frightened or annoyed.

Was this how it happened for Aulus?

Dad taps a lantern, revealing the perfectly ordered garage. He removes a bin labeled Snow from the shelves. He wrestles something from the bottom without removing other contents.

"This was his," he says, lifting a red JanSport backpack. The lantern clicks off as soon as he's sure I've seen.

My lips part with questions. My face must be beet red; a terrible, fearful heat floods me. We lay the bag on the concrete slab and examine every inch by moonlight. There's a Fisker patch on the large front pocket. I sewed that patch on the week before he disappeared.

I am aging a hundred years a second.

"He left it here," Dad says. And then quietly, "The day he disappeared."

"And you didn't tell?" This question is unnecessary. I already know he hasn't told a soul.

Uncle Warren asked me about this very pack last year. Well, not specifically, but the backpack was the first thing I thought of when he asked if anything was missing from the quattro. I described this JanSport bag, Aulus's wallet, a Casio watch we picked out one night at Walmart. Uncle Warren asked me to guess the contents and I'd said paper, pens, library books. Maybe his keys. School stuff. A snack from Quik Mart. Nothing of importance.

I hadn't been too far off.

"Why hide it?"

"You'll see."

Laid out now on the drive are two paper airplanes, two cheap pens from Dad's tax office, four pencils, a Matchbox Ferrari, a school binder, two library books—*Hot Rods Through the Ages* and *Dover Castle*—ChapStick, a prescription for antidepressants in Scott McClaghen's name dated three weeks before Aulus disappeared, a photo of the castle (that he must have stolen from Dad's pile), and two granola bars.

My name is written on the wing of the folded plane. A note. I've thrown away tons of these planes over the years. This one reads,

T,

Gave Homeless Richard a ride to the Dollar Store yesterday and he told me there's a group of college hippies living in the dugouts and tunnels of the old minor league stadium. Said they met on a private Facebook group for orphans. Think we should meet them and see what's up?

A

I understand why Dad didn't turn over the backpack. He didn't want to make Scottie a suspect or send the police looking in the wrong direction.

Dad slicks his ponytail into a tighter bun.

"We should get rid of this," I say.

He nods again.

With no discussion, I suggest we bury the thing.

Dad's got his face in his hands, thinking. We're crossing into unknown territory here. Legal. Illegal. Withholding. Tampering. There's a clear understanding between father and daughter that the witch hunt is not over.

"I'll do it," I say.

He sighs and returns the items to the pack. The zipper and the bullfrogs sing. Dad lifts a shovel from the wall of the garage and I think, *Trust is weird.*

The broken concrete lot of the Moose Lodge crunches under his tires. Aulus and I used to climb the roof of this very building and set off fireworks. The memories are so real I force my eyes to the building's brick.

"Two questions," I say. "Does anyone ever come here? And are you sure this building is off our property?"

"No and yes," he answers.

Three abandoned GMCs sit by the dumpster.

"Always here," he says without me asking.

Behind the lodge, Dad stays in the truck as I choose a particular spot on the wall, just above an old vent, and count twenty paces. I return for the shovel.

With the recent rain, the ground comes away easily, like cake scooped from a pan. As I dig, I remember Aulus's infatuation with the orphan group at the baseball stadium. I recall him confessing at nine or ten that he always carried a trinket of his father's. Abandonment meant many things to Aulus. To us both. I didn't go hauling around my mom's hairbrush or the gaudy orange necklace she left in the bathroom drawer, but I understand the compulsion.

He couldn't quite believe he'd been left behind, and he didn't want to become a person who learned to leave. So he held on to small things.

Dad has to know, as I do, that Aulus didn't run away.

When the hole is accommodating, I lower the pack into the mud basin. I can't see Dad from here, but he's there, watching me. The muscles in my stomach feel like they're actively deteriorating.

I rake dirt over the JanSport. I rub my palms on the thighs of my shorts and leave muddy streaks. This is a funeral of sorts, a messy affair. It's probably my imagination, but the clanking rivets from our tower's flags sound like a dirge echoing across the field.

I lift a final triangular chunk of grassy soil and fit it over the hole. After patting and tamping the area, no one will know. By the end of the week, the soil will undoubtedly stitch itself together like skin, and Dad and I might walk over the spot and ask, "Was it here?"

Back in my bed, I wonder which part of tonight was the dream. The part where I trusted my father or the part where he trusted me?

THE ELIZABETH LETTERS

Dear Elizabeth,

Four of us are in Sleeping Room; three of us are sleeping. I don't know if it's morning, afternoon, or night, but hello again.

We examined two more areas in Dark and the most exciting discoveries were an old washer and dryer, a bag of balloons, a leaf blower, and the missing queen of hearts. No screwdriver. No tools other than the knife. (I didn't ask where Tank hid the blade and I won't.)

We haven't had food in five Sleeps. Water in at least twenty-four hours.

There's not a wall in this place we haven't tried to knock down. The exertion depleted our systems. Zared spent an hour vomiting into our final waste bag. His face is screwed up like he wants to cry, but he has no tears. Dehydration. Rufus, in his very Rufus way, confessed he was dizzy.

"Maybe . . . yo, maybe I'm out too. We need sleeps.

That okay?" Then he asked me to drag the stuffed coyote beside his pool float, which I did. He patted the beast's head and flopped hard onto the float. After that, I fireman-hauled a nearly unconscious Zared next to Rufus.

I sat beside them, mothering them. These boys, they're my life.

The worst effects aren't physical. They're psychological. A colony of ants inside my brain, tunneling around, prepping for winter like they own the place. I don't know which thoughts to trust—Which are mine? Which belong to the ants?

Either way, while my snoring brothers float through dreamland, I've come to the unpopular conclusion that it's pee-drinking time.

In my above life, a man came into Quik Mart every day, roughly ten minutes after my shift started. I thought of him as a Richard or maybe a Tony, though we never exchanged names. Skin clung to his bones like Leo's dry-rotted book covers cleaved to their bindings—like they might slough off in a hard wind. He was early thirties, maybe late twenties, and had teeth that were no longer serving the function of teeth. A pair of navy cargo Dickies were attached to his waist with a bicycle tube.

Without fail, he pointed to the prices on the fountain drink machine. "How much do"—he'd lift a handful of coins from his pocket—"Sixty-three cents buy today?"

"A large," I'd say, even though the large is a dollar nine.

Richard—I suppose I do think of him as Richard—filled the Styrofoam cup, drank, refilled, drank, and refilled without meeting my eyes. I never met his either. I regret that. Now his thirst isn't so unique. It's up close. In tight. Between my teeth. Down my intestines. It curls my toes. If I could walk into Quik Mart I'd drink Mountain Dew until I threw up Mountain Dew and then I'd fill the cup again.

I am Richard.

We are all Richard.

So here we are.

Pee Drinking: Part III

It went down like this. Tank left to search for more tools, and I started the arduous task of waking the younguns.

"It's whiz-guzzling time," I announced. Then I cuffed Rufus's shoulder. "You're the guinea pig."

The Mason jar sat between our circle of knees and toes. The yellow-green urine glowed the color of fireflies. Rufus reached forward, gripped the jar, and flinched.

"I thought it would be warm. It's warm when you fill it up."

Zared laid flat on his back, shoving his dirty

feet at Rufus and picking at the skin where his eyebrows used to be. "Why does that matter?"

"I was gonna tell myself it was hot apple cider and now I can't."

"You're an idiot," Zared said.

I cut in quickly. "Rufe, you can imagine it's whatever you want."

Rufus pressed his lips to the rim. His nostrils twitched. "Eye of the tiger," I said, pounding my fists against the floor like we were in a bar.

"I can't, man." He lowered the jar, swallowing the lump in his throat, hating to disappoint me.

"You can." I don't want to waste the collection with a demonstration.

"No," Zared said. Droplets of blood gleamed from the picking job he'd done to his face. When he saw the blood, he pushed away from us and faced the wall. I could tell by the way his back bent and curled like a tree root he was made of thirst and anger.

Rufus ignored Zared and tightened his knuckles around the jar. Big tears swallowed his brown eyes. "I don't think I can." He wiped his eyes with his elbow, making tiny clear tracks through the dirt on his face. "Aul, would you sing or pray or something?"

There was uncomfortable silence and I wished Tank was back from his tool search. I don't pray anymore and I couldn't think of what to sing.

From his side of the room, Zared said, "If there's a God, he's forgotten us."

I tried to imagine what Tank might say if he

could rescue this conversation. Something like, *Doubt needs a voice.* Big questions are Tank's jam. I know you believe too, Elizabeth, and I hope that believing carried you through the horrors like it now carries Tank. But I'm just not there.

Tank appeared, staring at the Mason jar in the center of our miniature circle. Rufus stretched his fingers toward Tank like there was a gravitational pull but stopped short of touching him. I think there are some who would judge our intimacy, but you know what the absence of love does to a person. These guys, they are the reason I don't give up.

Tank surprised me with his next action. He hefted the Mason jar to his lips and sipped long and drank deep. "Your turn," he said to me, which was his way of saying we're all going to drink whether I play the hero or not. "Don't stand up until you drink that," he commanded. Then, overcome by emotions or committed to his task, he left to do more rummaging in Dark.

I started on the boys first.

"Ru-fus"—I used my fake parent voice— "God wants you to drink that."

He gave me the weak laugh I was hoping for. "That's low, bro," he said, but held his nose with one hand and swallowed.

One weekend back in tenth grade we talked about God and gods, faith, psychics, mysticism, shame, guilt, masturbation, abandonment, literally everything that crossed our brains. Like there was no such thing as a bad idea or a secret. It was weird the week afterward— knowing we'd gone there, knowing we'd let ourselves be seen—and neither of us got brave enough to go there again, but I think he thought it was good. This space, the things we're trying to say, feel like the Monday after that weekend in the tent.

203

"Have another," I urged. He swallowed more confidently. Without any urging, he moved toward Zared like a priest with prepared elements.

"Your turn, Z. It's not so bad."

Zared twisted his face toward the floor.

"You're doing this," Rufus said to Zared, then checked with me. "Right?"

"Right."

"Wrong," Zared said.

Rufus used a burst of energy to straddle Zared and flip him over. He trapped Zared's wrists and bounced on his weak stomach. "Get his head," Rufus urged me while he reached for the jar.

I watched, unsure. Do we make Zared drink against his will? My brain moved like Foucault's pendulum, steady on its course. Slowly, slowly, slowly, time ticked by.

"Stop, Rufe." The boys froze, the pause button pressed midaction. "Don't make him," I said.

Zared parted his lips, probably to thank me, but it was too late. Rufus poured the liquid into Zared's open mouth and the urine smacked the back of his throat. Some went down, some came up. Rufus triumphantly wiped the spit-up as Zared coughed and sputtered.

"Rufe!" I was angrier with him than I'd ever been, which confused him and me.

Our youngest retreated to his float, and I grabbed a T-shirt from the pile against the wall and cleaned Zared's face. He was sobbing. His words were hard to understand, and when I made them out, I was sorry I had.

"This is it." Sob. "This is it." Sob. "This is it."

In our old world, the one where I went to basketball games and Zared smoked weed in the bathroom, we wouldn't be friends. Here, I strapped him against me like he was my luggage to carry. His clammy skin met mine and I said what Mom said to me after Dad left.

"There's more." I said it again. Again. Again. Again. I repeated the phrase so fast the words stopped sounding like words. "There's more. There's more." I couldn't tell the syllables apart.

Zared lifted the jar to my lips. "Prove it," he said and I drank, hardly noticing the acidic taste. I kept my focus on him.

"There's more. There's more," I said, until one thing was crystal clear: the surest "more" left, maybe the only "more" left, was each other.

Elizabeth, maybe you'll never read these letters, maybe God has forgotten us, maybe the whole world has forgotten us, but we had communion today. And that's something.

Peace and Freedom,
Aulus

25

MAY

Our final day in Wildwood High School Tank and I sit, backs against the humming Coke machine in the gym, sharing a bag of Lays potato chips. The janitor's flat broom is tucked into the corner with us so every now and then we catch a whiff of adolescence. Below, on the sunken gym floor, fellow seniors play a vicious game of dodgeball. They invited us to join, but we've said no several times, despite our love for the game.

"You got your speech ready?" I ask.

"Yeah. Sure." He chooses a folded chip, which after years of sharing I know are his favorites.

"You could have declined. Still could," I say, though I'm not sure there has ever been a valedictorian who didn't speak at graduation.

"Maybe you could, but I can't."

I wonder—would I decline? I've pretty much declined this whole year. But for as long as I've known Tank, he's stayed obligated to himself over the expectations of others. And those expectations are high. His mom has wanted him to be valedictorian since kinder-garten; his dad made him add Ivy League schools to his FAFSA. He got accepted to Brown, but he's dead set on a gap year. Or he was. We haven't said much about the future lately.

"Tank, are you still leaving in August?"

He draws his knees closer to his stomach and looks away. That's a yes. A very guilty yes. "What about you?"

"I can't leave. Not now."

"You can. And you know what? You should. Aul would want you to . . . borrow the quattro and drive until it ran out of gas or do your insane Sasquatch mockumentary or open that dog-walking business." He laughs fondly, probably at all the marketing materials I created for a nonexistent company. "Gosh, remember when that dog place was all you talked about?"

"Those things aren't real," I say.

"Those things don't have to be, but something does. You can't just stay in Wildwood and take care of your dad and wait on Aul."

"But Dad trusts me." I explain the night adventure from the castle to the Moose Lodge and what it felt like to bury the backpack.

With no judgment, Tank says, "You believe him?"

"Yeah. I think I do."

"So . . . Warren?"

"So . . . Warren," I echo heavily, though research on that front has turned up nothing. Nick swapped vehicles with his dad and has been following Warren the last two days. Nick's bored out of his head watching my uncle drive from home to work, work to home with nothing in between.

"The man doesn't even eat fast food," Nick complained on the phone last night. "The only extra stop he made was for a Dairy Queen cake."

My graduation cake. For my awkward graduation party.

"You tell your dad about the train?"

I stare at the janitor's broom.

"You sure are giving up a lot for someone you only partially trust."

We return to watching dodgeball and both "Agghhh" when Colin Beasley takes a hard smack to the face that'll black his eye for graduation tomorrow afternoon.

Tank licks salt from his fingers. "If Warren did this, we'll get him." He wads the potato chip bag into a ball. He shoots for the nearest bin, but the bag flattens out and lands faceup on the concrete.

Tank stands, retrieves the trash, says, "Thanks for trusting me at least," and strolls off to meet Gladys in the library.

JUNE 1, 2010

We're on the football field. The smartly dressed crowd above us celebrates favorite graduates.

Tank does an amazing job addressing our class. He speaks eloquently on where we've been, where we're going, and how when we try to change the world, we can expect the world to put up a fight.

"Life isn't sink or swim. It's sink *and* swim," he explains. He nearly loses it at the end when he talks about us, his dearest friends, using the Swedish word *gemenskap*, which means a fellowship, and Tolkien's Lord of the Rings trilogy. He ends with, "Today, we depart on our own fellowship journeys, and it's my hope and prayer that on your way to Mount Doom each of you has company as good as

I've had. Glads. Thee. Aul. I love you. Always. Happy graduation, class of twenty-ten."

"Wow," Constance says when it's quiet enough for me to hear.

"He's really much smarter than he looks," Nick teases, which gives me the moment I need to wipe my eyes.

Constance dabs her own face dry. "Whatever he is, that was brilliant. Boy can preach."

Conferring the diplomas is next. Rows of graduates rise and file toward the dais. Gladys is near the front of the line. She lifts her certificate holder into the air and blows a kiss in my direction. I blow a kiss back that she can't see but I hope she can feel. A chorus of cheers and callouts continues to bat and bob around the stadium as each student passes the podium—until Principal Markum reads my name.

"Thea Donovan Delacroix."

The response is instantaneous.

"Booo!" and "Gemini blah, blah, blah." A gruff-voiced man coughs "Disgrace!" loud enough that Principal Markum asks—demands—the crowd to calm down. She says, "WHS will not tolerate belligerence or hatred," before she reads, "Matthew Carl Demos, cum laude."

Constance and Nick are my armor. Constance wraps her arm around my shoulders and I let myself relax.

"Fear mimics hate sometimes," she tells me.

"And stupidity," Nick adds.

"And stupidity," she agrees.

Shame rises like a zipper on a jacket. I say, "I didn't know he was innocent either."

"Even if he were guilty, you're not him," Nick says.

I don't blame the crowd. It's June 1st. There was a big debate on whether to move graduation, given the circumstances, but in the end Principal Markum argued that the invitations had been mailed and the calendar date secured since before Aulus disappeared. She told me personally that holding graduation on the first felt safer. Families were together. How much harder would it be for the Thief to strike when (a) most boys are with their parents, and (b) everyone is watching?

The town does not agree with her logic.

To them, the FBI returned the prime suspect to Wildwood on the eve of the Gemini anniversary. Over the last few days, Neighborhood Watches have formed and people demanded town curfews. Politicians bought up radio spots and hosted press conferences, each stating their big plans to "Keep Wildwood Safe." The press loved the infighting and gorged on the hype.

There are factions who want Dad jailed through tomorrow. Yesterday brightly colored signs popped up along the highway: Re-Arrest the Gemini Thief. Whoever is behind the movement, they're motivated and funded. Gladys's parents said a rogue Walmart buggy filled with stacks of the lawn placards and a sign reading Free—Take One appeared on the steps of City Hall.

Concerned citizens took one. Truly concerned citizens took multiple. Re-Arrest the Gemini Thief signs edge the lawns of Wildwood neighborhoods.

Including two houses on our street.

"I wish I could see my way to the other side of this," I say. Principal Markum is nearing the middle of the alphabet now. Tank's next.

"Thomas Michael Piper, summa cum laude." Her voice punches each name like there's a proud period after it. The stadium explodes with applause. Despite his friendship with me, Tank's golden in the way all good-looking smart boys are.

"You will. You are," Constance says.

Principal Markum is calling out the Ws now, and above us, the energy of the herd revs. Children wiggle against the bleachers, ready to discard suits and dresses. Mothers shift purses to their laps. Fathers hold recording devices steady, eager to catch the finale of their graduate's high school life.

"Let's go," I say, and by the time Principal Markum's voice booms, "I now present your Wildwood High School class of two thousand and ten," we're in Nick's car, cranking the air conditioning.

"You sure you're okay?" he asks.

He, like Tank, was valedictorian, and by all accounts loved high school. So, while he understands my decision to abstain from the processional, he believes I've been robbed of a milestone.

"I was never walking without Aulus," I say. I barely belong to the class of 2010 anymore. Wildwood High will have to be a watershed, coming-of-age, John Cougar Mellencamp lyric to everyone else.

Nick changes the subject and asks if I spotted Dana among the milieu of celebrants. I hadn't. I ask if he saw Warren.

"Uniform and all," he says.

When we arrive at the castle, Dad has three of the four card tables set up in the great room. He dabs sweat from his forehead with a handkerchief.

"I wanted to be done before you got back, but I got delayed. How was it?"

Three stacked chairs lean against his hip. Constance takes one, unfolds it, and lies. "Very nice."

"No hubbub?"

Nick answers, "Some hubbub. Be glad you didn't attend."

"Warren called. He'll be here soon," Dad says.

"Here now," Warren says from the doorway.

He's dressed in uniform, backpack slung haplessly over one shoulder, carrying a family box of Del's tacos, an ice cream cake, and a cooler.

"I say we eat cake first." And then a little lower and very earnest, he says to Dad, "Welcome home, brother."

I want to throw up.

Dad relieves Warren of the cooler. "Thanks."

Still balancing the cake box, Warren pecks me on the cheek. "Happy graduation, you. Weren't you starting kindergarten like two minutes ago? Hello *again*, Nick." The polite tone has an edge. Does he know Nick's been following him?

Constance lifts her hand in a wave befitting a queen. "Hi, Warren."

Warren calls up a hazy expression and tries out her name as though he can't remember it correctly. "Constance? Wow. Long time no see."

The lie is so impeccably crafted it nearly convinces me.

Tonight's guest list is a thing of strangeness. Discussed and debated multiple times, attendees currently will include: Griff and Ruby, Warren, Tank and Gladys, Leo Wittersham, Pattie McClaghen, Constance, Nick, and to make matters extra interesting, Dana. As soon as they're free from the official graduation ceremony, they'll trickle over with finger foods.

Dad makes a gesture, a lazy looping circle, and grins half-heartedly at Constance. "Crazy the things that come full circle; Constance showing up again like this?" That serves as her reintroduction. We all move forward in mild discomfort, each assigning ourselves random party tasks.

Warren saws a tiny sliver of ice cream cake onto a plate for me

212

and says, "Our secret," because DQ cakes are my favorite and I used to beg him to let me eat dessert first when I was a kid. I accept the cake and he steals a bite off my fork and I almost forget about the train. Almost.

Tank and Gladys arrive in separate vehicles, fifteen minutes apart.

Tank starts toward the food table and gets accosted by Constance, who swamps him with praise for his speech. Gladys waves me toward the bathroom. She drops a satchel of comfy clothes and collapses against the door the moment we're inside.

"Told Mom I was going out with Tank."

"You are technically *out* with Tank." I slide along the wall between her and a toilet that isn't attached to plumbing.

She picks absently at her purple toenail polish. "I'm not sure how long I can stay, but I wanted to see you tonight."

"Tank killed his speech."

"He did, didn't he?" She's beaming. We tilt our heads together, an A-line roof of friendship. I don't have to look to know she's crying too. This could have been—should have been—such a different year. "Speaking of unbelievable, Constance and your dad?"

"Pretty wild, eh?"

Leaning back far enough to see my eyes, she says, "And you and Nick?"

"I don't know, Glads."

"Tank told me he loved me from the stage tonight, but he's planning for August in California. Maybe I need to let him go." She sighs. "Despite that ever-positive speech, Tank's mad at the world. And can you blame him? Me. Aulus. Your dad. Wildwood's response. Ev-e-ry-thing." Gladys draws out the word and pokes through her bag until she finds a soft cotton T-shirt. She continues,

213

"One minute he wants to confront your dad about burying that backpack. The next he's accusing all those stupid sign people of being idiots. The next he's like, *I'm getting out of Wildwood and never coming back*. I asked him to let it go for tonight, but I'm not sure he will."

"He told you about the backpack?"

She shrugs like *Of course he did.*

Should I really be surprised? Last night Tank and I huddled on dry-rotted railroad ties in my backyard and let the dandelions tickle our backs and the mosquitos munch on our blood. He had lingering questions about my confession earlier in the day. Thirty feet away, Dad and Constance sat drinking wine on the back deck.

Tank asked, "Why would he hide that backpack if he's innocent?"

"Why would he involve me if he wasn't? He didn't have to do that."

"I know you don't want to hear this, but nothing keeps that blood on Chris Jenkins's shirt from being Rufus's or Zared's. Or someone else's for that matter. There's a real chance you aren't safe. I can't lose you too. I won't."

In my head, Tank is in more danger than I am. But when I brought that up, he laughed. And when I brought up the "Warren train theory," he laughed again.

"Come on. That's going nowhere. I talked to Nick. Warren's totally on the up-and-up. And what's the likelihood Corey's drawing is your train? Pinning this on someone other than your dad doesn't mean—"

"Except Warren's not a super-convenient second choice for me."

Tank slung a hand toward my dad, who was rolling castle blueprints and re-ponytailing his hair like a nervous boy in love.

"Uh, better than your first option," Tank said.

Which made me ask if I should procure a Re-Arrest the Gemini Thief sign for Tank's yard. He shoved me. I shoved back and asked, "If Dad's guilty, what do you make of the God-factor?"

"Saying God said so doesn't automatically hold currency with me. I want to believe there's some big fix for all this junk. Some purpose. But I'm not banking on that. Do you know how often I beg anyone up there listening to keep Aulus safe or take me instead, and, like"—Tank breathed so deeply my lungs ached—"he could already be dead. But I still ask. Still hope. Is that stupid?"

"I don't know."

"Me either, but I'm gonna keep doing it."

It was nice to hear him say that. Even nicer when Tank hugged me fiercely and shoved his mouth to my ear. "I'm sorry this happened to us," he said, and in the next breath, I said, "Me too," and rested my cheek on his chest.

I wore his hug like a second shirt.

Everything in life should be as easy as fighting with Tank.

Gladys loosens the straps of both sandals and rests her head against the bathroom's brick wall. Head lolled to the side, she licks her lips, the cherry color nearly gone, and says, "He's wound tight as a rod and reel. I've never seen him so likely to punch someone. We probably shouldn't leave him out there with your dad." She sighs as she tugs off her skirt and wiggles into shorts. I do the same and she reapplies mascara before we return to the great room.

Warren, Dad, and Griff are sequestered around a single card table, a set of paperwork before them. "Need you, Thee. Gladys, we can use you too if you don't mind," Dad says when she starts toward the open front door. The two of us slink over and share opposite corners of the same chair.

I check for Nick or Tank and Dad reads my expression. "I sent the boys to town on an ice run," he says. *Great. Tank and Nick, two guys, are alone, in Wildwood, on June 1st.*

"Now, Thea, we've been talking." There's a detached business tone to Dad's voice. "Griff had some ideas and we all agreed they were worth examining." I glance toward the papers. They're legal length with signature tabs mixed throughout. Dad continues, "I'd like to make some provisions for you in case I get rearrested and convicted. Dana warned me that innocence doesn't always mean freedom, and there's a lot of pressure in this case for an arrest. It's not going away. Is it, Warren?"

"The ceremony was . . . rowdy," Warren agrees.

"Are you planning on being rearrested?" I ask, temper growing by the second.

Gladys straightens and our chair rocks.

"This is a precaution," Dad says.

"What is?" I ask.

"Putting the castle in your name."

"And mine," Warren says humbly.

Dad nods his gratefulness at Uncle Warren.

Griff butts in. "I think that part saddles her with unnece—"

"And this is the harder part, Thee." Warren speaks over him. "Don wants me to temporarily assume your guardianship."

I can't form words.

"It's wise, honey."

Warren takes a deep breath. "I can't be your dad, but . . . I'll be there for you in a heartbeat if you'll let me. Ruby and Griff too, but . . ."

"We're not in a place to take you full-time." Griff presses his fingers together into a tight diamond shape and rambles about the growth of the WCC, money tied up in legal stuff, renovations for the guest room. He accidentally infers there's a reason Ruby's stuff is in the guest bathroom and then cuts that off. "Warren's got all that room and the means to finish the castle, which is important to your dad."

Which leaves Warren to ask, "What do you say, Thee?"

Everyone looks at me.

26

JUNE

I understand this transaction.

I'm being moved about like an object, like furniture swapped from one house to the next. But I can't say, *Hey! I'm not a chair. I'm not some stupid knickknack. I don't fit in a kitchen drawer or a closet or that dresser with the broken handle.* I can barely feel, much less articulate the painfulness of their decision. This feels like abandonment. Like losing my mother and Aulus all over again. I read these legal papers signing the castle and me over to Warren, and disappointment covers my heart with a concrete crust.

"I . . ." What's there to do except pick up the pen? This is happening whether I like it or not.

Gladys gathers the bottom of my T-shirt between us and squeezes the fabric into a wrinkled ball. Her fist presses my thigh: an unspoken *Don't do this.* The glow-in-the-dark train circuits my brain.

"Knowing the castle is in good hands gives me a real peace of mind," Dad says. Almost as an afterthought, he adds, "And you too, honey."

I click the end of the pen. Down and up. Down again. I'm so confused. One minute he's willing to sell to the Markums, and the next . . . I'm back in second place. Dad sees me as a fiscal responsibility, a commodity to lend or trade, a tax deduction. Warren doesn't. Griff agrees. Does it really matter which of my father figures is the Thief? I'm fatherless anyway.

I make up my mind. If I am the owner, I have more power. At least this way I can sell the stupid castle. Without making eye contact, I put the pen tip to the first signature line. The task is finished with the flipping of a few pages.

Castle owner. Check.

Parent legally changed. Check.

Scared to death. Check.

I simultaneously wish Nick had seen this transaction and am grateful he didn't.

Dad's relieved. Warren's laughing nervously. Gladys's hand stalls on my thigh. We've drawn a small audience. Constance and Ruby are following this strange deal from the hallway.

Constance says, "Sorry," and I can tell she fought Dad on this decision. Ruby also looks like she lost a war. *You can still stay with us too,* she mouths.

The documents are being folded into a manila envelope when Leo, Ms. McClaghen, and Dana arrive, small gifts and food in tow. The Markums are right behind them, and I didn't even know they were coming. Principal Markum hands me my diploma. "Thought you might want this."

"Thanks," I say.

Warren is the first to greet them. He explains to Dad, "I invited

Kev and Gina. Thought we'd make it a real reunion. Plus, they've been drooling over the castle."

Dad welcomes our new additions with ice cream cake and tacos. Regina Markum makes eye contact with Constance and smiles, but it's not a pretty smile and she's chewing her cross instead of food.

Head reeling, I shift attention to Leo. Aulus's uncle doesn't like Nick or me. Well, that's my assumption after our visit. We were fishing for details about the $500 transfers from Dad and set our hooks in tender skin.

"What do you care?" Leo said, looking up from a beaten copy of *The Stand*. He kicked his front porch recliner into the upright position. "Playing Nancy Drew out of familial guilt?"

Back in the car, Nick had said, "Sometimes grief is anger shaped." And I'd said, "He's just as likely to be guilty." And Nick said, "Thee," the way he always does when I'm stretching toward the ridiculous.

Leo's far more serene tonight. Puffy hands strain the seams of his jeans pockets. He keeps his chin down as his sister, my aunt, offers a half hug of congratulations. Puffy-faced and vacant-eyed, she waves placidly in my direction and says, "I brought some pizzas. I hope you all like pizza. Aulus loved pizza." She's clearly on something. "Your dad's been good to us." Her words are monotone, but I assume this is her *Don's not guilty* vote.

Leo takes her arm and guides them toward the food table. They pass Dana on the way, and he can't help himself. "Shouldn't you be out looking for my boy, secret agent girl?"

He's loud enough to make everyone stop eating midchew. Nick's sister, who since she arrived has been basically trying to mortar herself to the wall, puts her melting ice cream cake on the table and attempts to defuse Leo without creating a bigger scene.

To divert attention from the pair, the room reshuffles into odd social configurations. Ruby and Tank. Gladys and Aulus's mom. Griff and Constance. Dad and Warren, who stand in the kitchen hallway, locked in an unfriendly huddle. Warren carefully uncoils Dad's fingers and leans toward his ear.

"What do you make of that?" Nick asks.

A thoughtless answer slips out. "Maybe they're fighting over who pays my bills when Dad goes back to jail."

"Why would they do that?"

I might as well get this over with. "Because I am now the proud owner of this castle with my new papa bear Warren Burton."

Nick's cup slips from his grasp. Everyone turns as the plastic clatters on the floor. Without missing a beat, Nick says, "Sorry, folks. Gladys. Tank. Can I borrow y'all?" He waves the three of us toward the tower after tossing the cup.

The narrow chamber, which Dad and Constance have finished constructing over the past two days, smells like a lumberyard. When we reach the roof's open air, hot wind stirs construction dust into tiny tornados that cling to the bare skin below my knees.

Nick circles the stairwell opening. "Care to explain to them what you said to me?" He stops beside Tank, a natural ally in this fight.

Gladys, anticipating what this is about, steps in front of me. "Nick, Thea didn't have much of a choice."

"You know about this too?"

"I was a witness," Gladys admits.

Tank's lost. "A witness to what?"

"Oh, let me see." Nick doesn't spare an ounce of his indignation. "To Thea's dad turning over Thea and the castle to Warren. Yep, same Warren I've been cutting class to follow for the last two days because we think he's who? The Gemini Thief."

221

He cusses and Nick never cusses.

"Shhh," I say, hoping no one is on the lower balconies.

"Wait, what?" Tank demands.

Nick laces his arms over his chest. "Exactly."

"Guys, berating me is super unhelpful."

Tank digs at the concrete floor with his dress shoe and shakes a cigarette loose from the package. "Her dad signed over the two most important things in his life to Warren Burton. Call me crazy, but that sounds like he knows something we don't know. Why else would he take legal action? It makes me think long and hard about burying that backpack."

"What backpack?" Nick asks.

"Lower your voices," Gladys hisses.

Tank doesn't. If anything, he's louder. "Thea, Chris died with a key to this castle in his mouth."

"That was planted," I argue.

He presses on, building his case. "Your dad was in Baxter within hours of the body drop on I-40."

"Also planned. For the bell."

"And did the Gemini Thief also plan for your dad to hide Aul's backpack?" I try to interrupt but Tank barrels on.

"What backpack? Someone explain!" Nick says.

Gladys draws the short stick and she's kinder than either of the boys would have been about this alliance with my dad. Nick has a million questions, but he swallows them.

Tank's still going. "You won't convince me your dad hid that backpack for unselfish reasons. Maybe it was to cover his assets or someone else's. Family? Scottie McClaghen, maybe. Like . . . haven't you thought about the prescription bottle? Why'd Aul have it?"

"Because he always carries around something of his dad's. You know that."

"Yeah, except it wasn't old like all the other stuff. The issue date was new. Isn't there a chance his dad showed up, dangled a carrot to be in Aulus's life again, and when Aul said no, he snatched him? Now your dad's helping his cousin continue a mandatory father-son reunion." I start to protest. "Don't, Thea. I'm getting the backpack and handing it over to Dana." He starts toward the staircase.

That is such a bad idea.

"Yes," says Nick. "I agree."

"You're leaving right now?" Gladys is the one raising her voice this time. "During our graduation party?"

"Hardly a party," Tank works the cigarette between his fingers. "It's the right thing to do."

I say, "You're digging that thing up at Moose Lodge? In your dress clothes? In the dark? Great idea."

Tank points toward the moon. "You bet I am."

"What will that prove?"

Tank plows toward the doorway. He lifts his arms up in absolute surrender. "I guess we'll leave that up to Dana."

"Leave what up to me?" Dana asks from the shadows of the top step.

223

THE ELIZABETH LETTERS

Dear Elizabeth,

    Big moment down here. We reached a conclusion about the identity of the Gemini Thief.

    Rather than stretch out on the squeaky pool floats, Tank and I rendezvoused in the last space we lit while the boys rested. Other than the washer and dryer, it was another room full of trash bags. Tank patted the sacks and belly flopped onto the waist-high pile. We lay side by side, dust crawling up our noses until Tank started a sentence, paused, stopped.

    "What?"

    "I feel crazy," he said. "Do you feel crazy?"

    My answer released from my chest in a whoosh of rancid breath. *Am I sane? Do sane people wonder if their best friend is real? Do sane people find reasons to push, shove, make any physical contact to ensure they're not seeing a ghost? Do sane people go over and over the group conversations and check to see if Rufus and Zared ever interact with Tank?*

"Yeah," I said, the air between us stale with fear.

I was tempted to shove him. I didn't, because if he's not here with me, I'd wake Zared and we'd climb in the freezer, let the seal close above our heads, and drown in the heat of our own breath. Besides, if it were possible to wish people here, this room would be full.

I said, "I'll tell you what's crazy. We need Welder. How wacked is that, eh?"

Tank lifted a tank top that would fit a baby doll above his head, examining yellowed spots and mouse holes before flinging it against the wall. "Wacked. Totally wacked." He tugged another shirt from the pile beneath him. Found a stain in the armpit. Then sweatpants bearing the Rock Hollow Elementary logo, stained green and torn at the knees. He threw them. "Why do people donate damaged stuff?"

We were quiet and the quiet was so complete I nearly forgot what we'd said. But Tank hadn't. He licked his lips and the question came for him, from him, the way it had for all of us.

"Why are we down here?" Tank ripped a large sheet of plastic into confetti shreds. Dry-rotted black bits fluttered to the floor.

"Kicks. Giggles," I said. "In Welder's distorted view, we're loved."

"We're barely even watched."

There were cameras in the first bunker, but not here. Maybe we're some weird expensive experiment. "This

I'll bet you're well acquainted with why. When I think if it were Gladys or Thea or my mom, even one of my uncles, instead of me, whew, Elizabeth, I just can't. I'm sorry we share this experience.

person, whoever he or she is, pays to keep us alive. That's gotta say something about their psychology."

"Definitely. But, Aul, what's in this other than responsibility? Why risk so much for so little? Welder doesn't even spend time with you." He corrects himself. "Us. Doesn't spend time with us."

"You want me to explain the motives of a psychopath?"

"Could Welder be more than one person? I mean . . . this takes a lot of setup. And we were all taken in various ways. Drugs. Shovels. You said Rufus only remembers a grocery store alleyway and Zared's last memory was ice cream."

"We were also apologized to. Who shows that sort of remorse?"

On my first day in the bunker, I woke with the following note safety pinned to my shirt.

I'd considered co-kidnappers before and examined the shadowy body across the food slit for variance but never noted one. "Maybe," I said, because anything was possible. "Whoever he is . . . or was, he's methodical and smart."

Except for the steady working of our fingers ripping bags, we sat with that knowledge until I said, "You know what gets me? Other than being trapped, there's been no action. Zero. Sometimes I even think Welder wants to come through the food slit and hug us. He doesn't, thank God, but his body language is full of something that's less criminal and more paternal. But then Chris . . . That changed what I thought I knew. Welder took you for me because I was losing it."

"No way."

"I think so. I think it's my fault you're here. It's eating me alive. I need him to come back," I said.

Tank poked a hole through the tissue-thin T-shirt he was wringing. He tugged until the fabric ripped and he held pieces in both hands. He faced me, T-shirt tucked to his nose and mouth. "Welder's not coming to let us out, Aul."

"Hey, if you're going to be in charge of hope, you can't say stuff like that."

"I remembered something earlier, and it's not good," Tank said carefully. I did not have to say *Tell me*. "Don called the night I was taken."

Over the last month Tank had shared many details of the outside world. The rise of Justin Bieber. Wildwood adding a third school color. Leo driving the

quattro in the Fourth of July parade. He had even
described facts about Welder that he and Thea
listed in the basement of the WCC. He'd never told me
his taken story; he'd never remembered more than his
parked truck and bugs nipping his ankles.

"We were at the castle, celebrating graduation."
His breaths came in big gulps.

"Hey, calm down. Who is we?" I asked.

"Gladys, Thea, Don and Constance, Nick and Dana,
Griff and Ruby, the Markums, Warren, your mom and
uncle."

I didn't risk an interruption to ask who
Constance was.

"We were celebrating Don's homecoming and our
graduation." Details reeled out like fishing line on a
windy day. "Picketers. People yelling when Principal
Markum called Thea's name. Television coverage.
Hatred. Fear. Accusations. June 1st, you know?
Everybody in town was nutso even though most people
didn't believe someone else would be taken. I mean,
why would we?"

Tank had explained the kidnapping rhythm before.
Three to four boys taken for a year. Released. Wait
a year. Sometimes two. Ten years' worth of a pattern
and investigation.

"Okay," I said, hoping the memories would solidify.

"I told you Don was arrested and the DNA on
Chris"—he touched my arm as he said Chris's name—
"didn't match. Everything else in the case against
your uncle was circumstantial. His freedom was a win

for Thea, and we all wanted that. You're not going to recognize her when you see her."

"You must have been fairly convinced of Don's innocence. You and Nick wouldn't have let Thea go home with him if you were worried."

"Nick and I told Thee to stay with Griff and Ruby through the 30th and she wasn't having it. She was convinced Warren might be involved. She even helped her dad hide your backpack, but I"—he squinted and pressed his thumbs into his temples—"can't remember why. I don't think . . . I don't think I was on the Warren train either."

Tank heaved an entire bag of clothes off the mound and the bag exploded. "And now, after being here, that blood could have come on the shirt Chris was wearing. DNA doesn't exonerate him."

I know whose blood it was. I nodded. "You remember anything else about being taken?"

Tank covered his forehead with his arm. "Pieces."

Whatever he had realized or was processing, hurt him.

"Welder is someone we know. Isn't he?" I asked. Whenever Welder spoke to us, a pattern emerged that the voice machine couldn't hide. Early on, this detail felt circumstantial and dismissible. Rufus and Zared weren't local. Chris wasn't local. Welder couldn't be local. But when I concentrated on his go-to gestures— the way he sat, spoke, turned his chin when we begged for home—the specificity was familiar.

My dad and Welder sat in the same particular

way—legs crossed tightly at the knees, hips cocked sideways—but that didn't mean Welder was my dad. Another thing I noticed was that Don said "I'm zapped" when he was tired, and Welder once used zapped in a similar fashion.

"Aul, I'm about 98 percent sure Welder is Don."

"I . . ."

I let myself examine my uncle. If Don was responsible, these crimes would be nonviolent and obsessive. But there was no motive. Plus, he was so wrapped up in his stinking castle that he ignored his daughter. Why risk criminal repercussions to be a pseudo-parent to three or four boys? Unless he was building the castle for us. Unless the voice he claimed to have received castle instructions from was a marker of his diminished mental health.

"Hear me out," Tank said. "We found those balloons in Dark earlier and something jarred loose. I was in my truck, heading toward Wildwood, and spotted the Petersons' hot-air balloon flying overhead." He fell deep into the memory. "I'd talked to Don at the castle, but he called and asked me to pull off and turn around. He needed me to ring the tower bell and ring it right then. Another voice in his head, some gut-instinct instruction. You should have heard him, Aul. He was psycho lit over it. I told him to call Thea because she was in the tower right then, and he said, 'No, trust me. You're the one I need. I think your life depends on it.' He . . . I should have . . . Why would I pull off the highway on June 1st? I'm an idiot."

I caught his arm so he would stop driving his fist into his thigh and handed him more plastic to rip.

He said, "I can't remember anything after agreeing to come back to the castle. Except . . ." Tank smoothed his hair down and then up, like he was coaxing the memory by petting his brain into a docile animal.

"And he hit you with a shovel?" I guessed.

Head buried between his knees, Tank said, "No, there was, I . . . I . . . There was a towel or a rag. Someone covered my mouth from behind. I smelled grass. The hands were small, strong. I saw the wrists over my mouth."

Tank vibrated so violently he slid to the floor. I slid too. His eyes bored through my skin like a diamond blade. Without asking, he guided my hands over his mouth, reenacting the way Welder attacked him. My own wrist stung from the pressure he applied.

"This tiny bit of skin was uncovered, and a ponytail holder was *right there.*" With his left hand, he touched the narrow place between my wrist bone and hand.

The place where my uncle has worn a ponytail holder for years.

Elizabeth, I struggled to accept Tank's information even though he would not lie to me. Do you know how sometimes a truth will stare you down, wink at you, and you still don't know if it's hitting on you? Likewise, a lie might date you for months and you'd have no idea you'd been deceived.

To me, my uncle was always a man who built castles, not someone who trapped people beneath them.

Peace and Freedom,

Aulus

27

Tank barrels past Nick's sister and we track his downward footfalls, each step echoing through the metal chamber until the only sounds left are the wind snapping the flag and the bullfrogs claiming their territories. If we'd been talking, we might not have heard Dad call for Tank.

I walk to the tower ledge and lean over. They aren't in sight and shortly after, Tank's truck starts, Arcade Fire disturbs the air and he's taillights on the driveway.

"What's being left up to me?" Dana asks.

I have no idea how much or what to explain.

Dana targets her brother. "Nick?"

Nick freezes. If the backpack is as important as Tank believes, Dana will know sooner or later. I jump in with a version of the truth that might tide us over until Tank returns.

"It may be nothing," I begin. "Tank remembers where Aulus's backpack is. He's hoping to find something we've all missed."

Dana isn't having this explanation. "Uh-uh. If you thought you had a clue, you'd have had it in my hands last year. I've seen all your theories and you've searched for Aulus as hard as anyone. You're covering up evidence, and if you are, it's to protect someone. Now spill."

No one spills.

"They're protecting you?" she guesses, since Nick and Gladys haven't taken their eyes off me. Our expressions don't shift. She says, "No. That's not right. Your dad."

"No," I lie.

She doesn't *tsk*, but her mouth forms the shape; her chin cocks sideways. "You want me to believe Tank *suddenly* remembered an item that has been missing for the last year?" After tapping her watch for dramatic effect, she adds, "Someone talk or I'll . . . I'll arrest you all for hindering an investigation."

"Oh, whatever." Nick's voice is sharp and disbelieving.

His sister doesn't carry on with the threat. "For goodness' sake, your dad invited me." She reaches for me and I step back. "I'm on your side."

Gladys's face says she accepts this argument.

I put Dana through the gauntlet. "Sides flip."

Nick says, "Friends close. Enemies closer," like this might explain his sister's strategy.

She pops him on the shoulder. "Please. When have I ever been your enemy?"

He pops back. "I meant that philosophically."

Dana locks me in a bull glare. "You won't tell me about the backpack, fine. How about you explain why your dad signed you and the castle over to Warren?"

I don't bother masking my anger. "You told him he's not in the clear."

Dana wipes a hand straight down her forehead, nose, and mouth and shakes off the information, literally, like a dog tosses water after a swim. She makes a slow rewind motion with her index finger and says, "Okay, that's crazy, but before you start hating on me for helping, go back to the missing-suddenly-found backpack."

"When Tank brings Aulus's bag back, it's all yours." *If he finds it.* I gave him a decent description of the burial the other day, but it's still a fishing expedition. Dana parks herself against the low concrete turret Constance laid yesterday. When she's seated, she smacks the concrete on either side of her thighs. When we don't move, she repeats herself, smacking even harder. We bend obediently and join her. Down below, car engines start and stir the gravel patches. Dana says, "By the way, party's over. Your dad sent me up to tell you."

That's weird. I think it; Gladys says it.

"He called an audible. Said, 'Party's over!' because he had somewhere he needed to be." Dana blows air out her mouth slowly. "Plus, you four scampered off, and other than the castle, you're the main event." She smirks, but not with happiness. Her eyes roll toward the stars and she recounts a conversation she overheard between Dad and Warren. 'Your dad said, 'I can't believe you,' and Warren said, 'Nobody's perfect.' And then your dad said, 'You're a cop,' with a fair amount of indignation. And . . ." She shifts, searching the memory for precise words. "Warren asked if Don planned to tell Griff and Ruby, and Don rather aggressively said, 'Absolutely.'"

I try placing facts into the conversational holes. *Can't believe what?* Does Dad know or suspect Warren's the Gemini Thief? Is that why he was reminding Warren he's a cop? But, no, why would Dad tell Ruby and Griff that? There's a chance Warren told Dad he and Constance dated after they divorced. That, right after Dad signed over his castle and child to Warren, might have rattled his trust.

Nick asks, "How mad was Warren?"

"On a scale of one to ape, he rates a solid King Kong. Whatever Don's telling Griff and Ruby, Warren's not pleased."

"You didn't stop them?" Nick asks.

"For what? Raising their voices in an empty room? Don caught me eavesdropping and asked if I'd come find you all and I said yes. Oh, and also"—she gives me an apologetic eye roll—"Thea, he wants you to lock the gate when you leave tonight."

I feel like she rubbed jalapeños into all my open wounds.

"Trust me," Dana says. "You aren't the only one who felt like Don made an abrupt departure. Constance had a conniption, and that woman's barely capable of raising her voice, so it was something to witness." Dana swivels and peers over the wall. "They're all gone now. Down to just us chickens."

"Don say where he was going?" Nick asks.

"Did Tank?" Maybe Dana is fishing for details about the locale of the backpack, but it feels more like she's wondering how long we can expect to wait for his return.

"Shouldn't be long," I say.

We settle in to wait, discussing Tank's graduation speech, Nick's summer class, how we hope Pattie McClaghen's okay.

The clock creeps toward 11:00. With every passing minute, the night plays quiet mouse with us. No engine sounds. No closing doors. No footsteps in the stairwell. Even the bugs have gone off to their beds.

Gladys, who isn't wearing a watch, turns Nick's wrist toward her at 11:40, again at 11:45, midnight, and finally, 12:30. She's twisting each of her knuckles.

"Are you scared?" she whispers.

I blink my yes. Nick sits between his sister and me and catches

Gladys's question. Using minimal movement, he draws letters on my thigh. H-E-S-H-O-U-L-D-B-E. He starts the H of HERE and I say aloud, "I know." Because at this point, I'll trade Dana having more information for a normal pulse rate.

"Something feels off. I want to check on Tank," I say.

"The backpack could be *misplaced*," Gladys suggests.

"No." That's not how this feels. I don't have to tell anyone twice. Minutes later, we're bumping along the castle's driveway in Dana's Nissan.

"Which direction?" she asks at the gate.

"Right," we say together.

Dana flips the headlights to bright and asks whether she should speed up. I say, "No," as she spots Tank's truck parked deep in a farm equipment pull-off a hundred yards from the castle.

Panic snakes through my chest. *He could have pulled off and walked. The lodge isn't far. Half a mile?* This is the road Aulus disappeared from. This is the way he disappeared. Nick must also be wrestling with similarities.

"Tank might be on foot, Glads."

She shakes her head. We all know he's not on foot.

Dana cuts the engine and stops Gladys from getting out of the SUV. "Stay here."

"No," we protest.

"Okay, together. But you're behind me. Got it?" This is an order. She doesn't release Gladys's arm or unlock the doors until we agree verbally. Outside the Nissan, we're forced to wait for Dana, who shuffles through a bag in the back and produces a Maglite and draws her gun. The wide beam sweeps the bed of the truck. There's no damage to the frame as far as I can tell.

Gladys's muscles and mind must be in the same war as mine:

run toward Tank's truck, run away from the world. Insects fly through the flashlight beam, distracting me so I don't see whatever forces Dana to hold out her arm like a mom in a minivan. "What is . . . Something's written on the truck."

She inches forward, and though we are told to stay put, we follow. Nick is slightly ahead of Gladys and me. I squeeze his arm and pull him back.

Dana's beam catches two messy black spray-painted words: *Last One*

My lips part—my body wants to scream—no sound comes out.

The Thief left a final calling card.

Nick says, "That's new," but Dana shakes her head and offers information we've never been privy to before and shouldn't be now.

"William Theodore. Initial victim. Taken in 2001. There was spray paint then too. 'First One.' The Thief's declaring he's done. This is a victory lap."

To me, Dana has two faces. The first, visible only for seconds, is pure horror etched across every feature; the second is a business mask, downloaded from the academy.

"Don't touch anything," she says, and there's control and authority in her voice.

Gladys screams Tank's name.

You can't make that particular noise without love.

The silence that follows is its own horrific choir.

28

JUNE

Gladys is a wad of arms and legs and sobs. Nick and I absorb her, but she won't turn loose of her knees.

"I know," I say stupidly, patting the top of her head. "I know. I know. I'm sorry."

I wish there were a set of words for when there are no words.

"We'll get him back. I swear, Gladys. We'll get him back," Nick says.

She heard the same empty promises when Aulus disappeared. *How could this happen?* As soon as I form the question, I hate the answer. Aulus is gone because the world is awful, but Tank . . . Tank's on me. I'm the one who buried a backpack at the Moose Lodge.

Dana presses buttons on her cell. We listen as she reports the scene of a potential kidnapping. "Thomas Piper. No, Thomas. Tango. Hotel. Oscar. Mike. Alfa. Sierra. The kids call him Tank."

None of this makes sense.

Could my Warren have done this tonight? And if he did, why? Or rather, why now? Does Tank pose some threat, or is this crime *wrong place, wrong time*? Did someone else know about the backpack? There's no way Tank's part of some master plan. This kidnapping might have the *Last One* calling card, but it's unlike the others, from time of day to location to Tank's age and race.

Nick must be cycling through similar thoughts. Squinting at the truck, he mutters, "The Thief was right here. Right here."

Dana is on the same task, calling everyone who arrives with a badge to canvass the area.

I am tempted to dive deeper into my questions, but Gladys holds out her hand and the only thing I want to do is hold her and make my brain stop spinning. I bury my nose in my best friend's hair, breathe the strawberry shampoo she has used for years, and rewind all my mental clocks to safer times.

Us. "Graduating" from eighth grade. Us. When our greatest thrill was a first kiss. Or even better, being dropped off at Walmart with ten dollars from our fathers' wallets. Us. Buying makeup we didn't know how to apply. Us. Perusing the feminine hygiene aisle and reading the boxes, rather than shoving one in the cart when our parents weren't looking. Gladys. Choosing that first bottle of Kurl Karma, flipping the lid, passing the squatty container to me with total satisfaction, and saying, "Ahhhh. I want to smell like this forever."

She smells like Kurl Karma now, but the world's sourness overpowers the strawberries.

Aulus. Tank.

"I'm still here and I love you," I say, and Gladys's chin bobs against my chest. I squeeze Nick's hand until my fingers ache. He must be uncomfortable, but he doesn't complain. Does *Last One* mean he's safe tonight? Can boys in Tennessee and Kentucky sleep deeper now that Tank's their sacrificial lamb?

I ask Dana, "You think he'll still release the boys on the 30th?" hoping to heaven her answer will be good news.

A single siren wails in the distance. Help appears to be arriving from the left instead of from town. More sirens roar from other directions. They're coming. Yellow caution tape. Mobile light stands. Questions. They're all coming.

Dana closes the passenger door of her SUV and stretches blue latex gloves over her tiny hands. "No idea." She approaches the truck, each foot placed with consideration, leaving the scene undisturbed. With a gloved hand, she lifts the door handle. "Locked." Her eyes land on the words *Last One* again.

"Dana," I say. "You said Dad left the party before Tank."

"I said he canceled the party. I have no idea when he left."

"We heard him talking to Tank," Nick says.

Dana puts on her logical voice. "Thea, I'm not saying Don did this, I'm saying, look around. We're on your property. That's not a coincidence." She looks at me pointedly. "I'll have to bring him back in for questioning."

"What if Warren Burton is the Gemini Thief?" I ask before I can stop myself. I want to tell her Nick and I watched the video in her apartment, but I snatch the flashlight and stall. Shining light on the spray paint, I say, "Dad doesn't make his *t*s like that—"

"So a decorated Wildwood police officer, the one who became your guardian mere hours ago, took Tank?" Dana's skepticism drips like honey. She looks at me like I'm some crazy, desperate kid and maybe I am, but I need her to hear me out.

"Dana, Warren's in the welding photo too, and"—I almost make physical contact with the lettering as I examine the paint closer—"see the way the top line of this *t* arcs upward? Warren does that with the *t* in *Burton*. Dad doesn't arc his *t*s."

Dana won't let me argue. "O-kay. There will be a handwriting analysis, but the arc of a *t* is hardly a reason to accuse Warren—"

Bright blue lights flicker against branches and kudzu as a wave of squad cars dives onto the grassy banks, surrounding us.

I backtrack in my uncertainty. "I'm not accusing him. I'm asking the question. Your profile said—"

There's no time to discuss the profile. Warren is the first officer on the scene.

"Heard the call come over the radio. Started the Amber Alert," he yells to Dana. His mouth drops open, first with surprise, then in judgment when he realizes she brought us along. "You kids—" He bends and grips his knees, unable to finish. My impressions are skewed and he's a brilliant liar, but that response doesn't feel very cop-like to me. He looks as scared as we feel. And shocked.

"Where's Dad?" I ask.

"I . . ." He looks toward the highway. "He said he needed to drive around and clear his head."

"Call him." Dana uses her FBI voice. "Tell him to get back here ASAP. And, Warren, we need a timeline of when everyone left the castle."

"You're assuming—"

"That someone at the party or watching the party did this. Doesn't that feel true to you?" Dana asks, and Gladys grinds her fingers into her eyelids. Maybe this isn't happening and when we all wake up, it'll be 2009.

Warren inches in the direction of the castle. "It's possible," he says.

"Probable," Dana corrects. "This is Don's property. Tank left minutes before the party broke up. Everyone passed right by here."

242

"Maybe. Maybe not. I went left out of the gate. There's more than one cut-through road," Warren says.

To his credit, he doesn't sound or look defensive. More perplexed. More like he's processing the list of people who attended the party. Even though there's no good rationale, it feels more than reasonable to conclude someone at the party or connected to the party, or maybe even watching the party, took Tank.

Leo Wittersham is an unlikely suspect on many, many levels. There's no way he could sneak up on Tank in his loud purple Freightliner. We'd have heard him braking.

Kevin Markum has a welding helmet and is large enough to overpower Tank. Earlier in the evening, Regina and Tank tapped plastic cups and she said, "Congratulations on your commencement address," and he said, "I have a question for you," and they disappeared around the corner. A school principal? A shop teacher? Is that who commits a crime like this?

Ruby and Griff arrived and departed separately. When I ask myself if there's any chance the Holtzes took Tank, the case is crude. 1) Griff and Ruby were out of town the day Aulus disappeared. 2) Ruby has the required construction skills. 3) She used to travel Tennessee for work. 4) They've been wound tight as a rod and reel lately. 5) They're both physically strong enough to move bodies.

That said, they could take Tank from the WCC when there would be no evidence. Also, they're paying Dad's lawyer.

Warren. The quickest way to his place is Old Sycamore Lane. Could he have driven home and back to swap vehicles and had time to kidnap Tank? Not without premeditation and planning, but he's good at planning, owns a welding helmet, arcs his *t*s, and *chugga, chugga, chug*.

That leaves Constance, who is not a suspect in the slightest. I hope wherever Dad is, she's with him. A pastor's alibi has to rank way up there in the justice system. I check with Warren. "Constance left with Dad?"

Warren shakes his head. "She walked."

Dana responds the same as me. Indignantly. "Walked?" And then she says, "It's miles to town. And after midnight."

Warren slings a hand toward the farm equipment lane. "It's not far if you cut through the field."

"You've got to be kidding me," Nick says.

Warren's shrugging. "When I left," he says, "she was crossing the blacktop."

"Call Don," Dana says again. This time Warren makes a show of punching the buttons and lifting the phone to his ear, like he's mocking her request. Dana listens intently. "Do you hear that?" There's so much movement on the scene she yells for everyone to stop. "There it is."

Somewhere nearby a *brrrng* disturbs the country air.

I turn, expecting Dad. The only people around are other officers and Gladys, who lifts the blinking phone into the night air.

"This was in your car," she says to Warren.

29

Nick and Gladys are the sky above me. Someone's repeating my name. I can't ask what happened, my tongue's a slug. Nick understands and explains, "You passed out. Dana caught you."

I'm aware now of Dana's clenched stomach and thigh muscles pillowing my head. She reclaims her right hand and sweeps hair off my forehead. "Easy, you. Deep breath," she urges, and I close my eyes. The world swims.

"Warren?" I ask the back of my eyelids. "Warren?"

"Yeah, hon."

"Where's my dad?"

"I don't know, but I'll find out," he says. He turns to Nick and gives him a stern nod, a command. "Get her out of here and to bed. Call me first if she needs anything."

Why is no one asking about Dad's phone? I've no sooner thought this than Dana says, "Warren, the phone?"

"Oh," he says, as though the phone is all but forgotten. "Don

245

and I were together ten minutes before your call came through on the radio."

I test my ability to sit and Dana steadies me. "Where?" she asks Warren, and then, "Are you saying you're his alibi?"

"Or he's yours?" Nick says.

"You've got to be kidding. We were nowhere. That way." Warren thumbs toward the road, in the direction of his house. "We were parked in the weeds, having it out over Constance and—" His chin lowers in my direction. "I have no idea if I'm an alibi or not. I'm not even sure when you're suggesting the kidnapping occurred. It's very early in the case, Agent Jones."

The tension crackles.

Rather than say she's pissed, Dana's judgment is a set jaw, a searing glare. They don't even notice when I stand and test my shaking knees. When their staring match folds in Dana's favor, she checks her watch.

"I'm suggesting Tank disappeared from this truck, currently vandalized with the words *Last One*, sometime between 10:50 p.m. and 12:30 a.m. on the evening of June 1st or the morning of June 2nd, respectfully. Now, please suggest when you were with Don and how long this supposed argument over Constance lasted."

Warren leans against the front bumper of Dana's vehicle. "I'm not sure." He kneads his forehead like its finicky dough. "I went home, swapped the truck for my squad car, and intended to head into the station and pick up an extra shift. Totally wired. June 1st and all. You know how that is," he says to Dana, the friendliness back. "I'd already left for the station when Don called. He said he was almost to my house and wanted to settle things after our disagreement at the castle." *You know the disagreement*, his short pause

246

says to Dana. "I told him I was on the road, but I'd pull over. He got there. We made zero headway. The call came over the radio while he was in the front seat. He got out and ran."

"Ran?" Dana asks.

"To his car." Warren's not looking at anyone as he says this. His voice is thick.

"And then?" Dana prompts.

"He drove off."

"You didn't follow?"

Warren's chest puffs; he whittles Dana's question with an *Are you serious?* expression. "I came straight here."

Dana presses, and she's more cage fighter than investigator in her delivery.

"So what I'm hearing is neither of you have an alibi for the time in question? And that Don Delacroix, lead suspect in the Gemini Thief case, and your best friend, is on the lam?"

Warren, all six foot two of him, straightens. The car lifts with the absence of his weight. He arrives in Dana's space without invitation. Before she has time to realize what's happening, he uses an index finger under her chin to lift her face toward his. They're locked like two bucks in a field.

"Hear whatever you want, Dana, but neither of us would ever, and I mean *ever*, hurt Tank."

Dana steels her voice. "Then why run?"

Warren lifts his left hand, shows off a row of swollen knuckles. "Probably because I broke his nose and he didn't want you to decide he got his face battered by Tank. He's not stupid. He knew he had to be one of the last people to see Tank before the disappearance; he'd asked him to ring the tower bell and he couldn't explain why."

Dana's eyes drift to Warren's fist. Maybe she's thinking what

I'm thinking: *Is that really how you hurt your hand?* The only way to know is to ask Dad, but to do so, I need to find him.

"Can we leave?" I ask Nick.

He tosses a set of keys at his sister. "Swap me vehicles, Dane. I'll take the girls home."

Dana sends her keys soaring. Nick folds Gladys under one wing, me under the other. "I'll check on you," Dana says. Then she clasps her hands in a prayer motion, like a question, and says, "Long night ahead. I have to call the Pipers. The town's going to freak. We'll have to canvass this whole area, although he's likely long gone." Nick nods.

Drudging back through the clotted grass and sandy roadside to the SUV, we leave the blue flashing lights and Tank's crime scene.

"Home?" Nick asks, uncertain.

"Yeah. Drop Gladys and then me."

"I wish I could stay with y'all," Gladys says.

We both know she can't. Her parents are losing it. "I'll come over first thing in the morning," I say.

Gladys nods and we tumble mutely into our grief and dread. Every light in the Baxter house blazes beacon bright when Nick eases into the driveway. He says, "City on a hill," and kisses Gladys on the cheek.

I get out, wrap my best friend in a wordless hug that lasts decades and decades and would have lasted millenniums if Mrs. Baxter hadn't come all the way down the walk and used Gladys's first, middle, and last names.

"Tomorrow," we say at the same time, and then let go.

Back in the car, I say, "We need to find my dad."

"You need sleep," Nick argues.

"We need to find my dad."

Not home. Not the tax office. Not the WCC. Not Griff and Ruby's. Or the Markums'. Though, if he were running, hiding, he wouldn't go somewhere attached to him. He'd go to Scottie's, but I have no idea how to locate my uncle.

"Any other ideas?" Nick yawns.

It's well after two a.m.

"Maybe."

North of town, there's an old KOA campground with a spot along the creek Dad and I named Low Tide Hideaway. We—me, Dad, Scottie, and Aulus—camped there once. That feels like a million years ago. It's the only place coming to mind.

"If he's not there, we're going back to your house," Nick says.

I rest my temple against the window, letting my eyes close. I don't have more in me either.

The campground has seen better days. Abandoned, burned-out RVs, remnants of a miniature golf course, waist-high grass, and an empty blue concrete pool that skaters have had their way with. A heavy chain stretches between two leaning posts at the entrance. Nick drives around, the way many cars have before us. We enter the circles and circles of spotty gravel camping spots, and three baby skunks cross in front of us.

"All the way in the back," I say.

Nick dims the headlights and for once his automatic windows work. Whiffs of pot and Swisher Sweets cigars tint the air. Twitching, we turn nervously toward each other, aware there's probably an illegal pharmacy running a steady business out here somewhere. Nick drives deeper into the trees, using moonlight to stay on the trail.

249

There are parked cars in various turnoffs. Glowing red circles. Gray smoke. Flickers of movement as couples and addicts make sure we're not cops.

"There," I say when we reach the final circle.

Dad's Ram is hidden by brush and trees. "You're sure you trust him?" Nick asks.

I did. I do. I want to. I say, "At this point, does it matter if I don't?"

Long ago, fairy tales taught me that dark people and places in this world exist; every story I consumed said, *Expect dragons and trolls; thieves and cheats exist; witches and dark magic are out there; watch out, little one, they'll bring darkness to your doorstep and whatever you do, don't answer the door when evil knocks.*

None of those stories told me there'd come a day when I'd count the lock on my door as a cruel irony. Because here's the real truth: you can't keep darkness out if he has a key.

Why don't parents and storytellers understand that kids are smart and they can handle the truth? It might be a different world if we put children on our laps and whisper, "Honey, sometimes you can't tell a monster's a monster until it's too late, and sometimes you will love a monster, and sometimes you'll be related to a monster, and if that happens to you, you're not stupid; you're human, and love is still a good thing."

Nick takes my index finger and thumb before threading the rest of his fingers through mine. I think he's the one shaking until he sandwiches my hands between both of his and tucks them to his heart. My body is rattling.

"We can walk away."

"I owe Tank more than that."

"Thee, we can walk away."

250

"You can. I can't. He's my dad no matter what he's done."

We approach the Ram. "Dad," I call out. "It's me and Nick."

The truck's empty, so Nick and I follow the trail, the creek whistling from the gully below. "Dad," I say again.

"Thee?" he says, sadder than I've ever heard my name.

He's a hunched shadow, and as we close in, the details sharpen into a gloomy image. Dad's arms trap his knees and catch his buried face. His hair's loose and wild, the ponytail holder low on his neck. The wilderness has reclaimed the little clearing that once held a fire ring and tiki torches. Only the creek front is perfectly preserved, percolating and meandering, edging right up to the toes of Dad's boots.

"I'm so sorry, honey," he whispers.

He's crying and a bloody mess from Warren's punch.

"About taking off? Or Tank?"

"Both." Dad makes space on the log. He notices I sit closer to Nick, but I pray he's too tired and sad to feel the full betrayal of these inches. He talks. We listen. The fight Dana overheard *was* Warren confessing his relationship with Constance. The fight Warren referenced was the follow-up event to the same fight. Warren's story was pitch-perfect, right down to the timeline.

"So Uncle Warren punched you because you were angry about the Constance stuff?"

"No." Dad's head droops again. "Warren punched me because I asked if he took Aulus." He sounds how I've felt for months. "It has to be someone close to me. For Warren to have lied to me all this time . . ."

"I know," I say.

I think of Canada and nine years of lies.

He slides his eyes sideways in my direction. "Warren's relationship with Constance would have hurt me back then. Funny thing, I

251

wasn't mad about them dating. I'd just signed my castle and daughter over to him and there were a million times he could have told me the truth."

"We're all untrustworthy sometimes, Mr. Delacroix."

Dad inhales deeply, aware of Nick's gentle callout.

"Why'd you run?"

I'm glad it's Nick who asks instead of me.

"The call came over the radio. Warren asked where I went when I left the castle and I told him, 'Nowhere. I drove around,' and he said they'd likely arrest me again and I should consider running until after the end of the month."

"So you do or don't think Uncle Warren is the Gemini Thief?"

"Yesterday I'd have said I'd stake my life on Warren Burton. Today? Today the world is upside down again. The only thing I'm absolutely sure of is I didn't take the boys, and I was supposed to build a castle."

My father wades into the creek. Over and over, he scoops water above his head. The droplets land, disappearing in an outward ripple. He's thinking about his castle. He's mourning that he's not going to finish what he believes was asked of him. I mourn too. Not for myself. For him. I've learned many painful things this year, maybe the worst, right now: I want to save him and I can't.

I ask, "Do you remember the glow-in-the-dark train I played with at Uncle Warren's?"

"You loved that thing."

I say, "You weren't wrong to question Uncle Warren. The Gemini Thief gave a train like mine to the June Boys. If you want to finish your castle, all lies stop here. You tell Dana everything and we trust the truth."

30

JUNE

Gunmetal-gray haze crests the horizon on June 2nd as if it's any other day. Dad turned himself over to federal custody an hour ago. I'm lying across the hood of Nick's car, the engine warming my skin, while Nick paces my driveway and pumps his sister for current information. We should sleep; we're too tired.

"Right . . . I see . . . Yes, that's a complication . . . I'll tell her . . . Yes . . . Yes . . . I'll crash here. Constance is inside we think . . . Okay . . . I will . . . Yes, I promise. You too . . . Bye."

"What's a complication?"

"Warren's in the clear."

"Why?"

"Alibied out."

"What?"

"Also, they searched the area for Tank. Nothing."

I can't let Warren's presumed innocence go. "How did he alibi out?"

"All the other Junes."

I'm indignant. "And you believe that?"

He gives me a *You believe Dana too* look. "Hold up, Sherlock. You have a rogue memory that matches a traumatized five-year-old's Crayola drawing. That train's not one of a kind."

For the second time, I've gambled my father's freedom on Dana and she's failed me. "Warren stays on the suspect list. You were gung-ho Joe about—"

"You either trust my sister or you don't."

He doesn't speak to me like this, ever. He knows it, I know it, and he catches himself and sighs. He scoots close and lies back on the hood, close enough that when I roll toward him I see the line of sweat in the curls at the nape of his neck.

"You know I didn't mean that . . . Well, what I'm saying is . . . if your dad didn't do this—and I agree that he didn't—but it doesn't mean Warren did."

"Let's find a way to cross Warren off the list." I think for a minute. "Let's search for the train in his attic."

Two squirrels chase each other up an oak. Their little claws grab the bark as they skitter around. Nick stretches in the pause; his dress pants sag on his hips and his shirt creeps up his stomach, exposing a thin line of his tan belly. He's handsome in a disheveled, brooding way, and that's a far better thought than my anger.

He watches me.

The moment is jumper cables and engine sparks, energy where there had been nothingness. Though it's out of place, I smile. A single smile resets us. Every curl on his head is matted in wild paisley-like patterns and he wedges his fingers through the brown thicket around his temples. He's either going to kiss me or cave.

He says, "No. Absolutely not. Too dangerous—"

"Track this out with me. Dana says Warren is safe. We trust Dana. Why would you worry about me checking for a train that's likely right where I left it years ago?"

He raises his hand E.T. style. We press our fingertips together, leaving space between our palms. He whispers, "You didn't let me finish. Emotionally dangerous."

"Oh, please."

The pressure in his fingertips mounts, pulses. "You signed guardianship papers *yesterday*. Let's assume for a second Warren's exactly who he looks like to the rest of the world. Kind Warren Burton. Officer Warren Burton. Upright Warren Burton. You're inviting tension with the one person you're going to need if we can't get your dad out of jail."

"You going somewhere?"

"You know I'm not."

No, I don't. The universe steals all my favorite people.

He tilts toward me, strokes my hand, then my face. "Hey. Let's hash this out tomorrow when we're both more sensible."

Exhaustion swallows me. I don't have any more to give, and emotions are pouring out, magnetizing toward the only target in close proximity.

Later, as I lie in bed, a million things to tell him come to mind. *Thank you for always being here. Even in the terrible times. Even at five in the morning after my dad's second arrest. I love you.*

After three hours of restlessness, I take my tired heart to Griff and Ruby's. When I arrive in my godparents' drive, Griff is in the yard, dragging limbs to a blazing fire barrel. A column of gray stretches

255

high above the boundary pines. Quickening his step, Griff crosses the driveway and pulls me into a hug made of peat and smoke. He's wearing yesterday's clothes, which are far too dressy for the work he's doing.

"Tank—" I can't say his name without crying.

His mouth twists; his eyes find the asphalt. "I know."

My heart thumps. "Dad—"

"Warren called." Griff removes his cell from its belt clip and begins typing. "Actually, I'll let him know you're here. He was worried about you. We all were. Ruby was . . ." His eyes roll up in his head and I know what he's saying: Ruby was ballistic.

"Sorry."

"She drove around looking for you."

"She okay?"

"I don't think so, kiddo." He exhales. In that single exhale are hours and days of sleeplessness. His dirty hands and smoky clothes hold me close.

"Sorry," I say again. "I didn't mean to scare you guys."

The apology is weak. I want to ask how he has energy to pick up limbs and preen his yard after the night we've all had, but this is the shape of his exhaustion. Work. Work. Work. Bridle chaos with Midas effort.

"How much longer before you sleep?" I ask.

He shrugs.

"You?"

"That's why I'm here," I admit.

The house is night quiet. Day brightens the halls as I tiptoe past the bathroom and open the guest room door. Ruby is draped across the navy coverlet on the bed. She also wears yesterday's clothes and her hair is disheveled by restlessness. I linger in the doorway, tears welling in my eyes. She's asleep in this bed, *my* bed, because of me. For an instant, I long to be small enough to be lifted and held, the way Griff does with the kids at the WCC. The way I used to do when I was babysitting Tank's little cousin. Maybe Griff's wishing the same thing. Whatever's on his mind, he doesn't share. He gazes at his wife and then whispers to me, "Thee, honey, crash in our bed. I'll take the couch after I douse the fire barrel."

There are dreams of trains and jail cells and bunkers.

Of Tank, Aulus, and Nick.

Of duct tape and cinched ropes.

Before the alarm screams, a ghostly hand brushes *Last One* across my stomach in red paint.

I lie still for a long time, listening as Ruby futzes in the kitchen, searching for the energy to shower or fix myself a sandwich. Do I confront Uncle Warren? Do I beg Dana to share evidence? Do I sneak into the farmhouse and check the attic? Working the scenario gives me a massive headache.

I haven't eaten in hours. If only this were a normal summer day. Gladys, Tank, Aulus, and I would burn canned biscuits in the WCC kitchen, or if we had money, hit Waffle House for pancakes. Gladys is probably in bed too, drowning her room in the music her mother hates, picturing life without Tank. I know how dangerously far a what-if imagination travels when seized by worst-case scenario fears.

Not knowing feels like you're being digested. There are even days when I long for someone to call and tell me they've found Aulus's body, just to be released from hoping.

The day after the police found Aulus's car, I willed him to call. *This is all a huge mistake,* he'd say. Months passed before I adjusted to his absence. Phantom barbells clanked in the garage for weeks.

How many tickets? *Four. No, three.* Table or booth? Will someone else be joining you? *Yes. No.*

What are Gladys and I now? A table for two?

The injustice forces me upright. I borrow a sheet of paper from a bedside notebook and write:

The Case Against Warren Burton

- Ownslowned same glow-in-the-dark train Corey described.
- He's in the welding photo.
- He was in proximity to the castle during the window Tank disappeared.
- The tin *Last One* matches his handwriting.
- He has the cop know-how to pull off a crime of this magnitude.
- He fits the profile: single, white, male, under forty, who either feels powerless or has put himself in a career that accesses power and encourages trust with minors.
- He knows Dad well enough to frame him. Including knowledge of Dad's travel plans to Baxter and access to a castle key chain.

Solution: Search for the train.

THE ELIZABETH LETTERS

Dear Elizabeth,

Elizabeth, skip this section if you can't be my reader. But find a reader.

Have you noticed hate's often easy when it should be hard and hard when it should be easy? Like . . . open a history book of strangers who hurt people or animals and hate comes like we've opened our arms to a toddler waddling in our direction. But ask me to hate my dad, when I have genuine reasons, or my uncle, who must have kidnapped me and killed Chris, and I'll give you a million excuses before accepting the truth. We're wired with the queerest of loves, the oddest of hates.

I can't imagine how Thea felt when she found out what Don did.

By the time this letter reaches you, you'll likely be well-versed in some media character of the Gemini Thief and have accepted his guilt *carte blanche*. Same as Tank, who was now certain Don's wrist was his last image before succumbing to the drugs. When I said, "Anyone can have a rubber band on his wrist," he argued, "Yeah, but anyone didn't call and ask me to pull over and come back to the castle to ring a bell when there were four other people on the roof who could have done it instead."

Good point.

I forced myself to hold Don's guilt as truth.

No, not truth—fact.

My mom once said, *Truth is spandex. Facts are metal,* and she was right. But, Elizabeth, we were down here with him—dependent for months and months—and we didn't know, didn't suspect, not once. From where we sat, on the other side of the glass or across the food slit opening, Welder was a man in an oversize mechanic suit who brought food and water. The uncle I experienced for seventeen years of life was kind to stray animals, had no weird five compulsions, and helped me survive middle school. Yes, he was quiet, and yes, he was intense, but he was also tender.

And for that reason, while I accepted Don's guilt, I refused to feel stupid.

How crazy is it that I'm thinking another man in my life isn't who I thought he was rather than letting myself digest the fact that I'm dying?

After a long lounge on the pool float, I
needed to share more thoughts about Don.

Don was not what you'd call a logical
man. I mean, he tried to hide a *castle*. And
no matter how many times I said, "Uncle Don,
if you keep lying, Thea won't care that it's a
castle," he wouldn't budge. Castle building's not
exactly like secretly taking up scuba diving or
collecting antique cars.

Once, we were packing tools, sweating our
everythings off times five, and I asked, "Why
a castle?" He tilted his head to the wind,
wrestled with answers for a long minute, then
said, "Life's more fun when you learn to ask
how instead of why."

That explanation didn't sit well with me.
Not after my dad.

I pushed until he extrapolated. He claimed
God asked him to build a castle. No, it didn't
make sense. Yes, he'd been asked to do other
strange things. *Was he sure it was the divine?*
Not always. But this time, yes. The castle,
when finished, would change history, he said.

The day Welder took me, Uncle Don and I
were extending a cedar roof over the third-
floor balcony. He was on a ladder and I was
passing him hex bolts. I worked up my courage
and said, "Look, if you don't tell Thea, I
need to."

His anger was a sudden squall on the lake

of his face. I'd seen him mumble incoherently when construction went awry and knew there was no use communicating. He'd find reality eventually. Trying to give him distance and secure the ladder, I backed away and bumped the balcony ledge, causing the portable drill to fall. Drills aren't built to land on cement mixers. Horrified by the million pieces of DeWalt, I wheeled around and apologized.

He gripped the end of his shirt and stretched the fabric tight over his chest. His whole body was shaking when he said, "Aulus, you ruined the whole day."

I didn't know if the anger was rooted in the loss of the drill or in me threatening to tell Thea. Either way, Uncle Don raged his way through the castle, screaming at me until he was outside.

There wasn't much for me to lose at that point, so I called over the balcony, "I'm telling Thea." Then I left the castle, and not slowly either. I was passing the Moose Lodge when I realized, angry or not, crazy or not, I owed my uncle a drill, so I drove into Wildwood, cashed my work check, and bought the same DeWalt I'd demolished. Then I stopped by the house, endured Leo's grumblings about the Audi, and headed back to deliver the drill.

And the rest, Elizabeth, is a stalled
Plymouth Sundance and a shovel to the head. .

> Peace and Freedom,

> Aulus

31

JUNE

The crucial forty-eight-hour window crawls by with no leads or breaks on Tank's disappearance. The smoothness of the crime and the spray-painting in particular—which psychologists attribute to both mocking arrogance and a compulsion to finalize a predatory vision—match the case's decade-long frustration.

My father's being held.

Nick says the first arrest works against him being released. Under other circumstances, they'd maybe risk tailing him. But the real Gemini Thief would not be stupid enough to lead them to the boys, and they're hedging their bets that's who they're holding in lockup. Dana says they're interrogating him.

The only good thing: search-and-rescue efforts have become an elaborate operation. The FBI's focusing all its attention on canvassing Simpson County. A team of thirty agents is holed up in a roach coach motel on the outskirts of Wildwood, working the case. The first few days, they searched for boys. Five days in, everyone seems to think they're looking for bodies.

Constance, who thankfully is sticking around, stops me on my way out the door. There's a kiss brushed to my forehead and then she locks me in like I'm her baby. "You." She winks before she continues. "Please remember you can't solve this by yourself. You've got help everywhere."

I embrace her hard, trying to shove my love into her marrow and veins, and say, "I'll remember that if you promise no more *I'll cut three miles through this field of mice and snakes in the middle of the night*. Okay? Thanks."

She grins, we pinky swear, and I'm out in the sunlight.

"That was a nice exchange," Nick observes when we're in the driveway.

"We're . . ." I search for a phrase that encompasses Constance. "Pretty tight." At least one good thing has come from chaos.

On our way to Dana, Nick stalls at a stoplight and massages the steering wheel. "Tell me whatever it is you aren't telling me," he says.

I am thinking about breaking into Uncle Warren's and how that's technically a felony and how if you help and we're caught, your law degree, your future, is irrevocably damaged.

"You blame me, don't you?" he asks, pivoting slowly toward me. There's visible regret before he speaks. "I should have gone with Tank to get the backpack even though you didn't tell me about the backpack at all." There's bitterness in those words and he falls into a silence I understand. "And now everything you do or don't do— touch my hand, lean in or out, sit toward the window instead of the console—is this cosmic sign that I broke us all." He sighs again. "I'm tired, Thee. And then I feel guilty for the privilege of being tired. Do you wish he'd taken me instead of Tank?"

"Stop," I say. "I can't live through losing anyone else. Stop, and know I'm glad you're here. So glad."

When Nick and I meet Dana in the sad, untidy lobby, she looks dreadful. She's got a pizza box and a two-liter of Mountain Dew pinned to her hip and I've seen roadkill with better posture.

"I only have about twenty minutes," she warns as we walk through dripping air conditioning puddles to her room. Nick and I settle into the only two chairs available and listen to her babbling. "I'm not even sure why they got us these rooms when we're basically living out of the Wildwood precinct." She smells her pits and frowns. "Dang, I need a shower."

Nick opens the box, lifts a slice, and places it in her hand. "You need to eat, Dane."

Dana collapses on the bed, tilts the slice above her mouth, and takes a bite. We chew through one piece, two pieces; she takes a third, all without speaking. There are no cups for the soda so we share swigs. Dana wipes the grease from her hands on the comforter and scooches toward the pillows. The headboard rattles when she leans back.

"Your dad's holding up," she tells me. "I saw him late afternoon. He asked me to check on you and make sure you aren't doing anything stupid regarding Warren."

"I'm not. He's taking time off," I say.

Which I know because Gladys and I spent the day parked behind the old Rippee barn, sharing a pair of binoculars. There was hardly anything to watch except Uncle Warren hulking back and forth to his construction trailer, carrying lumber and tools.

"Personal days according to the chief," Dana says. There are no facial clues regarding her thoughts on this.

To hear Warren tell it, the days aren't optional. His chief said

266

something along the lines of "Burton, you're too close to this. Get your head on straight. Come back Friday." It's interesting Dana got a milder version of the story. Or maybe the sheriff's office isn't communicating fully after the invasion of the Feds.

"He calls every day," I say.

"Good." Dana sweeps her hair into a tiny bun, unfastens her belt, and riffles until she finds clothes that don't stink. "He didn't do this, Thea. Trust the evidence."

I argue, "Then why would he tell Dad to run until the end of the month? Wouldn't only the kidnapper know that timeline?"

Dana looks incredulous. "The whole world knows the timeline, and Warren loves your dad enough to try to save him from further destruction."

"Is there another suspect?" Nick asks.

Dana is halfway to the bathroom. "I can't tell you that."

Nick presses, "You know law enforcement often stops looking for the truth after a prime suspect is in custody."

Dana rolls her eyes. "Take the pizza when you leave." This should be our dismissal, except Dana leans through the bathroom door into the room, clutching her towel and sympathy, and asks, "Want me to tell your dad anything if I see him?"

"Don't mention the castle stuff if you can help it."

The castle's a complete cluster. As if we needed more difficulties, the police were dispatched to the property this morning. When the number popped up on the caller ID, my heart dropped out of my body until Constance and I listened to an on-duty officer explain there had been some trespassing and vandalism at the castle. *Some.* More like, a lot. The castle got tagged, inside and out, with *Release Our Boys* and *Execute the Gemini Thief* and *Wildwood for Justice*.

267

"Don's seen the report. We had to ask him if he had a clue who'd deface his property."

"And did he?"

Dana shakes her head and closes the bathroom door.

Nick pulls me out of the chair and walks me back to the car. When he gives me the casual hug I'm accustomed to, I don't let go and his lips brush the skin behind my ear. "I have an idea about getting you into Warren's legally."

"You do?" My voice is lower than I mean for it to be, sexier.

He slings the nearly empty box onto the Civic's dash. "Tell Warren you need to have a package delivered and you don't want it coming to your place or the castle because of the media. He'll say you can have it sent to his house. Then you have a reason to be there on Friday when he goes back to work."

"And if he doesn't say that?"

"Then I'll concede he's hiding something."

32

JUNE

Why I let Ruby order so much food when I'm not hungry is a mystery. Me pushing the grease across my DQ tray doesn't satisfy her in the slightest. Around the table appetites vary widely. Warren hasn't managed a single bite. Telling him about "the package" I'm having delivered to his house tomorrow would be easier if I felt I could read him, but he's here and far away.

I stomach another onion ring and endure Ruby's *That a girl* thumbs-up.

Griff's telling Ruby, Warren, Constance, and me about meeting with the lawyer. I'm not sure how we ended up at Dairy Queen, but here we are, crammed into a booth meant for a family of four. Griff salts his fries, says, "He's trying to expedite the FBI's release of exculpatory evidence and wants to bring us up to speed on what he's learned."

Warren says, "There's no way in a case this large, stretching over so many years, there aren't other suspects. But if the lawyer thinks he needs Brady evidence to win, it's because he can't cast probable doubt without supplying another potential kidnapper to the jury."

I wish Nick was here to translate the legalese.

Warren lifts an onion ring, ogles the fried circle with regret, and sets it back down. "And in this case, with Tank, that means the lawyer'd be pointing at someone who attended the graduation party."

Ruby pauses her burger midway to her mouth and turns to Griff. "But they're not doing that?"

Griff shushes the fear with an egotistical nod and that makes Ruby sigh with relief. She knows opinions are based on available information, not available truth. Everyone involved has a life they want protected from false accusations, same as Dad, and they're already taking heat for their association with him. Parents of my favorite kids have already pulled their WCC memberships. Warren told me yesterday that none of his ride-along partners have been all that supportive.

Still, I wonder if Warren's right or if Dad's lawyer misled him at Dad's direction. Dad had listened to me about the train, and he agreed the coincidence was strange, but he remains Team Warren 90 percent of the time. He'd said, "Warren looked me in the eye and told me he didn't do this. Plus, the FBI cleared him." My astute response was "So? The FBI cleared you too. They're not exactly batting a thousand."

Dad clicked through his rebuttals like a Rolodex. Finally, he said, "If I want people to believe I'm innocent, this is the only path there is. You're the one who taught me that."

I trusted the truth more when Warren was still on Dana's suspect list. Which isn't necessarily trusting the truth, I guess. Maybe it was cruel, but I told him he was naive to believe people cared more about facts than drama. Especially in Wildwood.

As if to prove I'm right, Lila Kate, who has slipped me multiple Blizzards when her manager isn't on shift, stalks our table and texts someone with fast-finger fervor. I'm probably being paranoid and her texts are about dinner plans or whether her husband has picked up the kids yet, but she's wearing so much open disgust that I wonder if old Lila Kate had a Gemini sign in her yard last week. When I lean toward Warren to ask about the package, she's straining in our direction.

"I had a package delivered to your place," I say to Warren.

His back straightens. "When does it arrive?"

"Tomorrow. Okay for me to come over and pick it up? The media are all over us at the house."

Constance exhales. "So true."

Warren stacks his condiment containers in a tiny white column on the table. "Why don't you let me bring it to you after work tomorrow?"

"Because it's a nozzle for Dad's pressure washer. I was hoping to get some of the paint off the castle—"

"Oh." He's relieved. "I'll take care of that Saturday, soon as I get off work."

"I don't mind."

"Are you kidding? Don will have my hide."

"So my faithful new guardian doesn't want me at his house?" I pour on the sugar.

Uncle Warren's cheeks blaze bright red. "Not until it's a little less bachelor pad, if you know what I mean. I've been crazy with the case . . . and I was doing some construction last week. There are tools everywhere."

I let him believe he's off the hook and excuse myself to the restroom. Nick answers on the first ring. After I tell him about

271

Warren's reaction, he says, "First of all, breathe. Then keep acting normal. I'll meet you later and we'll plan."

"My house?" I ask.

"Castle," he says.

Leaving the bathroom, I bump into Griff. He gestures to the parking lot.

"Bad news. Literally."

Multiple vans line the curb. The media zoo is lions today, prowling and hungry. In retrospect, Lila Kate's texts make sense. I cast a scathing look toward the register and wish I was wearing something nicer than a tank top. We dump our trays with no thought of the remaining food and assemble at the door like we're getting ready to dart into the rain. Warren lays his hand atop my head and squeezes gently.

"Mean it, kiddo. No worrying about the nozzle." Then to Constance, he says, "Keep her busy, please."

Constance nods and we scatter to the vehicles armed only with lowered chins and "No comment." Each stoplight gives me an opportunity to lose the tailing cars. I head downtown and hide in the public library book-drop lane. I don't wait long enough and two vans follow the Ram to the castle. They're camped beside the gate when Gladys arrives fifteen minutes later. They still haven't budged an hour later when Nick rolls up the drive.

"We should call them in for trespassing," he says.

"We've called in quite enough things lately," I say.

We bring our small meeting to order. There is little to no discussion. We all agree Warren's house needs to be searched. The primary question is how to pull off the expedition if the media follows me to Warren's. We agree to swap vehicles tonight.

Nick says, "You and Gladys take my car to Dana's hotel

room. She's working all night. I'll stay here with your dad's Ram. Tomorrow morning on your way to Warren's, drop Gladys at the Rippee barn to keep an eye on you."

"Where will you be?" Gladys asks.

"I'll head over to the WCC. That puts your dad's Ram far from the action and me near the police station. Hopefully Warren spots the truck and assumes you're hanging with Griff and Ruby. My gut says he's checking in on you tomorrow."

33

JUNE

The gravel road leading to Warren's farmhouse washed out in the recent rains, leaving a bare-bone rut that shakes the car. The creek's still swollen and sprinting toward the river. I think of Chris Jenkins. If this water was ever in his lungs.

Every jolt to the Civic produces memories.

Uncle Warren, ten years ago, shirtless in stars-and-stripes swim trunks, filling a plastic pool with a heavy black garden hose. The old waterlogged tire swinging from a skyscraper oak tree in his front yard. Black tire smudges on my pink shorts, which Warren meticulously scrubbed with spot cleaner. Adults do a million things to show you love that you don't register as love when you're young.

Warren does them all. And other things too.

The other things are why I'm here. A train. The arc of his *t*s. The way he deterred me from his house. Even the padlocked door in his kitchen, where once upon a time Aulus told me he was working to finish out Warren's basement.

274

Just being out here, my brain is a lemon shoved onto a juicer; memories eke like pulp. We stayed with Warren for three weeks before we moved into our Wildwood house.

Long after they put me to sleep each night, my father and Warren would either sit and talk at the picnic table in the kitchen or build something. On the talking nights, I'd creep to my perch on the bottom step and listen to them drink beer and curse my mother.

I remember Warren once saying, "Don't tell me that, Don. I'm a cop," and my father tapping his bottle against the table edge, responding, "That's exactly why I'm telling you."

On the building nights, there were hammers and saws, that ratchet sound a driver makes when there are no more turns to be made. The same sounds drift toward the Rippee barn this week.

I never saw what Dad and Warren built, and no amount of brain juicing pulls more substance to the surface.

When I shut Nick's car door, a deer munching on low-hanging branches bolts into the adjacent field. The old blue-and-white rope, tire long removed, sways in the wind like a noose. Knowing Gladys is tracking me through the binoculars, I turn toward the Rippee barn and put a thumb in the air. *Okay so far.* My head pounds with adrenaline as I stare at the white two-story farm-house. Its friendly parts: large dormer window with bright blue shutters, wraparound porch, rooster weather vane atop the metal roof. Its not-so-friendly parts: the brick cellar with the rusted door near the side porch, disconnected gutters, unpinned latticework that clacks in the summer wind, brownish-green mold crawling up wood siding to the roof. A house with two personalities.

There are no signs of traffic on the lane. Nothing to hear but crickets and my own beating heart.

I rub my hand over the bowed gray-wood table on the deck

and recall countless meals. Boxes of gas station–fried chicken. Over-grilled burgers. Warren's special recipe waffles with bacon and maple syrup in the batter for my birthday celebrations. It's strange how my acquaintance with his house feels like familiarity with Uncle Warren. And how maybe everything I've always believed is a fabrication.

There's a stone rabbit key box under the forsythia bush. When I shove the yellow buds and whip-like branches aside, the rabbit's gone.

I search everywhere and find the rabbit without its key on the first step of the cellar. I tug on the kitchen, front, and back doors, and they're all locked. Lucky for me, the bathroom window isn't latched. The picnic table scrapes long trenches in the grass as I drag it toward the house. Standing atop the wood, I lift the windowsill high enough to squeeze through and drop into the room.

I strain my ears even though I know he's not here. My heart is the only sound in the house. *Get in. Get out.* I head toward the kitchen.

Warren wasn't kidding. The house is a wreck. Clothes and bags are strewn across the living room floor, a pillow and blanket laid out on the couch. Two boxes of cereal are on the counter; a milk carton open next to them. There's construction equipment scattered all through the mud and laundry rooms. A stack of lumber sits in the entry corridor. I should go straight to the attic and look for the train, but that padlocked door to the basement won't let me. There are two locks now and I swear there used to be just one.

Several key sets hang on a hook by the window. None fit either lock. There are a few obvious places to check for more keys: four drawers beside the stove, the flour canister on the counter, the wooden bowl on the table. I find batteries, salt packets from

McDonald's, a tape measure, rubber bands long melted into the drawer bottoms, broken pencils. No keys among the madness. I've all but made up my mind to use the tire iron in Nick's trunk to break the lock when there's a sound behind me.

"Looking for something?" a male voice asks.

I drop the lock and it clangs against the door. Fear tiptoes up my body. The only weapon in sight is a pair of kitchen scissors, but I can't slide them off the counter without drawing attention.

"*Thea*, it's been a long time."

I stay still, considering my options. Run. Turn around. Pray.

"*Tsk-tsk-tsk*. Warren said you might turn up."

I make a hectic grab for the scissors and spin.

Uncle Scottie blocks the exit.

He has a gun.

THE ELIZABETH LETTERS

Dear Elizabeth,

Tank had a different reaction to Don being Welder than I did.

His emotions were visceral words, thrown rather than spoken. He landed punch after punch against the thin metal of the washer. I didn't warn about wasted energy or waking Zared or Rufus. I stopped writing long enough to scoot into his orbit and wait for him to stop.

"I defended him, Aul." Tank's lament came with another violent assault on the washer. "And now we're going to die down here." He roundhoused the dryer. The chinking ricocheted around the concrete walls.

I stayed propped on my garbage sacks. If there's one thing I learned down here, it's that rage needed a place in the room. Hatred wasn't trash to be taken out Monday evening and left curbside for Tuesday pickup. Emotions didn't end up in landfills. They lived here. With us. And somehow we coexisted.

"Reading people isn't like reading a chart or a graph," I said.

Whether it was my words or his exhaustion, the lashing stopped. He leaped atop the dryer and collapsed, chest down, sprawled across the two machines. In the half light, his shadow quivered, his lungs worked triple time. They were louder than his guilt.

Tank is brilliant, but Thea's one of his blind spots. If she wanted Don to be innocent, Tank worked to make him innocent.

(Sorry, I need to stop for a minute. My friend needs me.)

I slid across the pile of garbage sacks, forced Tank to sit up, and gripped his face with both hands. I said, "Don't, man. Just don't." For once, he laid his head on me and sobbed like Chris used to in the beginning. When his breathing calmed, I matched him. Long inhale. Long exhale. Long inhale. Long exhale. Again and again.

"Aul." He trapped his dirty knees inside his dirtier arms. "If Don's in jail, he's not coming back. We're not looking to make it a few more days. We need a way out."

I thought about Zared, how close he was to giving up.

"I don't want to die," Tank said.

"Me either."

I might not write again. We'll be busy or we'll be dead.

Peace and Blessings,

Aulus

34

JUNE

We are matador and bull.

"Put the scissors down."

"Put the gun down."

Uncle Scottie gives me the same *yes, ma'am* nod I've seen from so many born and bred Simpson County boys. As if I asked, *Could you check the windshield fluid after you change the oil?* He shoves the gun into the front of his waistband and lifts his hands in a *That better for you?* gesture. Hardly. He steps forward and I inch toward the kitchen door, wondering if I should run toward the living room or attempt to slip by him.

He pulls out a chair and sits. "You gonna put those Fiskars in me or what?"

I tighten my grip on the scissors and his eyes roll toward the chair across from him. "Sit, Thea. It's just me." I obey, the napkin holder a tiny wall between us. My dad's beloved cousin rolls his tongue over his lips and then says, "Want to tell me what you're doing in *Officer* Warren Burton's house uninvited?"

I tip my chair slightly back, putting as much distance between us as possible. "You first?"

Scottie pats the front pocket of his T-shirt and makes a show of checking the pockets of his jeans. "Let's see, I've got my invitation here somewhere." There's no humor stretching across those brown irises when he looks at me. "I'm searching for my son."

"You're about ten years too late."

He points a trigger finger in my direction. "Nice one. You learn that from your dad?"

"You're hiding out."

Lifting both hands in the air, like I'm the one with the gun, he says, "Caught me, Sherlock."

Is Scottie the reason Warren didn't want me here? "Why?"

"Because read-a-thon Leo and I own that"—he holds in a curse, but it's there on his lips—"flooded house in Nashville and Chris Jenkins drowned and my son is missing and I haven't exactly shown . . . What do they call it?" He snaps his fingers. "Moral fiber."

I want to punch the attitude off his face. "You investigating Warren?" I ask.

Scottie rears back. He doesn't laugh, but he's entertained. "Officer Bach. Oh, that's rich."

I flick my head in the direction of the locked door.

"What? Warren's keeping Aulus in his basement?" A sad smile creeps across my uncle's lips.

Something in me snaps. "I don't find anything about Aulus or Tank missing funny."

His expression melts as quickly as it formed. There's sorrow, maybe pain or even regret, etched on his face now. His handsome son hides among his aging features—broad shoulders, dark hair, darker eyebrows—and I find myself softening, aching that Aulus isn't here to see his father. The dad we always assumed didn't care.

"I'm here because my son was kidnapped." He readjusts in his seat, meets my eyes. "I'm helping Warren locate Aul. Clear your dad. Not that your dad's happy about it. He and Warren riffed pretty hard on it the other night."

I remove the Welder photo from my pocket and smack the print on the table. "You could be doing this together," I suggest.

Scottie lifts the photo. "Man, this feels like a hundred years ago."

"So you admit that you and Warren have welding helmets?"

His eyes raise, his eyebrows arch. "Yes."

"And you're in this photo?"

He shakes his head. "I took this picture."

I flip the image over, tap his name indignantly. "That's you."

"Uh, thanks, except I've never had that six-pack in my life. That's Griff Holtz every day of the week and twice on Sunday."

Griff wouldn't lie. "But Griff—"

"Not me, darling niece." There's depth and earnestness to the claim. "I couldn't get my act together to get a job back then, and even if I could've, Griff wouldn't have hired me."

I'm struggling to understand the implications of Griff lying.

"You're saying Griff has a welding helmet? That you and Warren knew all along?"

"Yep," he says.

I'm already standing up. "Come to the attic with me. Or don't come, but I have to check on something." I'm halfway up the steps before he's behind me, arguing that there's nothing up here. Turns out he's right about that. The attic is empty. No boxes at all.

"What were you expecting to find?"

"A glow-in-the-dark train. One of the released kids mentioned a train like the one Warren let me play with when I was a kid." The darkness of the room can't disguise Scottie's guilt.

"What?" I say. Fear charges through me again; I'm in an attic with a man I don't know anymore, and he has a gun.

"Thea, Warren paid me to empty this attic years ago."

"When?"

"I dunno. Before I left Wildwood for good. Aulus was like . . . seven or eight."

Scottie had the train.

"I dropped everything at the WCC."

The wheels turn; the situation crystallizes in a neat list of facts.

The Case Against Griff Holtz

- In possession of the train Corey described.
- In the welding photo and lied about it.
- Asked me to destroy the welding photo.
- In proximity to the castle during the window Tank disappeared. Also, was up all night burning stuff.
- Has freedom in his schedule. Owns an old ice cream van that could be used for transporting kidnapped children.
- Fits the profile: white, male, under forty, who placed himself in a career that accesses power and encourages trust with minors. Strong enough to lift Aulus or Tank.
- Knows Dad well enough to frame him. Including knowledge of Dad's travel plans to Baxter and access to a castle key chain.
- Hired the lawyer who has been unable to release Dad.

Scottie and I return to the kitchen and the welding photo.

"This is Griff?" I ask again, like the photograph might have rearranged itself while we were in the attic.

"Yes."

I pause. The next bit will be hard to say aloud. "You're not the Thief. Warren's not the Thief. Griff is."

Scottie nods. "That's the theory Warren and Dana are working."

We're interrupted by Gladys banging on Warren's door.

"Thea!" She's out of breath and screaming through the wood. The world must be on fire. Even seeing Scottie through the pane doesn't faze her. "We gotta go right now! It's Nick," she yells as I open the door.

Everything slows. Lurches. Slows again.

Nick is at the WCC.

Nick is with Griff.

Griff is dangerous.

35

JUNE

The seat belt metal burns the exposed skin between my T-shirt and shorts. In the back seat, Gladys grips the door's side panel, her fingers hovering over the window button like she's overheated and can't remember how to cool down. Uncle Scottie flies over county roads at terrifying speeds; the three of us pant like dogs left in a locked car.

"Tell me what happened," Uncle Scottie demands. When Gladys doesn't respond, Scottie snaps his fingers in the direction of the back seat. "*You*. Tell. Me. What. Happened. I need to call Warren."

Gladys gasps out the story in spurts. Five or six minutes before she burst into the house, Nick called. He'd called me first and I hadn't answered. The connection was so bad she'd only understood some whispered phrases.

Nick's voice: "Glads . . . train is . . . here." And then, far off in the distance, a man shouted, "Hey. Hey." Then Nick again, frightened, saying, "Griff. It's Griff."

286

Then *click.*

Gladys called back. No answer.

When I check my phone, there are three missed calls from Nick. The phone never rang.

"What do we do?" I ask.

Scottie tries Warren and when he doesn't reach him, leaves a message. "Warren. WCC now. Griff has Nick Jones. I'm on my way."

"What do we do?" I repeat.

Scottie's cheeks harden; his knuckles are white against the steering wheel.

"I'll kill him," he says. He's had time to work this up. I'm still fighting the psychology, aligning the Griff I know with the Griff who put Aulus underground for a year, aligning the Scottie who left his kid with the one driving the car at warp speed for a chance to save Nick. Aulus would enjoy the decency of the action; he'd love the rage.

I can't teleport physical matter, but maybe emotions are small enough to travel.

I send Nick courage.

I send him love.

I send him life.

Gladys fights Scottie's anger with logic. "You can't kill him, we don't know where Tank and Aulus are. The others—"

Scottie pounds the steering wheel and we swerve into the vacant oncoming lane. In the back seat, Gladys grips the ceiling handle with all ten fingers. Town's a few turns away. Scottie tries Warren again and when there's no answer, he throws the phone at my lap and instructs me to keep trying.

I dial and pray. *Help us. Help us.* A single image ripples to

287

mind and becomes sound: Dad's tower bell—the one he bought the night Chris's body was dumped on I-40—ringing and ringing and ringing.

Warren doesn't answer.

The WCC's playground is full of sliding, teetering, swinging happiness. Kids yell, "Ready or not, here I come," and chase each other from fence to fence. Today's a normal day for them.

We sling gravel through the chain-link fence onto the playground and Leah yells, "Slow down! These are children."

Scottie says, "Stay here. Keep calling Warren."

I pass his phone to the back seat. "911 instead?"

Scottie glances toward the playground. "I don't know what's best. Send the cops roaring in here and scare the bejesus out of everyone . . . But then again . . ." He shifts his T-shirt to hide the gun. "Go with your gut."

Scottie jogs toward the door and raises a casual hand to Leah. "Looking for Griff," we hear him say. Leah looks alarmed until she spots us in the car and waves.

Gladys raises the phone to her ear. "I'm calling Dana."

I cannot stay here. I keep jogging when she hollers after me.

Kool-Aid and snacks are on the lobby counter. No one is in sight. A chorus of singsong voices drifts through the halls. "We're going on a bear hunt," the leader sings jovially and the children repeat. In the closest playroom, a Jenga tower topples and laughter erupts.

These are the sounds of my childhood.

I force myself toward logic. The train wouldn't be in the basement; we're down there all the time. Nick must be upstairs.

Dust falls from the lobby ceiling fan. The building creaks. It's been years since I went to the second or third story. I ease open the stairwell door. Listen. Nothing. But there are shoe treads, close to the wall, disturbing the grimy wooden planks. Nick's shoes. My bravery isn't a deep well, but I inch up, again, again, again, pausing on every step to listen.

The second floor's empty.

I round the landing of the third level. Slivers of pale daylight work their way through the covered windows, casting grim shadows on the wide warped floorboards. *Has Griff already hurt Nick? Will he hurt me?*

There are more disturbances in the dust. How many sets of prints? Three? Four? I'm not sure.

I hear Griff and almost collapse against the wall. He's agitated. Anguished. I crouch, clutching the toes of my tennis shoes with trembling fingers. He first begs and then demands to be heard.

Nick begs back. "Hey. Hey. You don't have to do this. Tell us where they are and let them go. That's all people care about."

Griff responds, but the words are pinched, unrecognizable. Hysterical pleading and then, "It's over. It's over. It has to be over right now."

"Please don't," Nick says. "Don't."

There's a groan.

A sob.

I've been frozen, clinging to my hiding space in the hallway.

Assuming the standoff started when Nick called, they've been escalating for twenty or thirty minutes. That's a long time for tension to be this high.

I have a choice. Wait for Scottie or Dana or Warren, or go inside. There's danger and answers on the other side of the door that ask me to pause one moment and consider all the things I haven't done yet in life. College. Career. Marriage. Kids. And just as many things I put on hold this year to find Aulus.

Everyone, even my best friends, even my father, saw those decisions as a sacrifice. College applications, on hold. Friends, on hold. High school, prom, graduation, all on hold. But the thing is, I don't care. Some things require more than we have to give, and all I know to do is give and give and give and hope it's enough. I'm not sorry. I'd do it all again.

So this, the danger, it's not even a real decision. I turn the brass door handle and push.

I hear the unmistakable cock of a gun.

Voices run together like broken egg yolks.

"There's no other choice," another voice inside says.

I swing the door open, brace for a bullet. "Griff, don't hurt Nick. Please."

Griff is not the one who has a gun pressed to Nick's temple.

Even in the half light, I see Ruby's finger tremble against the trigger. At the sight of me, her mouth drops open in horror.

36

JUNE

Ruby and Nick are by the window.

Griff and I are by the door.

We are the room.

Ruby screams, *"Thea!"* with such force I am afraid she will accidentally take Nick's head off. Panic explodes through his face; he quiets every muscle with visible effort, forcing himself from tippy-toe heaves to flat-footed deep breaths.

Griff, eyes on Ruby, says to me, "You shouldn't be here."

Scottie must have started searching the basement.

I deconstruct my previous theory and try to fathom how Ruby—the closest person I've had to a mom for years—could hurt Nick. Hurt anyone. Ruby, as the Gemini Thief.

I don't know what I've interrupted, but that can't be what this is. I swivel toward Griff, begging for a silent explanation. Tears fall from his chin.

"Honey, let Nick go."

Agitated, eyes flying from door to gun to Griff, she says, "I can't. You know I can't."

Griff dumps buckets of love into two words. "You can."

"It's too late. Chris . . . ," she cries, and as she heaves, the gun jabs Nick's skull. His shoulders curl away from her.

"Hey . . ." Griff's hands are outstretched, pleading. "I promise you can. You always let your June Boys go, right? You take those boys to love them, right? Love them the way their parents don't. Help fill the holes in their lives. That's good-hearted"—*and completely psycho*—"and letting Nick go would also be good-heart—"

"Shut up!" Ruby taps the gun. Metal clicks against bone. "Shut up!" she says again, her voice rising.

A screech rebounds around the room. I don't realize I'm the one making the noise until the words empty from my mouth. "Why? Why would you do this?"

Griff pats the air in warning. "Don't. You'll set her off," he says. I can't tell Griff's involvement, but there's no doubt he's shielding me with his body.

He addresses his wife again. "Honey, let Nick go. Nick's not a June Boy."

"Neither was Tank. But Aulus needed him after . . ." She's not making sense. "Doesn't matter now. Dead boys. Dead boys. I should have fed them. I didn't feed them." Her tone flattens. "I'm dead too."

Griff inches slightly forward. "You're not. Warren said Chris drowned. His ribs were broken from someone trying to resuscitate him. Was that you?"

Her shoulders drop, the gun wobbles momentarily. "That was Aulus. All Aulus. I left them down there in the flood. I didn't know the bunker would leak. Fill. I didn't—" She's dissolving, the gun's shaking.

In her own way, she loved Chris and she's mourning his loss. While we have her attention diverted, I chime in. "Ruby, I know you'd never hurt Chris on purpose."

"You do?" she asks like a child on the first day of school, full of uncertainties.

"Of course," Griff agrees and nods at me.

"Absolutely," I say. "You are always kind."

"But I'm not," Ruby says. "I took them because I wanted them. I wanted to take more. Save more." She looks dead at me. "I even wanted to take you."

Nick's eyes dart toward the floor. He wants to duck under Ruby's grip. He might have been able to if Scottie hadn't arrived, gun drawn, letting fly a string of curses and threats.

We are right back in the danger zone.

Ruby's more rattled than ever. She stares at her husband, me, Scottie's gun. She says a single word, "Can't."

The sirens wheeze their arrival from the street.

I raise my voice over the noise. "Why not?"

Ruby pitches forward, her weight on Nick. "This isn't supposed to happen," she says, almost apologetically. She lifts Nick's chin with the gun. "Stop right there, Griff."

Griff, who has been advancing in baby scoots and shuffles, stops. "Honey, I'd never hurt you. Let Nick go. Tell us where Aulus and the others are. This will be okay."

"Please," I beg. "Are they still alive?"

"Dead boys," she says, her sadness profound. "And I only took him because you were back." She spits this accusation at Scottie. "He pulled me aside. Me. Showed me a pill bottle and said you'd showed up and wanted to be part of his life again, and then you disappeared. He wanted to search for you. I couldn't let him waste his life on someone as miserable as you."

Monsters don't always look like monsters on the outside, and maybe they're not always monsters, but this is a horrific thing Ruby has done, and done, and done, and done. Boys are dead.

I hear the billboards from I-65. *The Gemini Thief could be anyone. Your father, your mother, your best friend's crazy uncle. Some country music star's deranged sister. Anyone. Someone's stealing Tennessee's boys. Report suspicious behavior.*

The Gemini Thief could be the person who does your laundry and makes you mac and cheese and slathers you with sunscreen on the way into Holiday World.

She could be your Ruby.

"You wanted babies, didn't you?" Griff asks softly.

Ruby brushes sweat from her forehead with her arm. "Boys. I was going to have so many boys."

"And it's my fault we couldn't," he says. "My fault we lost Tony. I should have been there to take you to the hospital."

Tony? I've spent hours, days, even weeks at Griff and Ruby's, and I don't know a single Tony story. Dad never said they'd lost a child. I never noticed a gap in their two-person family. In fact, Griff used to tease me, saying, *Send that rascal home.* But now I see a couple who surrounded themselves with other people's children. I remember streaks of blue paint near the ceiling of my room at their house and Ruby lifting me to the bathroom sink as a child, brushing my hair, shoving her nose into the crown of my head and saying, *You smell like my dreams.*

"Ruby, I don't know about Tony, but Nick's parents love him.

His sister loves him. I love him. You don't want us to lose him the way you lost Tony, do you?"

Ruby says, "June Boys weren't lost. I borrow them. I borrow them for a year. I love them for a year. Half the parents of those kids downstairs would thank me if I took their child off their hands."

Scottie can't contain himself anymore. "You crazy bi—"

"Don't you dare judge me, Scott McClaghen. You don't even know your son and he's a marvel. I love that kid more than you ever c—"

Scottie lunges forward, but Griff wraps his arms around his old friend. "Slow down. Calm. Down. She's going to tell us where the boys are. Right, honey?"

"That's right." Ruby taps the gun against Nick's chin.

Nick's quiet. Sweating, but still. Everyone takes a breath.

Nick asks, "Are they here in Wildwood?"

Ruby nods.

Griff says, "Where in Wildwood?"

Ruby's finger dances on the trigger.

"Hey," Griff says again. "We're calm. No one's getting hurt today. Not you. Not us. Not the June Boys."

"No one's hurt," Ruby repeats.

"No one's going to get hurt."

"No one's going to get hurt," she parrots.

He's doing it, he's gonna talk her down.

Dana's voice threads the air behind me. "Ruby Holtz, lower your weapon and release my brother." The agent's body is tucked against the doorframe behind me, gun raised. "You do that and tell us where the boys are, and I swear we'll make you a deal."

A deal.

A legal transaction that would likely put Ruby behind bars for the rest of her life.

Everyone processes the offer.

When you love someone, even the smallest muscle move—a blink, an eye darting right to left, parting lips—speaks volumes.

Griff and I see her decide.

She'd rather join Tony than go to prison.

Griff and I yell together. *"Nooo!"*

Dana says, "Tell me where—"

Our words overlap.

"I'm sorry," she says in Nick's ear and swings her gun toward Dana.

Ruby's first shot is not the accidental result of trembling fingers; it is intentional and steady. The catalyst for the end.

Simultaneous gunshots, an eruption of sound and fury—I count one, two, three, four—and cries, bodies moving.

Nick drops to his knees, falls forward. Blood pools. His blood? Hers?

She's standing. Holding a place near her shoulder.

Two more shots.

A third.

The room quiets—there's hurried motion—but I hear nothing over the ringing. *The tower bell?* I wonder. *No, the gunshots.* This is such a small room.

Nick's lying on the floor. I scream, "Nick!" like I'm yelling across a football field. The haze fades like twilight to night. "Nick," I say, this time a whisper.

The pressure in my chest is enormous. I gasp for breath and fall. Someone's trying to wake me up. But if I wake up, they'll tell me what I already know. Nick's dead. I spent this year trying to save Aulus, and my obsession got Nick killed.

"Thea." I open my eyes a slit. Dana has blood on her face and hands. *Nick's blood. Don't die, Nick. Please don't die.*

Dana's face hovers, blurry and insubstantial.

"Help Nick," I whisper.

"Thea?"

I risk opening my eyes again. Dana's jaw shudders and I know that means Nick is dead. My head lolls. The blood on the floor pools toward me.

"Thea."

It comes to me that the pressure on my chest is Dana. She's jabbing her fist into my rib cage and she won't stop. I swat at her hand and feel the haze again.

"Thea, honey . . . Hey, stay with me."

I close my eyes.

THE ELIZABETH LETTERS

Dear Elizabeth,

Not dead yet.

I'll pick up with exit plans.

I guarded the buoyancy of my words when I said, "I have an idea."

Tank pummeling the washer made me notice the dryer, more specifically, a long metal pipe joining dryer to dryer vent. Running floor to ceiling, the rusted cylinder disappeared somewhere above the popcorn tiles and cobwebs. And I guessed, based on the vent work at the castle, somewhere . . . is outside.

"That dryer used to be installed," I said.

"Yeah." Cogs clicked into place.

"Dryer vent means—"

"That pipe goes outside. Which is great, except neither of us can fit through a five-inch pipe."

I said, "I'm appointing you to figure out something that will."

Tank seemed pleased with the assignment, but his expression folded toward disappointment. "You saw those sweatpants from earlier, right?"

"The Rock Hollow ones? Yeah, what do they have to do with this?"

"What if it's our Rock Hollow?"

I exhaled. "I don't care where we are anymore." That was a lie and we both knew it.

Tank said, "Let's say we manage to shove something through this pipe into the great outdoors. Then what? Someone happens upon an abandoned house or a building in the middle of nowhere and notices"—he threw a T-shirt at my face—"a pile of old clothes and thinks, *Man, I'll bet there are kids in this basement.*"

"You got a better idea?" He didn't. "Then use that Ivy League skull of yours and tell me what gives us the highest probability of pushing something through that vent."

"We need to be up there," he said, of the ceiling. "On a stable platform. 'Cause we have to punch through that drop-down stuff, remove the pipe on this side, and then figure out where it goes with some sort of snake tool."

"Well, I happen to have built a castle once. Stay here," I said.

"Where'm I gonna go?"

299

A goofy out-of-place grin took root. I
pictured Tank standing in the school parking
lot, tugging a cigarette from behind his ear,
cranking the volume on "Single Ladies," and
dancing until the girls were embarrassed
to be seen with us. The fall wind swept my
face. The air smelled of cinnamon. Vanilla.
Campfires. The cotton of my hoodie was soft
and warm around my neck and ears. I chewed
the sweatshirt strings and watched a fox
crossing the road, his ears perking at the sound
of oncoming traffic. I heard rain. I tasted rain
on my tongue.

We were free.

"Careful with that hope," he said.

"Careful with that doubt," I retorted.

Tiptoeing into Sleeping Room, I moved two
barstools without waking Rufus or Zared. The
boys lay on a single pool float, toe to head,
head to toe; the stuffed coyote "Bubba"
keeping watch. I returned for two more stools
and Zared stirred.

"Thanks," he mumbled in my direction. He
was asleep again, or pretending to be, before I
answered, "You're welcome."

Tank spotted the barstools and shook his
head. "Weight'll warp the dryer."

Unswayed, I straddled the chair over both
machines, needing to see if the ceiling was
reachable before we started construction.

The chairs were shaky beasts, but I got my knees on the seat of the uppermost chair and flung my hands wide like a tightrope walker. One hand found the wall and I inhaled. There was no resistance when I punched the first tile. Dust coated my hair and drifted to the floor.

"Nice," Tank said, wiping his eye.

Four inches above the ceiling, the vent passed through an exterior wall. I squinted. "We need the coupling off. I don't want to waste energy if we can't get the pipe away from the wall."

"Would the knife help? Use the end of the blade like a screwdriver?" He didn't wait for an answer. *We should have thought about that with the freezer lid.* "Don't fall," he added before retreating toward Sleeping Room.

Knife in hand, he returned. Rufus and Zared followed him like ducklings.

"You're hacking through the wall without us?" Rufus said, yawning.

Zared glided by, thumping the tip of the knife in Tank's hand with his middle finger. "He's keeping me away from the sharp objects. Right, Aul?" He made the joke, but he was grateful too.

Tank ignored the boys and said, "We'll have to snake something up the enclosed pipe

301

and then pray the vent isn't covered. They
often have external flaps to keep animals out."

Very carefully, Rufus joined me atop
the dryer. The chairs shook with his added
weight. I steadied us as Tank passed me the
knife. Using the tip of the blade, I loosened
both screws until they fell out of the coupling
and pinged against the concrete floor.

There was a fair amount of yelping,
hooting, and hollering when I yanked the pipe
away from the wall and stared into the
opening.

"What do you see?" Tank asked, standing
on tiptoes.

A true smile unclenched every muscle in
my body. "I see light."

Daylight, Elizabeth. Daylight. I wept like
a kid.

I'll write again when there's a plan.

Peace and Freedom,

Aulus

THE ELIZABETH LETTERS

Dear Elizabeth,

 Shall we agree I was better at constructing trash castles than at drawing them?

VENT
TO EXTERIOR

CEILING

BARSTOOL
STEPS

BUBBA THE
WILE
JUNE BOYS
MASCOT

· BOOKS ·
BAGS OF SHOES.
· ELECTRONICS ·
· BAGS OF CLOTHES ·

We collapsed at various points, our bodies demanding forms of nourishment we couldn't provide. Zared designated himself water boy and when anyone fell over in exhaustion, he pointed to the Mason jar.

"Good old 2 percent," he said. And because there was light shining in through the pipe, we drank. Not much, but a little.

After completing the castle construction, Rufus and I dragged "Bubba the Coyote" to the top of the pile, and the four of us stood atop the flooring of pool floats we'd made. Tank and I passed the jar like a stein. We drank it empty. In the unlikely event our bodies produced more urine, we agreed to play paper-rock-scissors for first drink. I think of Richard, the Quik Mart Mountain Dew, Leo's Big Gulp thermos, what it would be like to put my mouth to a water fountain at school and taste the metallic liquid one more time.

The daydream continued until Tank shook me. "Hey, stay with me. I need your help."

Tank and I made a plan.

1. Snake the pipe with coat hangers (which we have in abundance).
2. Put small messages that describe our surroundings and who we are into the balloons we found when we were searching Dark.
3. Fill the balloons with our handy-dandy helium.

(Orange-size balloons fit through the pipe. Grapefruit-size don't.)

4. Send up a test balloon. If it passes through the pipe, release twenty at a time, until we're out.

5. Stay close enough to the vent that we can call out to someone who might see the balloons.

We had 125 balloons of maybe, and maybe was worth more than nothing.

Tank snaked the pipe until he was fairly sure we gained five-inch access to the outside world. I released the first test balloon. The green latex floated up the pipe like a flying lime, blocking the light.

"Did it work?" Rufus whispered.

No one wanted to check even though we were all desperate to know.

Tank peered into the opening. "There's light again," he reported. We took that to mean the balloon was flying. One little green bird, off and away. Still, I held my breath until he shoved the coat hanger snake through the pipe. We waited for a pop. Tank turned around with a broad grin. "We're in business."

Rufus jumped up and down. I joined him and our whole castle construction rocked and shifted slightly. In Rufus's excitement, he slid along the trash bag heap while screaming, "It worked!" at the top of his lungs. When he landed at the bottom, he flapped, snow angel style, and cooed, "It worked, it worked, it worked, it worked." Zared followed and the boys rolled toward the middle of the room, wrestling, until Rufus finally pinned Zared, and they lay panting and giggling and happy. Tank smiled. I smiled back. We knew better than to wrestle.

We filled twenty balloons, wrote twenty messages, released them.

Tank kept his ear against the pipe, listening for any type of response.

"What do you hear?" Zared asked.

Tank didn't answer.

We waited as long as we could.

Zared asked again. Rufus chewed the skin between his thumb and index finger.

Tank's head cocked toward the pipe.

"Anything?" I whispered to him.

"I don't think so," he said.

"How will we know when to release more?" Zared asked me.

We decided to nap, and if there was light in the pipe when we woke, we'd release another twenty.

I'll let you know.

Peace and Freedom,

Aulus

306

THE ELIZABETH LETTERS

Dear Elizabeth,
    We released twenty more balloons.
    No one came.

THE ELIZABETH LETTERS

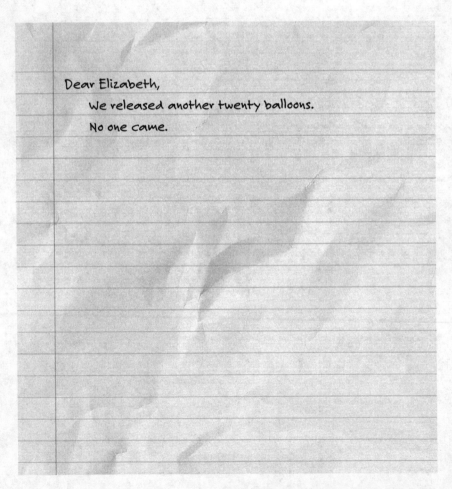

Dear Elizabeth,

We released another twenty balloons.

No one came.

THE ELIZABETH LETTERS

Dear Elizabeth,

We sat in a circle, Bubba the Coyote as our fifth, atop the trash castle. "I have another idea," I said. "We have three more sets, right?"

Rufus, who had laid the balloons out in deliberate color-coded groups, nodded. Green, blue, and yellow. "If we don't run out of helium," Tank said.

I hadn't even considered the air factor.

"What if we use the leaf blower?" I asked.

"To what?" Zared asked.

"See if we can send the balloons through the pipe with a little more oomph."

That turned out to be irrelevant; the blower only coughed.

"We're sure there are no more balloons?" Zared directed the question to Rufus.

Our scavenger dropped his chin. "Not that I know of."

I felt bad that I wound up the boys with the leaf blower. Their enthusiasm plummeted again with a lack of response to the fourth release of balloons.

Tank announced the light in the pipe was out. The night ahead would be long, maybe even dangerous. The wrestling. The moving. The work. Those physical activities were asking for a return investment.

"I miss the pee jar," Zared said as he stretched out next to Rufus. We piled ourselves atop the mound. No one wanted to be far from the pipe or each other.

"Who do you miss most?" I asked Tank.

Tank laced his hands behind his ears, rolled his face slightly toward mine and then back toward the pipe. "Glads. You?"

"Thea."

"You've been her whole life since you disappeared," he said.

And though he didn't intend for me to feel bad, I did. "Will you check the pipe again?" I asked.

He did.

Coal black.

Until light . . .

Peace and Freedom,

Aulus

THE ELIZABETH LETTERS

Dear Elizabeth,

Light filled the vent opening when we woke.

"Now?" Tank asked.

Everyone nodded. Morning, if it was morning, seemed like a time when someone might be capable of watching a strange grouping of tiny balloons rising over the trees and think, *That's weird; let's investigate.*

Rufus kissed a balloon and Zared said, "What was that for?"

"Luck."

I kissed the next and Tank followed suit.

They're gone.

Our hope was in the air.

We listened at the pipe.

Zared lost it first. He slid down the castle ramp and ran. Three rooms later I caught him. Neither of us were strong enough to fight. Our rib cages pressed and pinched each other; we drank air in gulps.

"Admit it. It's time to give up," he said.

"No."

Tank hurtled into the room, stopping at the door to watch us grapple. Zared was no longer the plushy boy from a year ago. He was bones and teeth. He was a beard with no eyebrows or lashes. In many ways, he was me, and I had no idea how to comfort him.

I looked desperately toward Rufus. "Tell me not to give up yet?"

Malaise folded Rufe like a piece of bread, but he did as I asked. "Yeah, Aul, yeah. Don't give up."

"Tell me we'll find more balloons," I demanded.

Rufus hesitated. "There are more balloons."

"Let's search Light and Dark for more. Go back to the helium room and—"

Tank interrupted. "Aul, we tried and it didn't work. That's not your fault."

"I know."

"No," Tank said. "You don't. I'm all for hope, unless hope stops making sense. And, brother, we've reached that point."

Zared and Rufus slunk to my side and sat down at my feet.

"Shut up," I told Tank.

He collared my shirt and dragged me away from the boys. "We're going to die and you need to make peace with the fact that you don't have to save us."

There were tears on my lips, on my chin. "You don't know that," I yelled into his ear.

"And . . . here's the hard part," Tank told me. "It doesn't make sense, it's not fair, and it's not our fault. Blaming yourself won't help. You're not gonna get your head around how and why this happened. Maybe up there Welder gets away scot-free. We don't know. But you can't punish yourself enough to punish him." Tank's hand—the one he slammed repeatedly into the washer—flopped listlessly into the air. The fingers were mangled, not to mention several sizes larger than his left. "You're afraid of what it means if you get angry, but you need to get furious or you'll never make peace with this."

I was whimpering. Zared had his arms around Rufus. I said, "Getting mad means it's over."

"It was over the minute Welder took us. Mad means you're human."

"Humans die."

He nodded. "Yes, we do. Now let's kick something to pieces."

"Why?"

"Because you need to."

"No."

"Kick something," he demanded.

"No."

"Kick something and yell your lungs out or I'll hit you in the face." Tank launched himself at me.

I turned my jaw, offered him an easy target.

He curled his knuckles but didn't throw the punch. "Come on . . . at least say this isn't your fault."

"But if I can't get us out of—"

"Stop."

"But someone has to—"

"You didn't put us here and no matter how hard you try, you can't make us fit through a five-inch pipe." He sagged but continued, "Earlier, when I was pounding the washing machine, you know what happened?" He didn't let me answer. "There was a voice in my ear and you know what it said, Aul? That we—you, me . . . Zared, Rufus, Chris, the others—are blameless. Not about everything, but this . . . this isn't on any of us."

"But I don't want to give up," I said.

Tank's eyes fluttered. "That might be a problem because I'm . . ." He slumped. I caught him before he fell, but only barely. The first thing I noticed was how heavy he was. Time down here has only whittled away his extra.

The second thing was how very unconscious he was. I eased the two of us to the cool concrete.

I held Chris like this.

You don't realize how warm bodies are until one grows cold in your arms.

I didn't know how to explain it, except—I want you to imagine that you go outside tomorrow morning and everything green—grass, trees, the bushes along the fence line, the weeds scattered among the concrete bricks, the vines curling up the porch, literally everything green—is gray. That is death. Death is gray.

Tank was not gray yet; he was a pinkish-whitish brown. The gray was not far off.

Rufus asked, "Did he leave us?"

Tank's eyelashes fluttered. "Sor-ry."

"You smell terrible," I told him. "You should really take a bath or you'll never get another date."

"You should," he said weakly.

I gripped his cheeks and smashed our foreheads together. "Brother, I need you not to die yet, okay?"

"I won't if you won't," he promised.

"If we can't find balloons, we'll make them, and if that doesn't work, we'll . . ." I looked toward the main room where the freezer was.

You might disagree with giving up, Elizabeth. You might even think our maker disagrees. And maybe he does. Or maybe he's the one who made sure there was an old freezer down here that'll let us airlock our way to heaven in a brisk terrible minute or two. Maybe he was saving us hours of kidney failure and nausea and torturous pain.

315

There were no more balloons. Instead, we cut several trash bags until they were the same size as all the other balloons, thinking they might hold air. The first disintegrated. The second: a tear kept it from inflating.

That's when I accepted it was over.

Using our last bits of strength, Rufus, Zared, and I shoved the freezer into the room with the castle and moved Bubba the Coyote to guard us.

We made an order. Zared first. Then Rufus, then me. Tank last, unless he's lying, and I suspect he is for my benefit. He wants this over for me.

Elizabeth, I am placing your letters in Bubba's mouth. Please don't hate me for giving up. I think Tank hates me. He's leaving the room as I finish this last letter.

I graffitied the wall one last time.

WE WERE HERE!

— JUNE BOYS

THOMAS PIPER
AULUS McCLAGHEN
ZARED PARKER
RUFUS COHEN

Zared sat in the bottom of the freezer, tucked into the smallest ball his gangly body would allow. He wore clothes for the occasion—blue jeans and a Pac-Man T-shirt. None of us looked better than Rufus, who donned a three-piece suit he dug from the treasured donations beside his bed.

One last time, Zared and I locked eyes. "Don't let me out," he said. "No matter what. This is what I want. Even if I scream."

He was scared. He was brave.

I was unable to do more than nod.

I didn't know if this or letting us starve to death was more humane, and I had no idea if I'd be able to pull their bodies out of the freezer without Tank's help. I wasn't sure I'd fit in there if I didn't move them.

Elizabeth, this was more awful than being taken.

"I love you guys," Zared said.

How many times had he told me he didn't love anyone? Thousands over the last year.

"There's no one else I'd rather die with," I told him.

"June Boys forever," Rufus echoed from my side.

He stopped me from closing the lid. I was momentarily relieved—hoping he might confess he had more balloons stashed by his float. But instead, he climbed in with Zared and they pretzeled their bodies into a lump.

Tank was probably at the door, shaking with disapproval. I did not turn and look.

"Ready?" I asked.

"Ready," the boys said together, peace and fear on each face.

I closed the lid.

Elizabeth, I closed that lid.

37

JUNE

I dream of castles and war. Curtain walls and keeps. Moats, dragons, drawbridges. Portcullises lowering. Arrows launched. Catapults flung. Armies without faces who want me dead and afraid.

The keep wall explodes and crumbles, and as it does, I dance in a cobblestone courtyard that's covered in ivy and purple flowers and fire.

Arrows pierce my skin as I stand atop the tower and swing on the bell rope like a child leaping over a lake, back and forth, back and forth.

Nick's there, sword drawn, calling, "Ring the bell."

I am the bell. The bell is me.

We are ringing, ringing, ringing.

I am spiked with dozens of arrows.

But I am music. I am hope.

"Ring the bell, ring the bell," I scream into the air.

Aulus and Tank appear in a cloud and fly to Nick and me. The

319

four of us ring the bell until the battlefield is quiet and all the fires are out.

There's a cadence to the quiet. A beeping. Like maybe the car door's ajar with keys in the ignition. I'm not driving. I'm not even in a car. My body's heavy; my eyelids obese. I let the **beep-beep, beep-beep, beep-beep** lull me back to dreams.

The beeping returns. *Ring the bell, ring the bell*, I mouth.

I am in Gladys's bed, no, can't be, her bed doesn't have rails, her comforter's orange—no, that was last year—her comforter's blue-and-green paisley and her sheets aren't starchy. I don't like starchy sheets. They're too white. I close my eyes.

I miss the bell. I wish I were a bell.

I am beeping. My lashes tickle the skin beneath my eyes as they flutter.

"Hey, you!" Dad's warmth floods me. He calls over me, "Nurse!"

I can't make sense of anything. *You're not in prison*, I think first. Then, *Why are you holding my hand like I'm dying?*

My tongue sticks to the roof of my mouth and I can't ask.

A cup and straw appear beside my lips. Constance.

There's such deep relief that she's here. I don't know why but I need the anchor of her warmth as I sip the water she offers.

Dad slides toward the corner so a man in blue scrubs with a massive Santa-length beard can lean over me and adjust the machine. The badge hanging from his neck reads Matt. *Saint Matt of beards*. No amount of reddish-brown hair hides his Happy Meal–wide smile. He adjusts the pillows behind my head, fusses with my IV, and swabs my lips with a little green sponge on a lollipop stick. The water feels marvelous.

"Welcome back, sleeping beauty," he says, staring at my pupils. "Do you know your name?"

I do. We walk through details that let him know I'm cognizant before he explains that he's Nurse Matt and "These are the very best accommodations Vanderbilt Hospital has to offer. If you see a tiny lady running around with red braids, that's Ruth, and she's the tech on duty today."

I attempt more words.

Matt swabs my lips again and nods to Constance when she asks if I can have another small sip of water.

Vanderbilt. Heart patient. Looking at my father, I telegraph the question, *How did I end up here?*

He understands. "Let's get you fully awake first."

That's when I remember Nick. I cough-whisper his name.

"Shhh," Nurse Matt tells me. "You'll be able to talk soon enough, but we just took out the tube this morning and you're going to be sore."

I sputter again. This time my eyes are full of tears.

"Nick's fine," Dad says.

I raise my IV hand half a foot off the bed and make a pistol. Ruby shot him. Oh, God, Ruby shot him. Ruby. The Gemini Thief.

"Nick's fine," Dad repeats.

I check with Constance, positive she won't lie to me.

"Honey, Nick was here an hour ago. His whole family was with him. It took longer for you to wake up than the doctor estimated. Trust me, he'll be back in the morning."

"Whether we want him to or not, right, Stancy?" Dad jokes, and I understand I've missed so many conversations.

Nick's okay. Matt dabs my cheek with a Kleenex. "You, my dear, have been through an ordeal, so you cry all you want. Crying heals soul wounds that medicine can't touch."

Even if this was bad advice, I couldn't keep the tears away. They're making it to the curve of my chin, rolling along my neck into the gown. Into bandages.

Thankfulness. Fear. Confusion. I have questions my body won't let me ask—*What happened at the WCC? Did Ruby give us the boys' location? Are Tank and Aulus alive? Is Ruby?*

Not knowing hurts more than the pinch in my chest. I wonder if I have broken ribs. My gown's open in the front. I wave my father away and Nurse Matt reads the situation perfectly. He draws the curtain around my bed and asks, "Should I stay and help?" The weight of Constance's palm disappears from my head as she turns to follow Dad. I wave that she and Matt should stay.

"You want to see?" Matt clarifies.

I nod that I do and Constance takes my hand.

Matt parts my gown and shows me my naked, injured body. Round half-dollar-size stickers attach wires to my chest and stomach in multiples places. Cords run from the stickers to the machine beside the bed. I feel ridiculous that I didn't realize the beeping was my heart before now. One hundred and twenty beats per minute. Matt taps the screen as I'm reading it and says, "Fairly normal. There's always some stress waking up."

A long, narrow, clear bandage zips up my chest. Two gauzes, tinted pink from blood, are attached to my right breast.

Matt hovers over one gauze. "You were shot here," he says and the second, "and here." "No exit wounds." He reels off paragraphs of procedures performed. He doesn't say *You almost died* but he explains that I was airlifted and had multiple surgeries, plus, I hear my father breathing deeply on the other side of the curtain and I understand I'm lucky.

Matt steps out of the room and Constance closes my gown, then pulls Dad toward her. He Velcros to her side. His eyes are sad but Constance smiles encouragement at me.

I want to know if there's permanent damage to my body, if I'm safe, but before we get to those questions, I can't wait any longer to find out about Tank and Aulus. I can't get any volume behind their names. "Au-lus? Tank?"

Dad is too large to hide himself in Constance's embrace, but he tries. I tap the side of the bed and mouth their names again.

My father offers me a terrible sadness and shakes his head. "We didn't find them," he says.

My eyes kick over to Constance. I need more. What does *We didn't find them* mean? Why are they here at the hospital when they could be out looking? I make a circular motion with my wrist to indicate searching and not being here.

Constance shakes her head and takes my hand in hers. "Honey, they stopped searching four days ago."

My throat cries like a dying bird.

Nurse Matt pokes his head in the room, notes my escalating heart rate, and says to Dad, "I'm adding some pain medicine to her IV soon. Should calm her down. I'll be right back."

Why would they stop the search? That doesn't make sense. The FBI should be increasing their efforts. I can't believe Dana gave up. I manage a single word from the barrage of questions.

"Why?" My eyes are heavy but I force myself to see this through.

Dad checks with Constance, who gives a weary, tear-filled nod. "Ruby didn't tell us where she hid the boys." *So? Double down, you idiots.* He continues, "Dana, well, she asked Ruby a question before she died. If the boys had water and . . . and they didn't."

So? I think again. *Can't the body go three or four days without water?*

"Honey." Dad rests on the side of my bed, his hip pressed against my gown, his hand on my wrist. When the mattress settles and everything in the room is quiet except the monitor, he says, "It's been ten days. We held a memorial for Aulus and Tank yesterday."

38

JUNE

When I wake, the hospital's a gaggle and a flutter. Parades of medical professionals lean into my room, checking monitors and the dressings on my chest. When they ask how I'm feeling this morning, I'm able to say, "There's some pain," and they give me broad smiles.

"My throat's sore," I tell the nurse who is not Matt. According to the whiteboard she's Jennifer and today's tech is Ricardo. Jennifer yanks the curtains to either side and opens the mini-blinds. Sun streaks into my room like it's allowed to be here.

"That's better," she says warmly, even though we now have a view of a lower flat roof covered in red-and-white pebbles and the Starbucks across the street.

There's a blue-tinted plastic hospital bag hanging on a hook by the door that holds the clothes I was wearing the afternoon Ruby shot me.

"Your dad is normally here around 6:30," Jennifer says as she gathers the trash. She pauses at the door to ask if I need anything and when I tell her I'm hungry, she brings the standard hospital breakfast, plus donuts from Dunkin'.

"I stole them from the lounge," she says, winking.

In the thirty minutes between donuts and Dad, I funnel through memories from yesterday. *Ten days.* Ten important days. Where I lived and Aulus and Tank died. I did everything and it wasn't enough.

Except that doesn't feel true or right or possible.

I do not remember my dreams from my ten-day sleep, the precise scenes, but bells echo into my conscious mind. One bell after another. Sweet and loud. They clang and clink, drowning out the woman yelling, "Nurse," down the hall, the talk news on the television next door, the footsteps passing over the tiled floor. I don't know how I know, but I'm sure of one thing: we have to ring the castle bell.

The castle bell is the bell from my dreams.

Dad and Constance arrive, matching coffee cups in the hands opposite their linked fingers. She's sipping; he's blushing at whatever she said as they enter my room.

"Hey, you're already awake," he says, delighted.

"They're not dead," I say.

His smile droops. "Honey." Everything from the slump in his shoulder to the crow's feet around his eyes says I am wrong. He releases Constance's hand and fiddles with the ponytail holder around his wrist.

"Tell him, Constance. Tell Dad they aren't dead." She's bound to know. She's holy and all that. "You hear the bell, right?"

Constance studies something out the window. She uses her pastor voice, the one that's soft as peach skin. "Oh, sweetheart, you've been through so much—"

I feel incredibly loved and incredibly dismissed.

"No! There are bells. We have to ring the bells." I am adamant, and the monitor beside my bed shifts rhythms.

"Easy," Dad says.

"You want me to be easy?" I cough the question. My throat can't go from ten days of zero to normal sentences without a protest. I take a sip and start again. "Easy. Even though . . . you're saying . . . Aulus and Tank are gone." Another sip. The straw spits water on my chest and I remember I'm wearing a gown that's slightly open in the front. I do not care. "And you had a memorial . . . for them . . . without me." It takes me a long time to string together the response and they both shake their heads the entire time. With pity. Maybe even with fear. Dad downs his coffee and turns to Constance for guidance. I close the top of my gown. Constance looks lost for words.

"You're wrong," I say. "You're all wrong."

"They're not," Dana states from the doorway.

Dana's head reaches the top of Nick's chest; they have their arms around each other's sides. Her hair is down the way it was last Christmas, but she's wearing exhaustion everywhere. This case is far from closed for her. Nick has cropped his hair close to his skull; the curls are gone. Their sadness makes them look more alike than their features.

"You quit?" I ask them accusingly.

Nick says no and the two of them part and encircle my bed. "Dana's searching for the . . ." He doesn't say *bodies*. "Them. We had the memorial at the request of the families."

But Aulus is my family.

Dana leans over the upper rails of the bed. "I'll find them." I know she will. "For now, we've moved from search to recovery," she tells me.

327

"They're alive. Please ring the bell."

"Okay," everyone says, appeasing the spike in my heart rate. But they feel sorry for me.

I kick everyone out of the room except Nick. I make space for him to curl next to me. We rest our heads on the same pillow. He scooches even closer, until he's propped on one elbow and covering me like an awning. He sweeps my hair, my very greasy hair, off my cheeks.

"I thought I'd lost you," he whispers. "We all did."

"I thought I'd lost *you*," I say back.

We are quiet for a long time. I can't say what he's thinking, but I'm drinking in the vein that thumps in his neck, the warmth of his living body, the precise shape of his upper lip.

Here's what I know: I got love wrong until now. I thought all these exploding emotions were the thing that proved love was love, but love—as I'm learning its language—is far less of a billboard and far more Braille.

The bells will not be quiet.

They're ringing, ringing, ringing. I don't want them to stop. They are a soundtrack of life and I attempt to tell Nick, and he hushes me with a kiss. It's nice to have a normal pulse of anxiety spike my brain: *Has someone brushed my teeth? I'm naked under this gown. Does he still love me if I'm damaged?* If he notices, he does a decent job of keeping his eyes above my chest. And when his gaze drops, he is full of questions rather than lust. *Am I in pain? Do I understand what happened to me?* Yes and no. We talk. When I ask about Ruby, I realize ten days have been very kind to the FBI when it comes to information. Nick walks me through the details.

"Griff is in federal custody, awaiting trial. Apparently he didn't have any knowledge of Ruby's behavior until the day we showed him the welding photo. He started piecing together the possibilities when he couldn't locate his helmet. He asked Ruby and her reaction was so off the wall he did his own investigation. He found receipts designated to the WCC for flats of food, bills that didn't match normal WCC orders. That led him to match the child cases Ruby worked in Tennessee with the Gemini Thief's locations."

"Why didn't he tell the authorities?"

Nick sighs, because we both know why he didn't tell. The woman he loved had been stealing and hording children for a decade. Substituting children for the ones they couldn't have. He blamed himself.

"Ruby didn't have a great childhood," I say, not making excuses but trying to understand.

"Griff says she was abused. Repeatedly. And in ways that . . ." He doesn't continue; he doesn't need to. Sadness runs like a train up my chest, the puffy scar, its freshly laid track.

Nick wipes away tears from my cheeks, says, "The court'll go easy on him. It's not like he knew for long. Dana will testify on his behalf. Sure, he knew Ruby was cracking, but he thought he'd have a better chance of keeping Tank and Aulus alive if he tracked her movements. But she never went anywhere. He's the one who took her down before she could shoot again."

"I don't remember that."

Nick says, "It's a miracle you remember anything. There was so much bloo—" I lay my finger against his lips and he shudders. He's seeing me on the ground. Dying.

To pull him from the image, I ask, "How did she get away with this for so long?"

For the most part, Ruby seemed on the curious side of normal.

Driven. Passionate. Sad—not sad exactly . . . like something important was missing—but fairly normal.

"According to Dana, women like Ruby are fascinating. There aren't many, but they exist. Most female kidnappers steal their own children from exes. Dana thinks Ruby probably had a god complex—a rescue-martyr type who believed she'd be a better parent than the kids had—coupled with other mental disorders. She's speculating Ruby was triggered by some kid when working with Every Child Now. Probably obsessed in a crazy one-foot-in-front-of-the-other way." He shrugs and pushes a hand through his hair. "Guess we'll never know for sure."

"And that's why the kids were returned and uninjured?" I ask.

"Dana says Ruby probably saw the community response or the parents' grieving and created her own set of rules that"—he uses air quotes—"'weren't *that* bad' when she started rationalizing her actions. One year with her and suddenly that kid is a star rather than ignored by everyone. Thing is, Griff knew she was off when it came to her childhood because she refused to talk about it with him in detail, but he had no idea she was . . . whatever she was. He feels crazy guilty he missed or discounted the signs, and no matter who tells him to join the club, he believes he should have known and encourages us to hate him."

"Speaking of hate. Warren? Does he think I'm awful for suspecting him?"

"No. He's been in and out of this room as much as the rest of us. You'll see. He's mad as hell at you for going into the room in the first place. Says he trained you better than that."

I almost laugh. Warren taught me to be brave.

"And Gladys?"

"She's not doing so great. You know . . ." *I know.* "Seeing you

330

like this hasn't been easy . . ." His voice cracks. "Once you're up and about, she'll do better."

These explanations don't soothe the ache in my chest.

"Tell me about the memorial," I say.

Nick kisses my cheek and says, "I will when you're better."

I'm grateful for his protection. "Nick."

"Thee."

"Will you trust me on something even if no one else does?"

"I'll try."

"Tank and Aulus are alive."

"Thee." This time my name is a protest.

"We have to ring the tower bell." I must sound like my father the first time he thought, *I'm going to build a castle.*

Nick is mildly apathetic. "How about we let you ring it when you're free to leave?"

"No. They'll die."

He squeezes my wrist. "I love you, but . . ."

Constance and Dad return in the middle of our fight. I am struggling for words, but I make them listen.

"You built a church when it didn't make sense. And goodness gracious, you built a castle, Dad. And you"—I stare down Nick—"you spent a year searching for a friend you'd only known for a few months. How come you all get to do crazy stuff that doesn't make sense? I'm not wrong about this. Or I'm no more wrong than any of you were."

Constance looks at Dad like I'm making a good point.

"Do you believe me?" I ask.

"The more important question is do you believe you?" Constance says.

And I do. I really do.

I've lost enough that hope costs less than grief.

39

JUNE

It takes four days for Vanderbilt to release me.

Sixty minutes to Wildwood. Another seven minutes through the stoplights.

Nick carries me up the castle tower in less than five minutes.

Four rings satisfy my soul.

I love this castle, love this tower, love Dad's relentless obedience to the vision I once despised. It must take as much strength for a normal man to walk a crazy path as for a crazy person to walk a normal path. I know that now because I am like him far more than I realized. I think of Ruby and cover the bandage over my chest. Nick rings the bell again, saying, "One to grow on."

I take my first deep breath since waking up.

"Now what?" Dad asks.

"We wait," I say.

None of us know what we're waiting for.

Constance and Gladys fidget, Dad and Nick stretch, I stare at the horizon and find myself talking to a God I don't know. *I can't see you,* I say. *I don't know if you're real, but I'm asking for a miracle.*

"Ring it again," I tell Nick.

He tugs the long braided rope and the old church bell spreads itself out like an auditory quilt over the county.

THE ELIZABETH LETTERS

Dear Elizabeth,

   This is my last letter and it will not be easy to write. There are things I need to admit. They're ugly. You already know my heart of hearts; I closed that lid on my June Boys. And not two seconds later, I heard a bell.

   The bell changed everything.

   But not at first.

   You see, I thought I made it up. Thought I'd made everything up—like Tank and this castle and my life. Just another story told to the boys at bedtime, maybe true, maybe fiction. Everything feels like fiction when you're underground.

   "Aul—you hear that?" Tank asked.

   "No."

   Because I'd reached the end, I told Tank, "There's no bell. There's no you. So you can go now. You're a true friend, a faithful brother, but I know you're not real."

Elizabeth, he smacked me across the face and shoved my chin up toward the pipe. "Listen to that," he said.

"To what?"

"That bell."

"You hear it too?" I touched his ears, the soft skin of his lobes. "You feel real," I said.

"That's 'cause I am." A smile claimed his face. "And I know where we are. Come on. Climb the dump heap castle one last time." There was no reason to argue with this smiling ghost. The freezer wasn't going anywhere.

"One last trip," I told him.

"One last trip," he repeated, like he was appeasing me, instead of I him.

He took another piece of garbage bag, tied a loop, and then shoved the helium spout through the hole. As soon as the bag was orange-size, he cinched the knot tighter. Miraculously, it held.

"How did you do that?" I asked. And at that very moment, I remembered the boys in the freezer and threw myself off the castle.

Tank spun me like a turntable. Compassion oozed from his eyes. Then something else followed the tears. Anger? I hoped not; I didn't want him to leave and I was fairly certain of two things: 1) Tank was a ghost, and 2) ghosts could come and go as they wished.

"Aul!" He squeezed my arm hard and said the thing that broke me and will likely break you too. "The boys aren't down here. I'm real. They're not."

"Yes, they are."

"I never met them." Slowly he shook his head and then tapped my temple. "They're in here."

I remember we've had this discussion before. Maybe more than once.

"Sorry," I said again.

"Me too."

Sadness has buoyancy. I pushed it to my toes and the pain ripped upward and lodged in my throat. It sat behind my eyes, hid under my cheekbones, built a house in my chest. I forced myself to hold the deaths of Rufus and Zared as something I lived through on the same night Chris died. Their bodies lay rotting in a bunker made to survive a technological apocalypse. Welder made me zip Chris into a suitcase and hand him out. And he dragged me from the water where Rufus and Zared had drowned.

I didn't mean to lie to you.

I didn't mean to lie to myself.

Rufus and Zared were my angels of distraction. My brothers. They walked into hell at my side. I tried to tell Tank, but he already knew.

"Cry all you want," he said. And when I was done— not finished exactly—but dehydrated, confused, and hoarse, I asked, "What happens next?"

"I don't know," he said, "but that's Don's castle bell ringing." I really wanted him to stop talking so I could sleep. I wanted to crawl into the freezer and not come out. "That bell's Thea, man. We rang that sucker when we were looking for you and the sound is distinct.

That's her. I'm telling you, she's ringing the bell for us," he said.

"You're sure?"

"Positive."

We released five garbage-bag balloons together.

We waited. We hoped.

The bell rang again and again.

Our ears were pinned to the opening.

The bell stopped and I slid down the pile and locked my hands over my ears. *Can I stop now? Is it over?* I lifted the lid on the freezer and Tank slammed it shut.

"You're really here," I said to Tank.

"I'm really here," he answered.

"And you never met Rufus and Zared?"

He shook his head.

"Do you hear a bell?"

Tank dragged me to the top of the heap and we listened again.

Four times the clapper struck the crown. *Ring-ring-ring-ring.*

"Do you hear the bells?" he asked.

I did.

40

JUNE

Dana spots the small green balloons first.

Nick squints against the sun. "Balloons?" he asks. "Tiny balloons?"

Dad says, "Over the . . ." Dad leans over the parapet. "Moose Lodge?"

"That's where they are," I say. It's not logical, but it is true.

Five minutes later, in the yard of the Moose Lodge, we find the first balloon skin and note. Tank's handwriting.

My name is Thomas Piper. I was kidnapped by the Gemini Thief. I am still alive and probably close to this balloon. Please search for me.

There's a second trash bag skin several feet away. Dad holds the message out for Dana to read.

She yells first. "Tank! Aul-us!"

"Thomas Piper, this is Officer Warren. Scream if you hear us."

Uncle Warren looks over his shoulder at Dana. "We searched here. Inside and out."

"Not thoroughly enough." She calls their names again. And then to us, "They've got to be close."

We each take up the cry. "Tank! Aul-us!"

Only silence answers back.

We spotted those balloons less than ten minutes ago. It can't be too late. I lie on the ground, ear to the mud, my stitches itching and pulling, and let the others scream.

The smallest muffled sound comes from somewhere near the building. I army crawl closer and wait for the pause after Dana calls their names again.

The same muffling of noise.

"Shut up!" I call to everyone. "Shut up."

A small vent is hidden behind a rusted air conditioning unit. I press my mouth to the hole. "Tank? Aulus?"

I can't breathe by the end of his name.

"Thea."

"Tank!"

Sometimes freedom sounds like a sob.

I am there when the FBI finds the bricked-in staircase inside the Moose Lodge.

I am there when they remove the cement and rubble.

I am there when Aulus squeezes through the hole. When he takes his first drink of water.

I am there when Tank crawls through after Aulus and says, "Thanks for not giving up."

I am there when my boys are carried by stretcher to an ambulance.

I am there as Aulus, skinny and pale, squints against the sun, pained by the light, and says to me, "You gave me back the sky."

I am there as I smile at my father and say, "No, he did."

EPILOGUE

THE FOLLOWING JUNE

Winter came like a lion at the end of 2010. For the first time on record, Wildwood High School missed ten straight days for snow. Students celebrated as the blizzard fell and cursed later when graduation was pushed back to June 11th.

Nick and I sit together on the bleachers. Warren and Dana are on one side. They're not "a couple." He claims he's too old for her, but Dana will wear him down, and let's be clear. He wants her to; he definitely wants her to.

Sitting between my sandals and Nick's loafers are Gladys and Tank. They're not a couple exactly, but they're friends. Good friends. Kissing friends. Being undefined is best for them at the moment. She's getting an undergraduate degree in child psychology from William Kenton and she'll never leave Wildwood. This stole spunkiness from her and gave spunkiness to him, and I think . . . Well, I think it is what it is. He needs to wander and never feel enclosed; she needs the anchor of home to fight her fears.

After Rufus's and Zared's bodies were found, Tank took the year to interview the other June Boys. We're writing a project together—with Aulus's letters, my journals, his interviews—to get our heads around this terrible thing that happened to the boys, my father, our community.

I even visited the first bunker and took pictures for Tank. (Tank won't do basements of any kind.) Dana drove Nick and me there after we convinced her we needed to see where Aulus and the others had been held. It took months to unravel the trail of Ruby's former clients at Every Child Now. She discovered Tanner and Lisa Wilson. The foster couple died in a house fire. Ruby must have been one of the few people aware they built a Y2K bunker in their field.

Warren quit his job, bought half of the castle from Dad, and is now running a new version of the WCC out there—Castle Care—complete with playground. He says the new WCC will hire Gladys when she graduates, same as Dad continues to hire Leo to truck in supplies.

I don't know what I'm doing with the rest of my life.

Everyone else has clear-cut paths and desires; mine come in temporary swirls and mismatched mosaics. Nick's heading to law school in the fall—Southern Illinois University—and I have half a mind to go along and half a mind to hike the Appalachian Trail or . . . go somewhere and help people. Maybe I'll try the academy and let Dana train me. Maybe I'll go film that mockumentary after all. Dad says it's okay that I don't know what I want. In the meantime, I'm volunteering at the castle.

The balloon under Nick's knees squeaks against the bleachers. I hedge mine with my dress pants. Principal Markum loved Tank's idea to release balloons when Aulus's name was called. So did Wildwood. Green balloons are everywhere. In the hands of the same people who put Arrest the Gemini Thief signs in their yards. On the laps of those who attended the memorial service for Tank and Aulus. They're tied to the wrists of those who showed up to help with castle construction. They're squeaky and noisy and in the way of cameras, but no one cares.

Our eyes find a young man in a black gown and a yellow sash. He nears the steps, spots the balloons poised to be released, and smiles. Not a happy smile exactly. Yesterday he told me, "Happy is a weird emotion. I don't feel it by itself anymore." And I said, "You will again someday," but the more I considered my response, the more I doubted its truth. Not because he'll never be happy again. He will. I believe that. But I think . . . The older I get, the more I hold multiple emotions at the same time.

Like . . . Take Ruby's death. I love her and I hate her and I'm sad she's dead and I'm relieved she's gone—some days because it means she's not suffering anymore and some days because she doesn't deserve to be on earth after what she did. Some days I remember she took Tank to keep Aulus alive, and some days I remember she never went back to feed them, and I always know she set up my father to take her fall.

And I find that's more normal than having a singular emotion.

I explained my feelings to Aul on the phone because I felt guilty for not hating her properly. But he said, "Sometimes I miss Welder. I mean, Ruby. And then, next breath, I want to dance on her grave. Literally dance on her grave."

And then he added, "But you know what I think about when I get stuck asking why I was taken, why Ruby did what she did, why a flood on top of a kidnapping? I remember your dad started a castle ten years before I needed it. And I remember you holding me when I first came out of the ground, saying, 'I rang the bell. I rang

343

the bell,' and hearing afterward that everyone else had given up. I want to figure out how to give that to someone else. I want to be a bell ringer instead of a June Boy."

I told him he was a bell ringer for Chris, Zared, and Rufus, but he couldn't hear me yet.

We hung up after that. I think I'll replay that conversation the rest of my life. Those final words: *I want to be a bell ringer instead of a June Boy.* Me too, Aul, me too.

There's a collective pause across the stadium as my cousin rests his foot on the bottom step of the stage.

"Aulus Edward McClaghen," Principal Markum says.

If a town could weep, its collective cheeks are wet.

Aulus pauses at the stage's edge and searches the bleachers for us. He points at a blood-red cardinal streaking the sky. *Yes, I know. I love the birds too.* Arms outstretched, he spins in a circle all the way to where Principal Markum stands. There's a chorus of laughter, sheer delight, and then the horizon blooms green with balloons.

I hold on to mine.

I'm not the only one.

Aulus's father stands near the long jump pit gripping the chain-link fence like he's not quite allowed to be here. When he releases his balloon, he watches it trail after the others, never quite catching up. He's been around this year. Warren says he'll stay that way, and I hope he does. Aulus needs him, but Aulus needs him to be trustworthy and consistent, and I'm not sure Scottie knows how to do that yet.

I text my father: Ring the bell.

I asked him to miss the ceremony to fulfill my request. Castle Delacroix is out of earshot, but even if I can't hear it, I want to know the bell is being rung.

As the balloons green the azure sky and a thunderous clapping storms the bleachers, I touch the zipper scar along my breastbone and marvel at my heartbeat. And then I hear them, same as I heard them a year ago.

"You hear that?" I ask.

Nick noses my ear and squeezes my hand. I squeeze back. "You feel that?" he asks.

My heart pounds. I am made of hope and doubt, anger and fear, sadness and joy. "I feel everything," I say, and release my balloon.

A FINAL NOTE TO THE READER

The Elizabeth Letters were written from Aulus McClaghen to Elizabeth Smart, who was abducted June 5, 2002, by Brian David Mitchell and Wanda Ileen Barzee and rescued by officers nine months later, on March 12, 2003.

BONUS SCENE

JUNE 2020

The following conversation between Tom "Tank" Piper and Constance Delacroix occurred after the ten-year anniversary of Tank and Aulus's 2010 escape from Ruby Holtz, better known as the Gemini Thief. Tom and Constance spoke to Constance's church plant, Wildwood United. Attendance totaled 319. Many familiar faces and former June Boys were present. Scattered among the first three rows were Thea and her daughter, Eloise; Dana and Warren; Gladys; Aulus and his friend, James; Scottie and Leo; and Corey Donahue flew in from Chicago.

Constance began by addressing the congregation. "Tom Piper needs no introduction to most of us Wildwoodians, but for visitors who have joined us today, Tom is the author of the bestselling book *Inside the Bunker: Stories of the Gemini Thief Survivors*. He's an associate professor of psychology at William Kenton, and if that's not ambitious enough, he's also the proud godfather of my granddaughter, Eloise. Would you all help me welcome Tom to Wildwood United?"

When the applause died down, Constance turned to Tom. "Tom, thank you so much for joining us today and for agreeing to this conversation of reflection and healing.

"Thanks for having me, Stancy."

"So, when the idea for this ten-year anniversary talk first came up, you jumped on board quickly. Walk us through why you are so passionate about telling your story."

"Bottom line: I want to help people. Myself included. Part of that process is to never under or over tell, or falsely re–tell, my story. When you've lived through a trauma, I've found that two stories often emerge. First, the objective story you lived through and second, the subjective story you tell yourself about what happened to you."

Constance clapped in applause to Tom's statement. "Don't I know it! And the two can be very different versions. Please share the story you told yourself about your experience with the Gemini Thief. Or even the story you've told yourself since you and Aulus escaped."

Tom leaned all the way back in his chair. His thick beard framed a knowing smile, a smile that promised he knew more than he could ever share in such a small window of time. "Perhaps the most helpful thing in a crowd like this is a warning to those people out there who have lived through their own traumas. When someone brings up Ruby Holtz, I'm still—even ten years later—tempted to compare my experience to those of my June brothers and minimalize it.

"I look at Aulus, who endured more than a year in the bunker, and I think about Andrew, Corey, Skates, and everyone else who made it thirteen months, and those who didn't make it at all . . . Compared to my few days . . . Well, that inner voice starts

350

riding me. 'Shut up, Tank.'" Tom knocked his knuckles against his temples and squeezed so the audience could feel the pressure of each word. "You have nothing to complain about. You're not the one who should be talking. You know nothing of real trauma. Real trauma is thirteen months.'

"Brutal, eh? But that's what comparison does. It tells you your story is no big deal compared to someone else's. Friends, that's a big fat lie. Trauma is trauma. You know how people say, 'there is no such thing as a small wedding'? Well, I think there's no such thing as a small trauma.

"Because if I told you I was attacked on the side of the road, held against my will, left to die in a bunker, and I'd be dead if it weren't for Don Delacroix building a castle in the middle of nowhere Kentucky—let me tell you what you wouldn't say: 'Come back when you've been in that situation for thirteen months.' We all know . . . even a day is heinous and atrocious.

"Minimizing trauma; comparing trauma is detrimental to healing. And you don't have to have been kidnapped by the Gemini Thief to have hurts that need healing. There is very real pain in this room." Tom stood and moved closer to the edge of the stage so he could make eye contact. He looked straight into the face of a woman, already in tears, and said, "Baby girl, learning to right-size trauma gives healing a starting place. Not a finish line, unfortunately, but at least a starting place." He went back to his seat and waved an I-get-carried-away-when-I'm-talking apology at the congregation.

Constance nodded. "You've said it. Anytime freedom is lost, there's a wake of devastation. Oh to find a world where every grief is recognized and respected and right-sized . . . I think you're right about healing starting there. Tom, because I know you and we've talked through all of this over the years, would you tell the congregation your thoughts on why this happened to you and the other June boys?"

"You want me to talk about how 'I'm supposed to find purpose in everything'?"

Constance offered a sympathetic and apologetic laugh. "Yes, if you will."

"There's a reason for everything. This is something I was taught in my upbringing. A family mantra. A Christian mantra. The thought process goes like this: if something happens to you, it probably happened for yours or the kingdom's betterment. In this mindset, a loving God looks at you like you're Job and thinks, go on and hurt Tank. This will serve my greater purpose and it'll make for a better story.

"And I have to tell you, I hate that idea and . . . people say it to me all the time in some form or other. Like . . . 'Would you have ever written *Inside the Bunker* if you hadn't been a Gemini survivor?' Well, no, of course not. But I'd have done something else, and we'll never know what that could have been now because this trauma showed up in my story. But make no mistake; I'm not better or more 'poised for greatness' because Ruby Holtz attacked me on the side of the road. I'm not, and you're not either. And I find it painful and re-traumatizing when Christians tell fractured, hurting individuals that God planned this for them and to 'just wait and see the good that will come.'

"Since Jesus lived and died and lived, I tend to believe He is the only child of God whom God orchestrated something bad to happen to, and that was something Jesus agreed to in advance, not yet as God's son, but as one-third part of the God-head, the Christ."

"You've been reading Richard Rohr." Constance gave the congregation a see-I-told-you-so grin. She'd encouraged her people to read the author more than once by sharing his quotes in her sermons.

"Oh yeah."

"So, you don't think there's purpose in everything? Or that 'All things work together for the good to those who are called according to His purpose'?"

Tank leaned forward in his chair and interlaced his fingers, then undid them—as if he'd seen one too many make that gesture and he already knew he wasn't someone who aligned with that all-knowing persona. Still, he spoke with confidence. "Oh, I absolutely believe the scripture. But . . . I believe there's purpose because God is loving. And because I treat God and my horrific experiences with the respect He and they deserve. I don't see my story like . . . God needed to me to get to point C so He orchestrated experiences A and B to get me there. This world is . . . unfair and God knows that better than any of us.

"But I still believe He is the author of life, and Satan is the orchestrator of death. Let me tell you: death was in the bunker with me and Aul. But so was life. That's the goodness in my head. That if I was going to be in a bunker, God wasn't going to let me go in there alone. I believe whole-heartedly He was there with Aulus, Chris, Rufus, and Jared, and I believe whole-heartedly that Aulus, the only survivor of that year, gets to grieve everything he lost in that bunker, and he doesn't have to hawk healing from a mall kiosk in order to live his best life. Or to be someone God can use."

Constance looked from Tom to the congregation, and then it seemed like she looked beyond them—maybe in the direction of her own pain. She said, "I so identify with what you're saying.

Trauma is confusing and many of us don't know what to do with pain, and we feel like we have to answer, 'Where it came from' or 'Why it happened' before we tackle 'What to do with it.' And when we can't answer the where or why questions, we assume God did this to us for one reason or another. That theology is incredibly painful and damaging and yet is often what we Christians promote. How many of us have heard or even said something to the effect of 'Pull yourself up by your bootstraps, God's teaching you a lesson.' I'm certainly guilty of pat answers. Maybe that helps one oddball out there, but on the whole, it can totally misrepresent a loving God."

Tom took the apology to heart. His voice cracked as he said, "Thank you for saying that." The strength came back, and maybe some anger too as he continued. "Pat answers are the worst. And it's nice to hear that someone else has questions."

"Oh, I have plenty of questions when it comes to God and healing. For instance: We pray about basketball games—go UK!"— Constance gave a little whoop that received claps and catcalls—"And expect Him to care about the outcome and yet . . . How do we reconcile a God we can ask for three-pointers and get an 'answer' and a God we ask for freedom from trauma or disease or healing for a baby and seemingly hear nothing? Not to mention those who don't survive long enough to attempt healing. It's hard to get your head around."

Tom shook his head. "Maybe we're not meant to get our heads around it. Maybe that's faith. Or maybe life is the effort of trying to get our hearts around it instead of our heads. One thing is certain: pain and questions are the common denominator of life. I say that all the time to my students." That image wasn't hard to conjure. Tom, in a William Kenton polo, khakis, and bright blue Vans like he wore today. He was handsome, with a countenance that pulled at everyone in the room—not by being bold, but rather by being humble. "We have more in common than we think," he said. "I don't know anyone who has been through a traumatic experience who isn't forged by the fire of asking, 'Where is God now?' For Jesus followers that question is often asked in anguish and for non-Jesus followers in sarcasm."

"Tom, after everything you've been through, do you still consider yourself a person of faith?"

"Absolutely. It's messy and confusing and beautiful and wonderful. Both the questions and the answers. But I know Aulus and I weren't alone in that bunker, and as I've wrestled with healing—and am still wrestling—I know I don't want to do that part alone either. One of my college professors once shared this quote, 'A man with an experience is never at the mercy of a man with an argument.'"

"Wow. Who said that?"

"He didn't have any idea and I don't either, but man, Stancy, I buy it. Honestly, I've wrestled with how to talk about Christianity these days. Because what it means in Western culture in the 2020s . . . can be sort of terrifying. For so many people *Christian* is synonymous with hate and judgment rather than love and belonging. So . . . I'm careful . . . You know . . . Not because I'm ashamed of Him . . . but because the width of representation associated with *Christian* can be crazy far off the way I move through the world. I find myself whispering *Christian* the way some people whisper *gay* or *divorced* or *Black*. Like I'm checking to see where the other person falls on the spectrum. 'Oh you're a Christian . . . One of these or one of *those*?'"

Constance laughed in her easy way. "This happens to me literally every day. When I meet someone new, I rarely lead with 'I'm a pastor.' Instead I start with, 'I do non-profit work,' until I see what I'm up against and what the person's preconceived notions are. That feels strategic in the world today. I'm not ashamed of Jesus, and I'm delighted to pastor—so the juxtaposition is super tough."

Tom started to speak and stopped himself—the look of concentration so deep it formed wrinkles between his eyes. When he tried again, he said, "I guess the thing I've decided is this: I don't have to stand here and convince anyone God exists or that I need Him. I can only tell people that He was with me in the bunker, and that's super hard to argue away, even with my million questions."

Constance glanced at the large digital clock against the sanctuary's rear wall and gave a slight nod to Tom that they should wind things down. A toddler's toy fire truck sounded off at the same moment. Giggles followed and Constance looked lovingly at the culprit and said, "Lincoln, I promise we're wrapping up." Everyone laughed again. "Okay, last thing, Tom. Over the last ten years, you've learned so much about captivity and freedom. Can you share with us the most important thing you've gleaned from processing your time with the Gemini Thief?"

"Boiling it down and getting real: There are bunkers everywhere, and it's an act of love to recognize the captives in our world.

"Whether it's the shackles of racial injustice or a woman who can't figure out how to leave an abusive relationship or the marginalized who feel they must stay silent or they will be judged or the young people who sell their bodies to get out of poverty or the elderly who need but can't afford twenty-four hour care. That's all captivity. Racism is captivity. Poverty is captivity. Abuse is captivity. People, we have to learn to recognize captivity even when it's not wrapped in a bunker and sealed by a famous kidnapper."

"You know, that makes me think about a chapter that's in the tenth anniversary edition of *Inside the Bunker*."

Tom smiled.

"I asked Aulus's permission for you to share something he said in that chapter because I felt like it was relevant to the conversation we're having here at Wildwood United and in the global church."

"Yeah, I'll never forget that. We were in Parnassus Books in Nashville, sitting on the couch in the middle of the store. One of the dogs, a silky little gray-and-black thing, was in his lap napping. I was reading a picture book, *The Hug Machine*, and Aul was reading Kevin Wilson's latest, and he just looked over at me and said, 'Tank, do you always feel alive?' and I answered, 'Not always. Do you?' And he said, 'No, but I'm learning how to sit peacefully in the same room with my past, and that's something.'"

"'Learning how to sit peacefully in the same room with my past.' Wow. There's something there for all of us, but what did that mean to you, Tom?"

For one long moment Tom met the eyes of his oldest friend. Aulus didn't do anything corny, but if you watched closely, you saw him nod and knew that within that nod was a lifetime of brotherhood.

Tom said, "Aulus's words were a deep reminder that my past isn't going away, which was what I'd been wanting. I kept wanting to wake up and miraculously be someone who never knew Ruby Holtz, and I'd try all these little tactics to believe in that non-existent and false story life . . . that I was above it, that others had it worse, that I needed to be strong, or that I needed to find purpose . . . But all those thoughts ever did was make me depressed. It wasn't until I let that time with Ruby Holtz at the bottom of the world sit in the room with me that I was able to grieve, not just my past, but the present and future."

The fire truck toy sounded again. This time, no one reacted. Everyone was locked in on Tom and Constance.

She said, "Say a little more about that difference—between grieving the past and grieving the present and future as well."

"Best way I can explain it: imagine your house burns down. You can't only grieve what you lost in the fire, you also have to grieve the fact that you have nowhere to live right now and that where you will live in the future will always be a different house.

"So, for me, I'd done the initial work of grieving what Ruby took from me back then, but it wasn't until Aul said he was learning to sit in the room with his past that I understood my grieving wasn't over. It'll probably never be over. Healing isn't closing the wound. Healing is living with the scars. And if you want to take that back to Jesus, you can."

"Right! Because He kept his scars."

"And we'll definitely keep ours. And that's not just okay, that's the example. So if you're sitting out there today and you've been waiting for your trauma and past to be erased, I'm not going to say that it *can't* happen, but I'm telling you it's flat unlikely."

"What is likely, Tom? What can we, those of us who have experienced deep trauma and pain, expect?"

"From my point of view, you can expect God to sit with you in all the bunkers. Whether He's represented in a friend, or an inner voice, or Scripture, or nature, or memories . . . He's there. He sat with me in the bunker Ruby Holtz threw me in at the Moose Lodge and the infinite bunker she made in my soul. And for me, that togetherness . . . That's enough to get me through. And I try to be someone who sits with others in their bunkers—so if they can't see God in that, at least they'll see someone loves them.

"That might not sound like peace to all of you, but it's where I am, and it's miles ahead of where I was. And I believe far too many of you understand exactly what I mean. I'm sorry for that. If I can leave you with one thing, it's this: you weren't alone then, and you aren't alone now, and you'll never be alone in the future."

"Amen," Constance said.

"Amen," Aulus repeated from the front row.

Tom looked at Aulus, and Aulus held eye-contact. Almost at the same time, they mouthed, "Thank you," to each other.

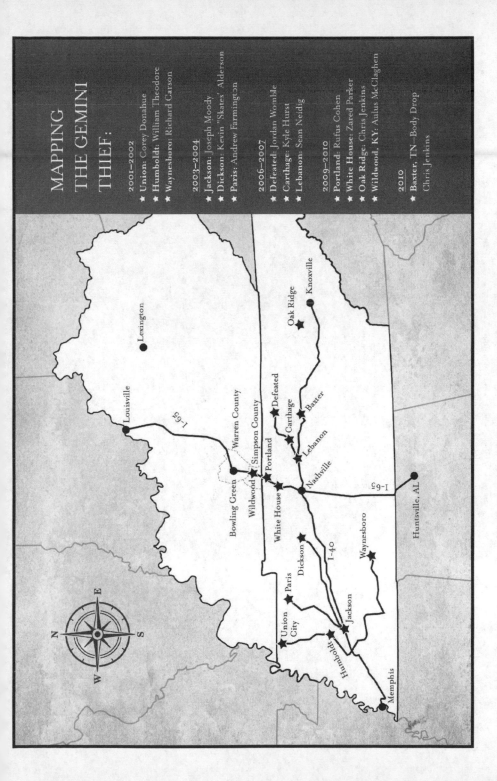

MAPPING
THE GEMINI
THIEF:

2001–2002
★ Union: Corey Donahue
★ Humboldt: William Theodore
★ Waynesboro: Richard Carson

2003–2004
★ Jackson: Joseph Moody
★ Dickson: Kevin 'Skates' Alderson
★ Paris: Andrew Farmington

2006–2007
★ Defeated: Jordan Womble
★ Carthage: Kyle Hurst
★ Lebanon: Sean Neidig

2009–2010
★ Portland: Rufus Cohen
★ White House: Zared Parker
★ Oak Ridge: Chris Jenkins
★ Wildwood, KY: Aulus McClaghen

2010
★ Baxter, TN–Body Drop
   Chris Jenkins

ACKNOWLEDGMENTS

A book has an author on the spine, but mine has a creative village as its soul architect. What follows is my attempt at heartfelt thanks to the village.

(Please note: Making sure you acknowledge everyone who helps transform an idea to a plot, plot to manuscript, and manuscript to novel is next to impossible. Inevitably, there are strangers and saints who provide inspiration, encouragement, and wisdom who go unnamed. And trickling into every paragraph and character are terrible and wonderful life moments that teach us how to be better single-soul organisms. All should be thanked, but I'm sure I've missed some.)

The June Boys came to life under the professional guidance and love of Kelly Sonnack, Becky Monds, and Jodi Hughes. Thanks are also owed to Amanda Bostic, Paul Fisher, Taryn Fagerness, the design and marketing teams at Thomas Nelson, and Rosemary Brosnan. Kelly carried me better than Samwise Gamgee and I love her more than I can say. The freedom Becky gave me to create *The June Boys* has been one of the most enjoyable creative experiences of my career. I work with the best of the best.

Three people got down in the mud with me during the writing process: Ruta Sepetys, David Arnold, and Ginger Knight. They read and read and read. *The June Boys* wouldn't exist without their kindness, intelligence, curiosity, love, and time. I likely wouldn't exist either. Thank you for making stories and sharing life with me.

At critical creative moments, Lauren Thoman, Mary Weber, Kristin Tubb, and Alisha Klapheke stepped into the fray and offered advice this story soooooo desperately needed. Ladies, meet me at Panera, and let's write books as long as that bartender's class and better than the kitchen sink cookie.

This past season of life, thanks to Karen Hayes and Ann Patchett, I've been a children's bookseller at Parnassus Books. This job taught me to love the book industry in a fresh way. A huge, huge thank-you to every coworker who loved me, asked about my writing, and laughed when I tried to sell *Hug Machine* to all who passed through the children's sections (seriously, go buy a copy of that picture book!). Special thanks to Stephanie Appell (champion of children's books) and Niki Coffman, who convinced my brain I could work retail.

I benefited from countless cheerleaders over the course of drafting this novel. I'd be remiss not to mention their names: Erica Rogers, Ashley Herring Blake, Shelby Ijames, Katie Corbin, Katie Cotugno, Shelli Wells, Paige Crutcher, Sarah Brown, Amanda Borchik, Meg Fleming, Mary Uhles, Julie Stokes, and the incredible SEYA bookfest ladies.

My earliest reader on this novel was Julie Alexander. Her comments and reactions shaped the manuscript, and I owe her a massive thanks and probably some guacamole. Near the end of story construction, Sarah Arnold, Keltie Peay, Megan Miranda, and Gwenda

Bond read. There is nothing like having your novel read. But especially those first nervous reads. Ladies, thank you for sharing your enthusiasm.

If you've heard me speak over the last year, there's a chance you've heard me mention the importance of mental health care. It's about getting in deep and dirty with your soul, being honest, showing up, and doing the hard work. All of which is impossible without educated and loving professionals. These are mine: Christen Johnson, Leah Bowen, and my integrative trifecta: Lauren, Katie, and Emily. If you're in the Nashville, Tennessee, area and need support, please check out Sage Hill Counseling, the Center for Hope and Healing, and Tennessee Integrative Health. If you're elsewhere, ask until you find someone right for you, or google like your life depends on it. (Because it just might.)

Mom, Dad, Matt, and my whole wonderful family: thank you for loving me for me. You gave me the gift of working at the estate, and that has transformed my writing and soul in immeasurable ways. I love you.

Carla, Christa, and Ginger: you came and found me in the pit and fed me Thai and Paleo and cookies and trail mix until I could breathe again. You wrote Post-it Notes, voxed, cried, held, worked, boated, loved, and shared the puppies with me. I love you. Gnome sayin'?

To God, may you receive all the glory; this and all belong to you.

Lastly, to the readers, you will always be my better half.

DISCUSSION QUESTIONS

1. When someone you love is absent from your life, how do you typically respond?
2. Is there ever a time when lying is justifiable?
3. More often than not, we want our parents to be heroes and discovering their fallibility is deeply painful. Discuss a time you were disappointed with your parents' behavior.
4. If you could receive a return letter from someone famous, whom would you choose to write?
5. Have you ever followed a gut instinct that didn't make sense to anyone else? If so, what happened? Would you do it again?
6. How difficult do you find continuing and completing tasks without emotional, relational, or spiritual support? Name something you are currently trying to finish that you wish more people would cheerlead?
7. Is the experience of sharing difficult pieces of your personal story easier with family, best friends, acquaintances, or strangers? If you need help, whom do

you ask first? Do you feel there's a limit to how much help
you can ask for?

8. Is forgiveness more difficult with certain people? If so,
    why do you believe that's true?

9. A village of adults surrounds and loves these main
    characters. Name your village.

10. Do you have seasonal obsessions or passions? What are the
    benefits of pursuing a task or objective relentlessly? What
    are the pitfalls?

ABOUT THE AUTHOR

Photo by: Carla Lafontaine

Court Stevens grew up among rivers, cornfields, churches, and gossip in the small-town South. She is a former adjunct professor, youth minister, and Olympic torchbearer. These days she writes coming-of-truth fiction and is the community outreach manager for Warren County Public Library in Kentucky. She has a pet whale named Herman, a bandsaw named Rex, and several novels with her name on the spine: *Faking Normal, The Lies About Truth,* the e-novella *The Blue-Haired Boy, Dress Codes for Small Towns*, and *Four Three Two One.*

CourtneyCStevens.com
Instagram: @quartland
Facebook: @CourtneyCStevens
Twitter: @quartland